W9-CJR-698

Ania Malina

Lawrence Osborne

CHARLES SCRIBNER'S SONS
New York

To Karolina

My thanks are due to Mrs Susan Rose for allowing me to write this novel at her house near Panzano during the winter of 1983.

Library of Congress Cataloging-in-Publication Data

Osborne, Lawrence, 1958–
Ania Malina.

I. Title.
PR6065.S23A8 1987 823'.914 86-26167
ISBN 0-684-18790-6

Manufactured by Fairfield Graphics, Fairfield, Pennsylvania

First American Edition 1987

CONTENTS

PART ONE

Unsent Letters

nr Beaumont-le-Roger

My little M.,

We slept in the village for two nights and are now back in the open . . . a small hill covered with conifers and elms where we congregate in a shallow trench under the pines, cooking beef tea and shooting at a long, straggling arterial road in the distance. On the other side is a wood and they are in the wood. We live for, and dream about, this road finished with dark tarmac and bordered with shimmering lime trees. On the first day we noticed the odd vehicle moving along it: a bicycle, a staff car, a civilian truck. You understand, it is our duty to shoot all bicycles . . . a single shot knocked it over and it lay in the road across the body, its front wheel uplifted, spinning, and the spokes glittering in the sun. This was our first triumph. The other vehicles passed on in alarm and we could not hit them. Only the bicyclist lay all day in the summer sun until the wheel was still. I thought that he began to give off a faint silver steam; perhaps the tyres were burning in the sun and the tar melting around him. I could swear there was a cloud of dust or thin, transparent smoke rising over the surface of the road. Through binoculars it seemed like the light steam over hot water.

There is sporadic small-arms fire in the morning and again towards evening, but nothing is accomplished. At night I count the stars of Charles's Wain and look for the big fiery stars my father taught me about . . . Alpheratz, Altair and Capella, the head of the Charioteer, burning blue and white. A red illumination blots out the Milky Way over the enemy wood, another village burning, but it reminds me of a big city and I think of boulevards and newspaper stalls and ice-cream vendors in neon (only the wood cuts us off from the network of streets governed by traffic-lights, the glare of cinemas and late bars). The bullets make their own nocturnal glow, a cheerful parabola over the pine trees and sleeping guns. If only I had my city shoes I would walk over into the wood and pick up a cocktail.

Now I have unpacked my kit and laid out my rounds neatly about me like toy soldiers. The camp is asleep and there is no light. I like to disarm myself in secret, to unprepare myself and lie down in the middle of my junk, a tortoise sliding out of its shell, unbuckled, unclipped, unfastened. It is warm and you can sleep naked if you are not seen to be unready. I smoke on my back and the stars of Andromeda are overhead between the pine-needles. A little moment of anarchy, a second of star-gazing. It is wonderful to lie down in the dead needles under the cold currents of air that puff up suddenly in the night-wood.

Several of us have gone near the road now, creeping up at night. If we creep by the fences, over the wet furrows, behind the brambles and wild strawberries, they do not see. The road is like the river around the edge of the world, impassible and unimaginable. Nothing can move upon it. It stands out of its frame of trees with nightmare lucidity, we can see the myriad cracks and pores in its mauve surface, which seems to be the normal, palpable compound of pitch and creosote oil but set apart in the incertitude of hatred. There are tall flowers rising out of the grass between the trees, red trumpets, yellow corymbs and floating umbels of white blossom. The moon illuminates the prosaic and untouchable cracks and there is a dark greasy patch where the bicycle fell. It is magical, this barrier of tarmac and flowers, where the will of a nation has erected its furthest limit. There is no sound in our motion – in our condition of secrecy we admire, on our bellies, their potent invisibility. And often we are seen returning and a sharp observer fires a rhetorical shot into our backs, so hopeless it is almost a gesture of friendship. So we sing the song about the whore they all know and love . . .

Vergiss mich nicht

it says, with jovial nostalgia.

I am sending you a little drawing of the road which the censors will not suspect. I have drawn in the horizon of trees as well as I can, and the contour of our hill. X marks me, as always, lying on my back involved in the harmless ecstasies of tobacco. I am waving a handkerchief for you, though you cannot see because of the screen of trees. The Watcher of the Road is waving to you in his mode of invisibility. He sends kisses upon your brow and strokes your Minoan hair with his hand. He sends you the blessing of God and the benediction of all His seraphim . . .

Jamie

nr Vimoutiers

Dearest Maria,

As I know you will have read in the newspapers, the historic offensive against Falaise eventually succeeded and we are moving eastwards in the direction of Rouen. We are still in the countryside, however, though things have changed for us . . . we are in a farm near the Lisieux road (beds, fresh eggs, milk) and a little removed from action. The soldiers with me mutter songs about the Germans, but without personal hatred, and I watch occasional transports on the road without anticipation. A column of smoke went up yesterday beyond the road, a black undisturbed smoke ascending vertically in the shape of a tornado, the insignificant trace of a destroyed aeroplane or some ground barbarity we are too distant from to hear. I was eating the marvellous eggs and did not pause to consider.

The farm lies in a small cluster of fields encircled by far-off hills, the ghostly highway to Lisieux and the fringes of lush Norman woods. The fields are scattered with yellow mustard and poppies, pieces of semi-oxidized machinery and a few fragments of grey military clothing. The outhouses are empty, we found no one when we came. The soldiers play cards in the kitchen – exuberant with a kind of savage guilt – and we pass our days hiding ourselves away from the slaughter. It will not last, no longer than the games of cards. I should sing a lament over the soldiers, having seen them disarmed, humble in their shirt-sleeves, knowing also that they will last no longer than the games of cards. Their bodies, originally white and wiry-English, have become thicker and darker; they wash together like ancient hoplites at the well and I watch them, remaining apart at the open window that overlooks the courtyard, noticing the nuances of each body, the distribution of each individual's muscles and the nonconformity of the calves and buttocks hardened into distinct variations of a single communal beauty. They smoke cigarettes and dry in the sun, sprawled over the massive paving-stones (stones as massive and powerful as they), enjoying peacefully the evaporation of the water from their wet skin. If only for this ritual of anointment and self-display I could wish this sojourn to perpetuate itself for ever.

I admire them as I grow distant from them . . . they are savage and unconscious in conversation at table, distorted by accumulated private hatred, not hatred against the Reich but against this elaborate interruption of normality. But I am accountable, I am the gear that sets the war in motion, accelerating or decreasing the speed. I am the wheel to their cogs, the clue to the machine, and they are set against me – an antagonism natural to the fighting-machine. It will be better if we are eventually split apart by force . . . this primitive organization will only kill us.

Now, as I am writing, the men are under the window greasing their weapons: knives, cartridges and rifle parts are spread out around them on a square of dry grass, and they are happy in the presence of their tools. It is hot and I can see the faint blue reflection of the sky in the tight skin of their shoulders and in the fragments of metal. Over the road behind them – which I can see and they cannot – a motorbike is gliding through intervals of shadow and harsh sunlight, the fields soaking up the noise of its engine. *Ave atque vale*, I say, and keep away. But it will return with orders and the long arm of the national effort will snatch us from this dream. The Myronic discus-throwers and wrestlers will put on their boots and trudge back to the road to Lisieux. It is a scene so foreseeable – they will whistle 'Lili Marlene' and count time to themselves, each one individually, to regulate the muscular clock, and then with an oath to Wodin they will wet their bayonets with a dab of saliva and do their work. But that is tomorrow. Today I look at their azure shoulders and the swift agility of slender, muscular fingers.

If you were here, of course, I would take you back towards the west – I would have the courage to do it – and we would dance out of it all. We would take a ship to the United States and disappear into the imperturbable continent. This is also a nocturnal vision of mine . . . the night-lights of that continent glimpsed from an approaching ship and the smell of wharfs deep down – a simple, ancient smell alien to this familiar death struggle – and the smell of the great belt of native grass and concrete behind. And we would be there together, dancing under the deck lights. It is a lovely dream, but reality is Vimoutiers and the sound of falling aircraft, the road that will not disappear and the sudden bitterness of these men. I cannot change it and it will not change of its own will, so I am doomed to act. And there, my elf, is the rub.

Jamie

Hôpital St Lazare
nr Laon

Dearest Maria,

Finally, they have taken me out of the front and, with the assistance of a small eye injury, have found an excuse for leaving me here. I have made myself insignificant for them and I have been designated some small duties. My eye is still bandaged and the children in the wards where I have to work are afraid of me – also because I speak with an accent and still wear my uniform. I work with a Swiss doctor named Kessler, who is civil and dry, but otherwise there is no one to talk to.

Yesterday in the children's ward I saw someone who reminded me of you, a girl from Laon with a broken leg – there are many of them from the demolished factory areas in these towns. She was reading American magazines lying under a blood-bottle, her plaster leg elevated about six inches above the mattress by a slender chain. She was Nordic and small-throated, fair-skinned and blonde. Her mother had been to visit, neatly infiltrating her ordered hair with paper roses, and had left two cubes of dirty sugar in her lap. The sugar was so pathetic I wanted to talk to her and give her some company. We had an amusing little conversation.

She explained to me, to begin with, that the bomb which had destroyed their house had fallen sideways into her mother's bedroom.

'Elle a creusé le plafond, monsieur, comme ça . . . ' and she slapped her forearm with her palm as if killing a mosquito. She had been in the garden, pulling up potatoes, and the bricks had rained down among the family geese, killing them at random. 'Mais la bombe, monsieur, c'était épouvantable, ça m'a fait peur. Elle a tué toutes les oies. Elle a creusé le plafond.'

Her mother, ten minutes previously during her visit, had tied up her fuzzy, coppery hair into a tight, reserved chignon, leaving only a rim of wild frayed fibres around her face.

She held her palms together in mock-prayer.

'Mais, ils vont payer, monsieur?'

I nodded and assured her that they would.

'Oui, c'est sûr,' she went on, 'ils ont fait sauté les murs en plus. Ça c'est pas gentil!'

She had cut out some of the pictures from the magazines – large gleaming photographs from *Life* and cinema periodicals: a portrait of Eisenhower, a Polynesian queen, a still from *Drôle de Drame* showing handsome Barrault naked in a luxury pool. There were also carved outlines of automobiles spread over her knees, filled in with crude faces in red crayon.

'Elle a creusé le plafond, vous savez,' she continued, lazily cutting open the imaginary faces as if exacting an imaginary revenge. Around her the roomful of children was asleep, fixed in plaster, doused in anaesthetic, dulled with morphine. Far away the Americans were bombing, the rumble of motors and falling rubble echoed over the farmland, reaching even the shuttered wards of the hospital. But the children had fallen asleep, leaving only the cinema fan with her photographs of film vedettes. She had rounded smoothly with her scissors the ear of Barbara Stanwyck and was detaching the head from the irrelevant image behind it.

'Les briques, monsieur, ont tués les oies, les poulets. Imaginez-vous, monsieur, une telle catastrophe.'

The glare had started up from the distant city, filtering through the blinds, and the bands of brandy-orange had settled upon her torso, the white cylinder of her leg and the flat images rucked up in the blanket. The girl with her tireless analytic scissors was hard and watchful. She told me, with some caution, that her name was Ania – pronounced Anya – that she was fifteen years old, that her mother was Polish and that she had been born in Warsaw, and that their house in Laon had been utterly demolished by the explosion . . .

'Une telle catastrophe, ma mère est devenue folle.'

Curiously, as it became darker I noticed oval bruises on her arms and a blue line encircling her throat and faintly touching a clavicle, half-concealed by the hospital shirt. Pieces of splintered wood had flown into her back and thighs, leaving a rash of tiny savage cuts. One bandage reached up to her ear from behind, indicating a tear in the shoulder blade. Our conversation turned to gangsters.

'Vous aimez les gangstairz?' she went on, lifting up from its frame of palm trees and the neon cafés of a Californian boulevard the idolized bust of Stanwyck. 'C'est superbe, cette "Itz curtainz Walkie". Mais je ne comprends rien du tout.'

'C'est fini pour toi, Rockie.'

Her eyes were wide open, wondering at the explanation.
'Mais c'est la mort, enfin?'
She fell silent and opened a *Vogue* in her lap – an old yellowing number from 1938 – leafing through the outmoded designs with quiet disinterest. The brutally transformed destiny of the gangster had begun to haunt her. Is a hood's death so flat? The evaporation of a gangster cannot be so banal . . .
It was night and the nuns had begun to comb the rows of beds. I rose to go and laid my hand over her hair-line, lifting a coat of sweat.
'Salut, Ania. La prochaine fois, je t'apporterai des magazines.'
She glanced up with the exquisite politeness of the precious Infanta Doña Margarita in Velázquez's 'Las Meniñas', who looks with oblique aloofness at her adoring parents.
'Au r'voir, monsieur. Bonne nuit.'
She could not see in the darkness, but still I could hear the sound of her scissors curving, the sculpted paper falling away and a glossy confetti drifting on to the tiled floor. The town was burning behind the lines, maybe fifty miles away, with the soft regular sound of an electric generator, dissolved in the invincible slumber induced by modern medicine. The white starched bonnets of the Holy Sisters floated past me in the dark with an odour of iodine and soap, and a candle appeared far away at the end of the ward, lighting the desk of the night-watch with its mess of bottles and virgin swabs.
My boredom was interrupted for the first time on that day and I am now resigned to this war and will wait patiently for it all to end. Meanwhile I add more kisses to the thousand you have already received and swear to rescue you one day from Bulldog Island and take you off to Esmeralda in a boat made of green leaves and Liquidambar.

Jamie

Hôpital St Lazare

Dear M.,

In the last two weeks here I have become the candyman of the East Wing (children's ward), a kind of small-footed military

Santa Claus with the whitest fingers they have seen in so long. I distribute my candies and flowers around noon, hard on the heels of lunch. I am now an effeminate pirate with my wounded eye, and a figure of fun. They have tamed me and incorporated me into the antiseptic routine of life.

Ania is still here, her leg is healing in its bizarre mode of suspension. I brought her *Vogues* and cinema reviews which she has proceeded to cut up into three categories of images: perfect beauties, strong men and elegant machines. She draws faces over the cut-outs, calls them *les Caractères* and gives them individual names (Robert la Lame, Nana la Naine, and so on). We make up stories around these collages and exchange interpretations of her faces. There is nothing left to do as – so Soeur Emmanuelle tells us – the mother has disappeared and the Holy Ones do not know why or even where she has gone. There is no one now to do up her braids and bring her sugar. She does not seem to notice, the magazines interest her more, and this mystifies the Sisters. And she is a strange child . . . I am the only adult who has gained access to her conversation (through the unconscious bribery of glamour magazines) and the only one who may see her collages. For my part, this little game is beginning to entertain me.

Apart from these self-imposed pleasure-duties I am sick of it here. They do not seem to know what to do with me. Probably they consider me 'fatigued' or shell-shocked or inoffensively traitorous. There is another Englishman here in the military – a Captain Vellors – who is my antithesis . . . fierce, dependable and assertive (and in the manner of these lions he is stony and rugged on the exterior and hysterical, vain and sadistic, with a strong sense of disintegration, on the interior). I suppose they compare us . . . he with his monocle, I with my wad of sterilized bandage – *pile et face* of a pirate race.

Kisses

Jamie

Dear M.,

As you see from my address I am firmly established here now, and while the front rolls eastward I pace the length of disinfected corridors in my superfluous soldier's greenery, saluting the medical and military personnel, inspecting store-rooms, stock-taking, distributing, supplying, arguing. I tick off instalments of penicillin and morphine, bandages and plaster-of-Paris. It's a doggy life and I am unconscious of how I perform. The doctors ask me for stories over coffee and opinions of the campaign, then proceed to haggle over supplies. *La barba*!

Yesterday a handful of bombs fell near us to the south. The children were alarmed until I appeared with my candies. Ania, however, was calm and refused my gift with exaggerated politeness.

'Je ne mange pas les chocos,' was her comment.

I had some chocolates for her (through Kessler) and an apple. I try to cover up these marks of favour from the other children and the nurses. I must include her only in a general itinerary around the beds . . . Santa Claus cannot have preferences.

She has moved her bed nearer the window, as the interior of the room depresses her. Now she can see the soldiers in the opposite wing, who wave at her and write her messages backwards on the window-panes. They address her as 'Fais-la-Boudeuse' in these telegrams, as she makes no attempt to respond. She writes nothing back, she does not smile. Our conversations, on the other hand, have developed. She calls me 'Monsieur James' and shakes hands with me with amusing formality.

It is possible that the mother does not come through lack of money and the shame of not being able to deposit her precise maternal doses of dirty sugar. I have learnt from Kessler, the Swiss doctor, that the French father was killed in 1939 in the first days of the war and as a result Ania reverted to her mother's maiden name. Before coming to France the family had been living in Poland where the Frenchman had been working. Her sister is in Paris, concealed from view as a result of some predictable disgrace. We talk about the sister who leads, as I gather, *la vie en rose*. 'Sylvia' is not traceable, but the family receives from time to time small packages with the mysterious aroma of wealth. The packages convey a quantity of luxurious items as monstrous in this age as Leporello's list of seductions. The mother was bitterly wounded by this, as you may guess, sensing behind the haul of nylons, fresh meat and black-market fuel the condescensions of a German officer. No address ever came; that would have been indiscreet, considering her new profession. The mother ceased to use her name at table, substituting it with *la pute* ('La pute nous a envoyé des bas de soie', 'la pute nous a écrit', and so on). Even if Sylvia is a whore at the blossoming age of seventeen, Ania is devotedly awe-struck. She keeps a wad of the silk stockings under her pillow and she preserves the wrappers of the chocolate, folded up with the foil and pressed into immaculate, sacred tablets with their hieratic German texts and images of walnuts and cocoa flowers. Elsewhere she has sheaves of blonde hair in a biscuit tin, sister's sequins with pieces of material still threaded through them, and small squares of silk from her most glamorous dresses. She doesn't show me all these yet, she is still shadowy about the sister because of Mama. It is an illicit worship.

Also, I have seen a photograph of Papa in his military kepi sitting on a futuristic white concrete bunker (a Maginot tomb) with a long lazy piece of grass in his mouth, as if it were a day on the river. He is compact and elfin with a delicate pedantic cleanliness and perfection of dress, and his helmet is slung prettily on a rifle barrel behind him. He is not like a 'Papa', more like a smug, squinty country cousin sharply conscious of the strange attraction of his neat shapely legs and his insect-like trimness. There is a round cheese in the grass by his side, reminding me – oddly – of a Brueghel peasant. Behind the bunker the rich, glossy elms and larches of the pre-war summer, idealized and softly intense, stretch up into a sepia sky. Poor Papa, *Papa misérable*. His life is detached and summed up in the cruel aphorism of this grubby snapshot. The simplicity of the pose is made ugly by the certain death only a few weeks ahead. He is content for nothing. The bunker will not, after all, save him – a useless, graceful bunker of talented design, like a suave pod of vanilla in the peaceful earth. I did not want to sneer in her presence, or point out with my expert fingers the obvious deficiencies of the bunker that will murder and entomb her father. She is very proud of the bunker, smooth as an egg, because he is part of it, it is part of his world in the photograph. She is incapable of believing that it will betray him.

Last night there were scattered fires on the horizon – the last paroxysm – and I lay in my room with the light off watching through taped windows the glow of the conflagration, smoking *pour faire des mirages*, lazy and contemptuous . . . I am no longer part of the great endeavour. Ania, for once, slept through it all without waking. This was the only thing that made me glad. We are near the apocalypse in Germany and everything will be wiped clean. Then you, Ania and I will take the big liner west and drink cocktails in the Marine Bar from Le Havre to New York and arrive drunk in the splendour of an American dawn, throwing confetti and dancing, as I have said, under the deck lights . . .

Jamie

Hôpital St Lazare

Chère Maria,

Berlin is burning tonight and we are sitting – the doctors of the establishment and myself – around the radio set listening to the agony. During the day soldiers poured in from the east in horrible combinations (injuries have an ingenuity all their own). Thank God I am out of it.

We are smoking together in a kind of primitive ecstasy like senatorial Guahibos – and this, in fact, could be the Rio Negro since everything is in darkness, a swamp of the Casiquiare, depopulated but rich in Carib fish. There are many speeches in the air, floating through the night, flickering through the radio like the chatter of jejune flies. The doctors know that I am a *soldat raté* and are accordingly interested in my psychology . . . I am the howler monkey the scientists have caught in the jungle and keep in their company, fed on bananas and insects, for the purposes of observation. If I were intact and wholly sane I would probably have to drink with the officers. As it is, we smoke together like a bunch of old Indians and I like it like this.

I have struck up no friendships among them with the exception of the Swiss man, Kessler. He is one of those savage middle-aged men with faces like open blades – hooks, armatory ridges and screws. He reminds me not so much of any article of machinery as of a Megasoma beetle with its giant horn. But he is the crystal mind among them, witty and unfoolable. I am attracted to his judgments – always too hard and acid, but somehow never wrong in the end. With him at least I can discuss the cosmic role of howler monkeys . . .

During my round of the East Wing this evening I noticed a letter by Ania's pillow, something from the soldiers. Now they are getting through to her in this way. I was furious when I saw it there, I wanted to forbid her, but she was asleep and I did not dare take it from her. I cannot imagine how it got there. Now I am afraid for her, someone could easily crush her: in the end, her fantasies are fragile. I will speak to the Sisters and put an end to this fooling.

Now we are in the middle of autumn the beech trees around the hospital are disintegrating in a dull anthocyanin fire, the leaves crumbling downwards in inverted flames and washed up in brittle dunes over the stones, steps and kerbs. The mornings are haunted by dark blue light, frozen and contentless, and the grass is browner, tipped with orange. I have some precious circumscribed time in which to do banal things – bark rubbings with Ania, flower pressings, insect catching, water-colours (you see that Ania can now walk in the garden). You must not be disgusted with my insular leisure because cities are burning and the men are burning in them. I have no compunction. I do not feel it in the marrow, as warriors say. Also, you must not tell Mother and Father . . . I cannot tell anyone yet that I am passing the war procuring Parisian reviews for a fifteen-year-old girl in a French hospital and taking her to make pretty pictures out of tree skins. But that will come. In any case, they might return for me and I will have to fight in the belly of the German whale . . .

As I sit here smoking I remember a day at Bamburgh chasing dragonflies with teacups and you singing:

> On the top of the Crumpetty Tree
> The Quangle Wangle sat.

It was by a pond . . . and afterwards we went to the fields for butterflies. What connection does this have, lepidoptering Maria, with the burning of Berlin?

Jamie

I resume, dear M.,

Yesterday was the day of masterpieces . . . the healthiest children and your J. repaired to the gardens and the children, like a flock of medieval apprentices, arranged themselves in a circle around the perimeter of the English Garden to draw a girl named Chantal – a complex composition of enormous sheets and long wrinkled hair, a religious subject something like Titian's 'Magdalena' with eyes uplifted in expiation . . . very funny and subversive, considering her size . . . more like the other kind of *madelaine*, a child's fairy-dusty biscuit. As you may have guessed I produced a long study of Ania wrapped in a dressing-gown under a hazel tree instead, because the shadow had caught her in a pretty way. I painted four or five girls who were sitting together in the same block of darkness (the permeable glazed darkness which is the effect of bright sun), the faces bent downward and reflecting like pale vegetables the colour of the grass and the coarse grey wool of the hospital shirts made smooth and dolphin-like by this near-winter atmosphere. I painted A., sitting in the middle of them, four or five times. She came to look at it afterwards, trailing her own sketch of a smudgy Magdalene through a bed of decaying summer fuchsias, uneasy and ill-looking, her lips softened and blurred with accidental charcoal smudges and with rolled crumbs of eraser rubber sprayed over her shirt. I pointed her out in my group picture with the handle of my brush: 'Flora, la Belle Romaine'. She saw that I had Italianized the setting of trees and bland lawns sprinkled with garlanded amphorae. She was annoyed not to see a perfect reproduction of the infant biblical whore in her massive sheets. That the florid, overcoloured *contessa* at the centre of the barely-sketched adolescents was her annoyed her even more.

'Il est laid, enfin,' she muttered (her habitual *enfin* draining my mouth of saliva). She was perplexed by the imperfect temples I had added, and the vases of studded putti. If it had been a precise cinematographic image of her own age, she would have acquiesced, allowing the flattery to caress her. But the legs were not shaded with nylons, her waist was not gathered in towards a miraculous vanishing point and her hair was not carved and persuaded into solid glittering blocks of curls. It was an insulting misunderstanding. She sensed the possible saintliness of my portrait and her mouth curled upward slowly with ferocious will. No gentleman would put his arm around that waist or trace the course of future diamonds around that neck with his finger.

'Laissez-le comme ça,' she advised, a crack in her voice.

I bowed before the futility of it, laying down the palette in the grass.

'C'est raté,' I agreed.

The children were swarming indoors, throwing back plucked flowers into the beds of black earth and the square pond with its streaked stones, casting sly glances at us and humming, as if to disguise them, tunes the soldiers had taught them:

Imini pimini
Francesca da Rimini

Despite her disappointment Ania stayed with me, sheltering herself from the others but ignoring the portrait which I was longing to cover up. She does not want to exhibit her mutilated walk to the other children . . . even in this reborn movement, timorous and clumsy, it is easy to see the craving for sexual grace. The healing leg has an awkward stiffness caused by the swellings. She tries to manipulate it with her hip, but the hip will not swing until the back of the knee can straighten out. Her face is pale with effort and her fists are always drained of blood, sharp-knuckled. The ankles are twiggish and colourless next to the poplar leaves sodden in the grass and shifting over the terraces. I told her that she looked cold (it was almost evening), that she should cover her throat, that she should wear socks in autumn.

'Vous êtes vraiment le bon papa,' she replied, grinding the stalks of charcoal in her palm into a grey moisture. She turned on her feet. 'Bonsoir, Papa.'

In the evening her disgust softened. She has not heard from Sylvia and there is chaos now in Paris: the suave mistresses with the lap-dogs of last year are being shaved on soap-boxes and probably Sylvia is there enduring an inevitable humiliation. In any case, Ania waits without showing any orthodox sign of despair. She displayed to me more than once her symbolic wad of stockings – the nylon of dreams – with hard, synthetic hope in her eyes. If anything has happened, I will have to make it known . . . I too have begun to shun the despatches.

This, of course, does not include your letters, which I always recognize by the red ink and the outsize letters sloping to the left. You must write me some lyrical descriptions of home life to warm my heart. Until next time I hold you under the arms and kiss you a hundred times.

Jamie

Hôpital St Lazare

My M.,

A letter has finally arrived from Paris for Ania: a friend of Sylvia (unnamed) who writes with a kind of numb discretion to tell her that under the auspices of one of the underground armies her sister was nearly beaten to death during some mock *auto-da-fé* at Créteil, spat on like the martyrs of '89 and tortured with broomsticks, I think she said. Ania was nastily shaken. She must have reconstructed the scene to herself countless times during the night, for I found her hysterical in the morning, tearing the sacred chocolate wrappers to pieces like a heretical Aztec smelting down the sacerdotal golden tablets of her ancestors. I stopped her and she was red-eyed and incoherent. So it is finished. The mother and sister have disappeared into nothingness and she will be alone to join the refugee roads.

The rain has come and the drawing classes are at an end. Ania has gone back to her tattered *Lifes* and *Vogues* and will not speak to anyone. The war has receded so much further, the sirens are heard only faintly at night, but everyone is awake . . . I have my photographs to look at, pinned above the metal basin: Maria in Spanish frills, Maria as Papagena, Maria on her head illustrating with her legs the shape of an astronomical constellation. My dim icons. Your aggressive haircut survives in the first picture, you are still the Samoyed Cossack, domesticated only by a lemon-ice. I see no reason not to turn over these images again and again . . . I have come to enjoy shaving over the basin, remembering the summer of 1935.

Kessler came to me yesterday towards the end of the afternoon as it was growing dark and I was sitting by the fire in the kitchen near the store-rooms. He discovered me unshaven and in shirt-sleeves, my vision disunified, drifting over the empty curd-coloured walls. I was cold in the room, my daydreaming had gently steamed the windows, hazing over the grey walls and copper trees that shimmered behind. I had made a golden tea with swirling deep green particles, nursing its heat in my palms and breathing in a steam that reminded me of Tamil Nadu and the hills of Sikkim and Darjeeling. Kessler saw my dreams immediately, asking if I had some tea to spare. He was dressed in his white apron, against which his hands seemed etiolated and fowl-like, as if belonging to a human being of the future. So he sat with me in the cold, bringing his Megasoma's head close to mine, with the brow like armatory ridges and the curved horn of nose, brutal and superior. But there was something soft in the eye, as if he wanted to tell his secret. He drew up, confidingly. I thought his life-story might be brewing, for he began with his childhood . . .

We drank our tea together using a first-aid bucket as a primitive samovar. Kessler folded his frozen hands into his apron, doubled over in an intensely brooding position and began to rock gently over the aromatic steam of the bucket as if the fumes had intoxicated him and opened up his memory. He began.

His father, he told me, had been a butcher in Zurich and the venerable doctor began his life on earth in an atmosphere of hanging meat and bloodstained refrigerators. It was a long story, this infancy, a lengthy description of indignation and revulsion. It was as if he wanted to exhibit a starting point for his career as a doctor in some pre-conscious twist of his character, a great tragic revolt dating from his childhood. As it happened, the rest of his life's story was of no interest to him and he switched suddenly to the war and his work – at the age of forty – with the Red Cross. I cannot decide whether I was bored by all this, but I was too tired to raise any resistance.

As he talked I saw the grey lines over his throat reaching down into his reptile's chest . . . the crack-marks of continual concentration. No one can notice what he does not notice – impossible to outdo the speed of his calculations, the agility of his retina. He had summed me up quickly in the first few minutes, smelling decay as his upbringing had taught him to. And then the stalking began, the crafty circles of irrelevance that would bring me unknowingly back to myself. He wheeled out the barbs of a dry doctor's necrophilic humour . . . a history of anaesthetics, a history of toe operations, a history of salvarsan – the arsenic compound, once a famous cure for syphilis – and of neo-salvarsan, or '914', its descendant. He wrote with glee the extraordinary formula on the window-pane and his breath came over me, a wave of mint and dark tea, hot and vaporous, drawing me into his laugh. He wanted me to think him an evil man, a man made clairvoyant by the butcher's trade. We smoked my cigarettes and I told him my stories of the fighting in Normandy. I smoked down three butts and was finished (I was not in the action for long), leaving him delighted. The account of my blunders gave him belly-deep pleasure. He is one of those who claw at the edge of things, feeding from the debris that falls his way. That I was a failure in the field confirms in some way his existence here.

Next topic, when the tea was hot again: the patients. He spins out eerie and abnormally detailed accounts of the children, many of whom I had never even noticed – Sophie with the 'long throat', Monique with 'the hair of a Semitic heroine of Delacroix', Annicke with her 'elongated feet'. And finally, pinned to the end of a strangely pornographic list, comes Ania, as if fished up for a crowning effect. And what does he notice? The limp, the sexually straining limp twisted into an unsuccessful fluency. And that, he finds, is the charm of it. A sweet, staggering voluptuous limp, the crack in a lovely child. He pricks me to see my behaviour. He is avid for signs of jealousy, but he discovers nothing. And when we had returned to the subject of disease and Kessler had reeled through the histories of several of them, I rose to go to Ania and save my soul. I hope sincerely that this is the last revelation of K.'s inner world that I have to endure.

You must write to me more often and send more of those infantile photographs (my walls are still too empty). I in turn will send more drawings, including one of Ania, and a view of the hospital. For anything more substantial you will, alas, have to wait.

Jamie

The hospital

Dearest M.,

As February draws on we are beginning to see the end of our

isolation at St Lazare. Far away, the Reich is collapsing inward like a circus tent. The radio describes to us the catastrophe, but before our eyes the world is springing back to life in a mass of details . . . the interlude of abstraction is dying away. Some of the children are already leaving for their villages. The soldiers are aching to get to Paris, to be expert *boulevardiers*, to be academicians, to pick up old entanglements, to find what has been lost. Ania is more dry: she hopes for nothing. She will find a brutalized, shaven-headed sister, she will disengage herself and begin again. That, she tells me, is the plan. Yet, by the effect of some inexplicable thaumaturgies she still expects to become rich, in an inevitable manner which dispenses with the necessity of hope. The broken pavements and Occupation mud will give way to gold-fields and she will only have to pick up the nuggets, as simple as harvesting cucumbers, and she will be happy evermore . . .

Meanwhile the hospital and its gardens are sunk in winter, the endless grey interior walls are in their proper element. All through the building (vast and symmetrical as a scholastic's incubus) the sour, toneless parquet and the spiteful wallpaint, faintly grey as a goose's belly, increase in darkness, mirroring each other in surfaces as vacantly reflective as celluloid. The beds of flowers, cut in the shape of half-moons, parallelograms and tidy spheres, are only dull geometries of turned earth, barren and odourless. The wood has been stripped down to a carpet of leaves the orange of carotene, into which the phantasmal forms of convalescing soldiers are permitted to wander in the afternoon, solitary bundles of green wool and faces turnip-white, a bolgia of ghosts threading through the red foliage as if enduring the floating leaf-like fire of the *Inferno*'s Third Round. I watch them occasionally from Ania's bedside, brooding like lonely duellists or vegetal eremites of a northern winter. A. draws them from her bed, transforming my vision of tortured monks into a grim carnival of exiled knights. She, of course, has names for them all and a story for each soul. Into these fresh imaginary receptacles she pours her fantasies of cruel action, simplified and emptied of accidental barbarity, as stereotyped as the marble cavalry of a Greek frieze. Her dreams must be filled with this violence, with Amazons and Rockies and Tamerlanes. But there is no trace of it in her face as I watch her sleep. Her skin is paler now, the structure of her face has changed. Her puppy-fat is ebbing away in a sudden maturation, her adolescence has been hastened on. Her system is on the brink of the next stage and she is being transformed as she lies in her bed, a restless chrysalis. The novel darkness of the night sky, the absence of fire, the silence of the air have rocked her gently into a new world. She sleeps now with the savoury odour of domestic incinerators – damp leaves and decomposing bark – contained in the long triangles of blue smoke that rise up from the wood and drift over the hospital until late at night.

I should tell you of another conversation with the Swiss doctor about Ania, a conversation of a very different nature from the first – in fact, it is hard for me to connect the two in any way. In our talk last night, Kessler was suddenly paternal, admonishing, conciliar. He was talking in this manner:

'You are not, after all, her doctor. You are not any kind of blood relation. You have, of course, no "rights" over her. You are not entitled . . . now, if you were her doctor . . . '

He lit a cigarette (we were back at the white tin samovar with its red cross), leant his spiky beetle's body backward until his eyes were struck and ignited pinefrost-blue by the bare bulb.

'If you were supervising a certified sickness, something detached from her personality, then . . . then . . . '

He formed a lancet with two hands.

' . . . then, alter Bursche, you could – friendship would be possible. But I say it again, you are in a doubtful position. You are not even (arching of surprised eyebrows) a doctor.'

Despite his dubious logic, I understood the truth of his complaint, knowing that he was unwilling to state that truth openly. I did him honour, dipping into the bucket to scoop out his tea, leaving him my silence to dance upon.

'It's not for me, Kamerad, to give you warnings . . . (and these "Bursches" and "Kamerads" are a brittle intimacy in his nasal accent), it is not for me to do so, but it is best for me to say it. You have no jurisdiction over Ania. Minors (he made this word bite) are a special case. In the eventuality of the mother or the sister returning to reclaim the child, your presence would be somewhat superfluous . . . '

I bowed, further indicating my submission, and he delivered his final admonition.

'Remove yourself a little. You forget that children also have eyes.'

However, in a certain way she seems to be dumb. She is caught between two ages and is master of neither, drawn into her own confusion. I will not entice her out. My conversation with Kessler went on and it is not worth reciting it all to you – you have some idea of his observations. No doubt he is right. Yet I cannot decide whether he is attempting to defend the hospital or himself. He is too eager, too clear-headed.

Ania sleeps now on her side, crooking her leg like a sleek compass across the metal bed, dreaming face downward into the coarse pillow, her arms hanging to the floor in the form of drooping liana. Before, her sleeping position was petrified by the plaster leg so that she was always on her back. Now she turns in her sleep and at dawn her feet are thrust out over the edge of the mattress into space, faintly blue at the tips. The rooms are colder now, they are hardly heated even in winter. The overhead bulbs reveal our breath. The administration is saving coal and electricity and so we eat, sleep and live in a satanic castle of unlit corridors and frozen rooms. The children are miserable with the cold . . . the morning ritual of kisses and candy is over. There is a kind of dull hatred in them. When snow came yesterday there was only silence to greet it. And Ania was silent with them, always positioned in an attitude of exclusion, her back sullenly curved against intruders like a cusp of a hand around a candle. And she does not move, even when the sun carves up the nereidic silky head into heraldic stripes and cubes and lozenges of shadowed hair, and the Infanta's cheek is zigzagged with light, and the sun in her ear is locked up in a golden puzzle of cartilage. She will not turn to me. Her torso is bent over her knees, the curl of a foetus.

I put down coffee and warm bread (a rare gift) by her bed, not daring to lay my hand – as I used to – over the moist hair-line, and creep away through the sleeping beds, not daring to speak . . . I remember that children also have ears . . .

But now I must break off and count syringes. I must tell you that my eye has almost completely healed and that I am wearing a ridiculous pair of hospital spectacles made of copper wire, which make me look like Herr Himmler. You will laugh when you see me.

Kisses

Jamie

L'Hôtel du Brésil

I

When all was done and the warm loaves were laid cross-wise like swords upon the table, emitting a faint steam, the cups scrubbed, polished and laid out opposite each other, a mouthful of milk foaming in a Chinese-style jug between them, and the towel-burnished knives distributed in a heraldic symmetry around the table, then I could shave myself. But even so, the pocket mirror was nailed to a beam in such a way that I could continue to watch the smoking bread and the coffee bowls with their stencilled designs of plum boughs and bamboo bridges solidify in the air of six o'clock. My aubade was the last tick of electric lights, the first motor engines and the boots of grocers on the cobbles of an empty alley. The blue and green street sign visible from our window, nailed to a wall of ochre-covered plaster, revealed the word 'Aboukir' with its memory of a blue Egyptian bay and the sound of cannon. I would lower the razor gently into its suds, twisting it clean in the purity below, and my cheeks would be eggshell suave, with a faint grain. I would commence again upon the troublesome growths around the thyroid mound, nicking, circumnavigating, while the steam rolled up into the cold air, smelling of flour and crust. I genuflected before the mirror, sketching the cross with a lathered finger . . . anointed, my jowl fleshy-clean. I would just have time to wipe bare the razor, fold and encase it, tip out a basin of grey, frothy water laced with blood, dab perfect the delicate thyroid cartilage and ignite the rings of gas jets under the coffee before she awoke and rose up into the dull ether of morning.

If I parted the door of the adjoining room, breaking open the sealed chamber, a feminine odour would steal up out of the chaos. A clock would be ticking inevitably in her slumbering closed fist, and the foot always there as I remembered it, bluish and uncovered. The room was a rough cube of white walls, two shadowed by fingerprints, a third stained by the pipes and the fourth punctured by an image of the Polish Black Virgin defined in muddy gold. The odour did not vary, and the morning was above all this regular and essential phenomenon: the odour of apple soap and the swell of nocturnal sweat beneath. She would not stir until the sun was up, the Virgin set guard above her like a black mastiff, the fruit-soap and musty diaphoresis embalming her until she was ready. Regaining the window overlooking the street, I would read the newspapers and count the pigeons on the hoods of other windows. But even here there was a permanent fragrance . . . the basin was always left full overnight with an aromatic lather trembling on dead water. Her tread left traces on the only carpet, an ovular rug depicting Aesop's fable of the Stork and the Jug. Even the bare iron taps of the bidet smelt of too-sweet apples saponified in tallow and almond oil. Soap and ash were the perfumes of our mornings, the latter derived from minute quantities of cigarette ash that made me think of the Dead Sea fruit and the poison of Sodom.

The fragrance of a commercial soap which only an adolescent would use, the plum boughs and glittering blades, the humid aura of the loaves, the gold of the icon and the yellow lunar surfaces of plaster walls were the atoms of this world. They are fixed together in my memory by the word 'Brésil', the name of that small hotel . . . a word denoting the red wood of the *Caesalpinia sappan*, the East Indian tree, and then the great triangle of tropical rivers and forests, the wild country which I have never seen.

From the street the vestibule seemed endless, like the corridor of a penitentiary. The establishment had stated its claim in the jungle of hotel insignia in dripping handmade letters in the style of Guimard. Blood-red and dangerous, the words 'Hôtel du Brésil' marred, like the signature of murderers, the rue d'Aboukir.

Ania was curiously attached to the leaning windows of this street, filled with cacti and geraniums, and the disengaged pipes hooped to shadows of rust. The street was a food market, the canopies of the shops were bossed with the heads of snails, swine and horses rimmed with gaslit silhouettes, so that at night they were like Egyptian gods blazing over their own flesh. She worshipped it all. She would run in from the street glorifying the essence of cabbages and holding like a courtier an Algerian orange to her nose. She did not flinch before the grandeur of the Brésil. The stench rising from the drain before the front entrance did not provoke hesitation. She picked herself lightly over this old-style ditch, over its curse of dismembered rinds and ground cigarette butts, barely touching the insignificant rectangle of swept space before the threshold, and plunged into the corridor, which even I was nervous in, with no sign of the sudden infantile fear that used to overtake me there.

But sometimes I would watch her more closely and then I could see clearly that she would pause in mid-step, so quickly that sometimes I almost missed it, at the moment before entering, and look with the speed of a lizard over her shoulder, back across her path, over the crowded stalls and the streets full of possible pursuits. It was not that she was being followed. It was a moral reflex: she paid tribute in this way, every time she entered the hotel, to the illegality of our cohabitation. It was a nod of guilt before recommencing. Perhaps the gaslit horses of the *chevaline* reminded her of watchful divinities. I noticed this habit grow over a period of three months. Her head would flick leftward over her shoulder and she would shrug slightly in the same movement as if stooping under a blow. But when she had climbed the four warping flights of stairs, pushed open the door with the point of her foot and was before me, carefully arranged with her oranges and bare arms and the yellow fuzz of curls flattened with sweat around her ears, then it was impossible to remember the confession of guilt, the flick of the head and the primeval stoop of the shoulders. She was normal Ania, who had just begun to smoke and who dominated the centre of the room as if her graceful exhalations would confirm her physical superiority (when she smoked she would put her weight on one leg, making the small hip bulge, and turn her face upward to receive a flattering blow of light).

When the bread was laid thus cross-wise between us it was a sure moment of peace. So I waited for it gratefully. My cheek was then ready for her finger and the dry, scaled lips. It had to be perfect before she would consent: the loaves must steam, the cups must be polished white as sharks' teeth, the blades and metal hilts must mirror her, the ivory handles must conduct the warmth of her hand, the butter (artful curled butterflies in a bowl) must melt on the bread, the conserve must have seeds, the coffee must have naked grains dispersed by drops of cold water, the linen must crackle under her arms, the sunlight must not slant too heavily across her throat or interrupt the serenity of her vision. She would sit quietly, illumined with the greatest possible generality, and incline slightly over her breakfast . . . she tested the coffee and spread the grains along her lower lip with an invisible precision.

She had to know that I had made it well, and only then would she begin to talk to me and nibble her pastries.

Before her rising, then, I would sit with the global information and the smudged photographs of dreary data spread out over my knees and listen to her breathing in the room with the gold icon, the vibration of a flap of cartilage somewhere in her nose or throat. The odour would seep out, the bed would strain under gentle convulsions. If I wiped the steam from the glass of the window I could see, convulsed in the same sleepy agony, fat and fawning Verron the grocer, opposite, dragging out his sodden, splintering crates of cauliflowers and carrots fringed with earth, stabbing his potatoes with price tags and hurling bright balls of spittle fragrant with tobacco into the drains. We would nod to each other. Seeing the window above the shop, I would think of Madame Verron coiled in mammalian splendour under a gold Virgin, respiring softly like a dolphin under a froth of quilting. We would nod, early-birders. Verron would hook up his lip and form a soundless greeting with a sad simultaneous wink. He would motion with his finger, the little finger of the left hand extended upward with comradely complicity: 'She's there.' His eyes would roll. They were beaten to a pulp, doggy and Latin-brown, in sloping orbits, smoothly liquid as the oil of nuts and marbled with gentle amber. He reminded me of the boy prostitutes I used to pass every night on the rue Houdon, who tagged on to my arm for a second, arching their spines, tipping forward the head in a lush greeting, and then were gone at the sign of a single maledictory word . . . his greeting was the same damp secrecy and dazzling momentary intimacy wired up to the same crafty eye. He waved, splaying his hands before turning away, and shrugged with philosophic charm . . . 'des haricots, la vie'.

As he turned the clock would begin to ring in her half-sleeping hand. My reverie would be overturned, I would be seized by a slight panic: perhaps the table was not perfect, perhaps the blades of the knives were misted with finger-prints or my thumbs, stained with newspaper ink, had left sordid oval traces along the brims of the china bowls. Something would anger her, she would not consent. It often happened that she would become angry and sweep out into the bars. At night it was glorious, this out-going, she was like a ship with its wake of phosphorescent sparks when the water is tropic, leaving the insolent fire of her cigarettes in the air. But in the morning it was wrathful and brusque, the passage out was a sullen movement of sleepy perspiration and stale flesh. I would then find her alone in the Oasis, knocked up with the bubbling, milky cocktails she adored, 'grasshoppers' with mint and cocoa or bland Kahlúas whisked with cream. They liked to serve her . . . sometimes her lips smelt of something harder and I would have to pull her away, her nails hooked into my arm and my ear bleeding. Then she would swear to kill me during the night. But softly, under her breath, so that I would not hear.

2

By the time she had risen it would sometimes be nine o'clock. Already three hours would have been wasted. I would commence my breakfast again and take care to relish – it was the normal compensation – the resistant cluster of curls like bunches of grapes that swung down to the level of her collar-bone. I would watch, with routine pleasure, her fingers curl around the Chinese jug to lift it over the coffee, the weary partition of her section of the loaf, the timid sips, the methodical collection of fragments of crust that had fallen on to her dressing-gown. But even this nervous domesticity took months to achieve. It was not easy. At first I was tender with her. In our first room I brought smouldering almond croissants to her bed every morning enfolded in transparent tissues. I would tear off the wings and immerse them in coffee (she liked them damp and semi-bitter), feeding her as they feed baby whales. Or else it was *madelaines, coeurs de pamiers, chaussons aux pommes* and miniature *tartes tatins* which crumbled over her chin and broke into a buttery dust that stuck to the grease on her lips. Later in the day I would encounter these flakes at the back of her mouth and the taste of butter on her fingers. They made her lips sweet and rancid and even at night her mouth made me think of a baker's oven. I laid winter irises by her coffee. Even at the hospital I had found blue anemones, chicory and cornflowers. I was a serious romantic with blue flowers, absolving a centaur's guilt.

This peaceful and humble breakfast ritual began in our first room in the rue Cécile. The room itself was an abomination, combining the profane and the divine by its proximity to the shabby Gothic church of Ste Cécile, adorned with living gargoyles of tramps slumbering on its ledges, and the fruit-like cupola of the Comptoir National d'Escompte de Paris, which cast a beam of shining pride – in the form of a golden pineapple – into the depth of our darkness. Here there was a balcony where Ania could display her elbows to the street and where she could lean from our haughty tower and shake out her hair as if she had risen from bed behind Japanese screens, in the perfume of laziness, in a private order of faithful cats and whispering maids. Behind her would lie newspapers filled with crumbs, and a purple lampshade over the bed would make visible, with a dry light, the detritus of a full moon's pleasure. The walls were lime-coloured lawns of imitation velvet and the cheap metal of the fixtures – door handles, light switches, towel rails – was cold under the fingers. The plastic tiles, like a vast photographic jigsaw of a parquet floor, were cracked and curled up savagely at the corners. The first night we slept there, I saw her mouth quiver at the sight of the flames of mould flowing downward from the painfully visible complex of pipes. Her eyes sought out the source of each river of corruption. Her gaze dilated with disbelief: my promises had been a lie.

Yet it is impossible to overcome with disdain the importance of these temporary habitations. I had no nostalgia for my father's English house, dull-red as the blood on a butcher's counter, spreading endless banal roots into his soil as if afraid of the speed of the earth's rotation, heavy as a bull's flanks and still with chill nobility. The hotel room has no history, it is destructible, assembled from scraps and pieces of string. It has no reality in terms of memory and custom, which is why I embraced it. From our balcony I looked down with detached contempt at the yellow crockets and spire-lights of Ste Cécile, clustered together to preserve a vagrant power. And from the Brésil I felt myself raised above the fundamental alimentary commerce and the congestion of voices. In every room it has been the same . . . in the rue Thimonnier, in the rue Greneta, in the rue Marie-Stuart, the rue Riboutté, the rue de la Tour d'Auvergne, in the avenue Trudaine . . . shifting stage-prop bedrooms. The greased pipes and shabby photographic illusions of the Hôtel du Brésil summarized a domain of which we were the children. I saw my chains holding me to this world, spun out of warm sheets, crumbs of sweet pastry and the loaves laid with exquisite solemnity cross-wise like swords upon the tables . . .

3

During my first eight weeks in Paris after the war I lived with the Abbé Davergne, a friend of my father's, in the rue de Rochechouart. My father allowed me a small flow of cash: a lump sum was determined in advance and thereupon delivered in four initial instalments. I had written to him explaining the nature of my situation and my future plans, indicating the desire 'to study'. The money arrived in large finger-soiled envelopes bearing a typewritten address but containing no personal greeting or instructions. It was a sign that a period of my existence had just come to a conclusion.

At the end of the war I had been posted to Austria, and had lost contact with the Hôpital St Lazare and its inmates. But by the end of my first month in Paris I had located, through the charity organization of Davergne's church, Ania's mother, Maria Januszewska. She was living in the streets near St Denis, a member of the refugee army. I waited for her at the church's soup-kitchen, erected every day at dawn on the pavements, but when she appeared on the third morning she was unrecognizable as the discreet and enigmatic sugar-donor of the Hôpital St Lazare . . . unrecognizable until a priest presented me to her and her face turned up and I saw a shadow of the genetic ancestry I had memorized in Ania's form. But she did not remember me or the hospital. We sat in the small square, whispering together among the birds . . . she was planning her return to Poland, a plan that had become a desire with the intensity of an opium dream. She had begged the authorities for money, she had begged her daughter Sylvia, who had disappeared once more. She gave me Sylvia's old address near les Gobelins. She told me the apartment had been ransacked and partly burned, that Sylvia had come herself to ask for money, her head shaven and scarred, with missing teeth, but still – said the yellow-eyed mother – 'like a whore'. The encounters between the members of this family had now acquired the ferocity of those between rival animals in a prehistoric cave. The mother foamed (silently with inbred control) when she discussed her offspring. Of Ania she knew almost nothing. She had gone back to Laon in order to take her away. Ania had not been there, she had been discharged . . . She, the mother, was herself sleeping in the squares, it was not her duty, she said, it was not 'in her power'. She had even searched for her husband because – she touched my arm as if touching a sensitive nerve – 'that was the first duty'. Her Frenchman with his kepi, indolent helmet and sly yokel face. She had found out – again a proud tap against my limb of English wool – the name of the cemetery, or at least the village nearest to it. She pronounced the name softly, with great difficulty – linguistic and emotional – drawing it out like a self-contained prayer: St Quentin.

The apartment in the rue des Tanneries where Sylvia had lived with her German lover was boarded up from the outside and a note was scrawled over the wood in red chalk: 'Maurice, je t'attends chez Sylvie, Simone.' The apartments were ranged around a narrow spiralling staircase. There was no smell, no sound. I rang the bells around me. The apartments were empty and there was no concierge. On the jambs of the ground-floor entrance dozens of messages were scribbled in chalk and the charcoal of fragments of incinerated wood. I had not seen them on my way up and Sylvia had left her address there, enclosed – by some aggressive irony – in a cupid's heart. She had moved to a diagonally opposite corner of the city, a small street near the place de Rome. When I arrived she was not there, and I saw through the dusty and fractured windows an empty room unrelieved by light or colour. I returned later in the evening and the room was still empty. I wrote a short letter to Sylvia and left it under the door. In it I explained the disappearance of her sister and my desire to find her. I wrote down a short account of my career in the war, to tell her who I was. When I called two days later the concierge was waiting on the street holding my letter, which she returned with elaborate condolences. Monsieur was assured that the blonde lady of foreign name was not there, had indeed moved on, would surely not come back to her house, had left, certainly, an address, but was not definitely to be expected to, was not – he was assured – to be found in that *quartier*, was not . . .

I posted the letter to Sylvia, being convinced that she did not want to be seen. She wrote back after a week, a brief precise letter in English which I remember by heart:

Dear Mr Lovecraft,

I received your letter yesterday and am so sorry you have been troubled. It is best to ask the hospital again for Aniuszka or Mama, who you have seen. You must ask the hospital for her and give her my kiss. I will be most recognizing to you.

Sylvia Januszewska

The letter was written on cardboard and the pen had punctured the surface many times, lending pathetic stress to certain words. I imagined Otto, her lover (her mother had told me of him), with cropped hair and dressed in a greatcoat, writing it out for her in his battlefield English. By now the address would have changed again and they would be in another suburb or huddled in a freight train bound for his native Bavarian village. I did not reply to thank her for her familial emotion. She would come back, when her face had healed and her hair was thick and golden once more, and her plump baby had copper curls and laughed ga-ga on her knee and she had become a fat handsome wife, once more pulling a trail of desire after her, a radiant wake of lust, and they had forgotten her political crimes.

And now Ania had vanished. The city had at first presented itself to me as the raw material from which I was to piece together her identity, its chaos being only the scattered parts which could be put together or pushed aside to reveal her. But the puzzle fell apart, the configurations of addresses, street plans, telephone numbers, parks, cafés and streets remained as they were, the arbitrary secretions of the city's history, containing no mark of her presence. In desperation I stayed with Davergne until November, trying unsuccessfully to apply myself to his library, and then returned to my familiar, effervescent habitat: the hotel. This time it was the Hôtel de l'Océan in the rue Mayran, with a big bright *bar américain* and a view of the square at the end of the street with its ash trees and flowering chestnuts.

It is strange, when I think of it now, that she was sent to me. Even when I know, as I do, who was behind it, it strikes me as unnatural. I failed and Kessler succeeded. A week after Christmas she came herself to the door of my hotel room with a note in one hand written by the good doctor. This letter I also remember well:

Hôpital St Lazare

December 19

Dear Lovecraft,

Allow me to tell you everything, if you will forgive this abrupt intervention . . . I realize the pains you have put yourself to.

Ania Maria, as I told you, went to Paris last summer. This I assure you. We omitted to ask her for the addresses . . . there are many children and we forget these details. We assumed that she would live with her family. You could not find her with these persons – it is regrettable – and have wasted some weeks of your time. Now, she appeared here on the morning of the eleventh of this month, in a terrible condition, and will say nothing of her movements between last summer and the present time. She had bruises around her face, small cuts and abrasions on her thighs, her left ear was badly torn and bleeding profusely on her arrival. She said she had been on the train from Paris during the night. I asked her about the cuts, of course, the injury to the ear being savage and ugly. But even after convalescence she would not talk. She carried with her a small military canvas knapsack containing a rolled-up winter coat and an old doll which the nurses had noticed the year before. She had no money with her . . . her mind seemed to be falling apart with cold, hunger and the pain from her ear.

That, my dear Lovecraft, is the whole story. We cannot keep her here, you understand – you must find something for her. It would be useless for me to give suggestions. If there are any complications, you should write to me immediately.

When I visit Paris I will not fail to call on you. In the meantime I trust things will go well with yourself and Ania and send you greetings for Christmas and the New Year.

Yours etc.

Wolfgang Kessler

The letter had a strange effect on both of us (I saw, by nearly invisible signs, that she had opened and tried to read it), due to the unexpected phrase 'yourself and Ania' with which it concluded. She did not enter the room while I read, leaning back against the frame of the door and noting in her mind its upholstery and accessories. She waited for the phrase to strike. Kessler had done this with great delight, with proleptic malicious pleasure. The thought passed – while folding with officious secrecy the rain-spattered letter – that he had arranged a fate for both of us, that he had held us apart and tied us together at a precise time with relaxed and unassertive authority.

She had materialized from a magic box, the contraption through which guinea-pigs appear and disappear with inexplicable graceful cunning, traversing simultaneously the media of time and space. She had again descended to the state described in Kessler's letter . . . there was a gap of several days separating her arrival and the date at the head of the letter . . . her hands were scaled with small fresh scars, the new coat donated by the hospital was already frayed, maculate with grease and worn with a sense of dark, arrogant experience. Her masculine shoes – outsize tap-dancer's instruments – were in a state of tragic incoherence. I motioned her into the room, closing the door behind her. Because of my amazement I could not separate the details of the image she presented and saw only a dark hollow inhabited by the bluish punished flesh, the vestige of an ancient limp and the contentless gaze which she projected, unaware of its power. But my attention was not needed. She strode to the bed and laid herself out with the symmetrical formality of a mummy and fell asleep for two days and a night.

When she awoke, I had her coffee ready and a small phial of perfume laid in the saucer, wrapped in cotton wool and a membrane of paper the colour of the flowers of Levant Cotton.

4

During the winter I had no exact idea of what to do with my adopted child. The mother succeeded in returning to Poland after having – I am sure – laid a pauper's wreath on the little white cross that was her husband. Sylvia vanished into the fog of Northern Europe. Ania Januszewska was left alone with me, and I could not resist keeping her once the bond was formed.

After two months at the Hôtel de l'Océan I was obliged to move down to the Hôtel Montholon-Lafayette in the rue Riboutté, and from there a little further 'down' to the Hôtel de Bâle in the rue Papillon, with a tortured façade of crooked windows. My father, seeing no attempt on his son's part to falsify or conceal his *dolce far niente*, informed me in an unusual handwritten communication of his decision to cancel the financial agreement we had made and to send me one more instalment, after which – he scrawled with livid irony – he would await 'further proposals' on my part.

Meanwhile I found a room for Ania in a church dormitory in Aubervilliers, a pure white cubicle so bare it seemed an imitation of divine light, and filled it with presents – mirrors, carpets, toiletries, *abats-jours* and coverlets. I sent her the smaller articles wrapped in the same paper coloured like cotton flowers so that the stupidity of signatures and written formulae would be unnecessary . . . a material message would be better, heavy with luxury as an icon. There would be no indirect spiritual terms between us, there would be a brutal and immediate contact through the invisible medium of money. I acted by instinct, I was not trying to 'buy' her . . . there was no transaction. I had only perverted money from its natural vocation and constructed a means into her imagination.

But at first she made many mistakes. At the end of the first two weeks of gift-making she came to the Hôtel de l'Océan in a fury, having, for the first time in her life, ordered a taxi to take her through the city, and having dressed in a deadly manner for confrontation. She had used her table of new cosmetics. She had bought a black suit with the money I had given her, had searched out a little brittle false jewellery and even a cigarette holder made of brown, cracked ivory. Her colour was calculated with painfully naive consistency, the garb of psychological war – not a single spontaneous button. It was laughable: black, the colour of death, of judgment and condemnation. She slipped past me as I opened the door and strode over to the window, one hand supporting with affected habitude the elbow of the smoking arm. I noticed from behind the used thinness of the short jacket, her tight yellow chignon twisted around a wooden pin, and the elevated leather heels with their brash reflections.

'You', she said in French, 'are quite wrong about me. I want to make this clear immediately. You are quite wrong. You cannot buy me with these things (she plucked her skirt outwards with rhetorical contempt). Yesterday you sent me three parcels at different times, one by private taxi . . . quite unnecessary things . . . a watch, handkerchiefs, hats, scarves . . . and I am pleased to have them, and grateful, but in two weeks I have become uncertain and I am afraid. You cannot buy me, I mean, I will not be "maintained". I like these things, we understand that, but I am saying this to make the situation clear.'

She strode in an elliptical circle around the room, leaving a wash of tobacco odour. Her fury had emptied itself in the first words and a gentle confusion descended over us.

'I am not sure', she said more softly, 'if you understand me. I can't remember who you are . . . I remember you from the hospital and your chocolates and magazines that you got from Paris. You are a friend of my mother's, I think you said, you know my sister, you are an old friend, an old friend of the family . . . '

I lay on the bed, in the centre of her meditative revolution. The black shoes fascinated me with their sleek brilliance and creaking novelty. They forced her to walk with excruciating elegance.

'You have been very kind, very nice, monsieur Lovecraft, you have saved me for the moment. No, it is true (I had smiled sly self-derision) . . . it is true. And seeing you are an old friend of the family, it is terrible for me to accuse you, I am grateful, on the contrary, I realize . . . '

Her confusion melted into embarrassment. The time was ripe to touch her shoulders and regulate her pulse, question, reassure, take her hand and contrive compliments. But instead I had to laugh.

'It is true,' she shouted, 'I become confused in French, but you understand, I am not joking with you. I came to tell you you cannot buy me. Enough. Now I'm going home.'

The next night I took her to an old wartime cabaret called La Lune Rousse which had once been a favourite with the Germans . . . she told me with pleasure that her sister had probably been there. She insisted on parading a necklace of false onyx and an imitation pigeon's blood ruby on her right hand. Both went unnoticed in the darkness, and likewise her red lips and eyelids coloured like opium poppies met a thankful oblivion in the dim interior. She wore the same second-hand suit (she had saved money to send to her mother) as if to heal the small scar of the previous day. But the cigarette holder did not reappear and the pose with the smoking arm dissolved into infantile excited gesticulation. Only the tone of her flesh, raised to the level of artefact by a cloak of powder, possessed a natural authority.

To buy her trivial doses of alcohol seemed inexplicably significant to me at that moment: I was aware of her innocence, I tried out different substances and mixtures on her, enjoying her dependence. There was a total whiteness, an ingenuous emptiness to fill.

'This is?' She would pick up a cocktail and shake up the colours. 'Is this another whisky?'

'No, this is a Vermouth Achampanado . . . ' I repeated 'Ach-amp-an-ado' and she laughed. 'It is lime, seltzer water, sugar, cracked ice and French vermouth.'

The words flowed over her and into emptiness, but the sounds, and their association with the pale tints in the tall glasses, made her smile.

'They drink it in South America,' I added and her eyes inflated.

'In Brazil?'

And when a showy jeroboam of champagne arrived she touched the pewter foil over the neck as if it were real gold, a mark of the liquid's rare value. She tasted, tipping the strange glass with horrible affectation, and was visibly sickened by the fizzling sweetness, whispering, 'It's ambrosia.'

As the intoxication worked itself into her I became more aware of the significance of this experiment: she had permitted me to take possession of her . . . vicariously, through the chemical spirit of alcohol. The array of cocktail names and the fabulous titles of wines – I made her pronounce Pichon-Longueville-Comtesse de Lalande, Leoville le Clos du Marquis, Egri Bikavier, Tokaij Essencia, Schloss Bockelheim Kreuzbach and the beautiful names of sherries: Manzanilla, Amontillado, Amoroso – had become fragments of her world-to-come, a narcotic shimmer. She held them in reserve at the back of her mouth, making them dissolve blissfully again and again.

'De-za-ley,' she murmured to herself, when the shrill suppressed laughter began to gain a hold over her, 'De-za-ley from Switzer-land.'

When I moved from the Hôtel de l'Océan to the Hôtel Montholon-Lafayette I did not tell her immediately. Meanwhile I wrote a series of pathetic-filial letters to my father. It is a scene as old as prostitution. I composed a portrait of prodigal remorse accompanied by reformulated intentions of heart-breaking complexity and irrefutable detail. He warmed and demanded more letters. I wrote them without scruple. In the last week of February, the money came with a letter of partial forgiveness.

I had moved to the Hôtel de Bâle by the time the cheques came, and had made a needless economy. But as the schemes by which I had earned my money were fabrications, and the handsome umbilical cheques were certainly the last of their kind, I tried to save money and build up the fantasy that was the condition of Ania's consent. The first enchantment, I knew, had eaten into her heart.

I took her to other clubs at this time, the Lapin Agile, another Occupation haunt, the Casquette Noire, and even to the pompous and unenjoyable Lido on the Champs-Élysées, where Ania – assuming the gestures of discrimination – squealed and pointed in imitation of my irony.

She often ate a particular large ice-cream, a 'mandarin mountain', and the ground almonds stuck to her rouge as she sucked on a long spoon, coquette, the men admiring the paper flowers in her hair and her false stones, heliodor and aquamarine, her odour of lemon rinds and lavender. With the 'mandarin mountain' she drank peppermint milkshakes and fizzling water. She found scraps of watered silk to wear, an old dash of bitter glass diamonds, turquoise drops for her ears and lazulite rings. Someone stopped her by the cloakrooms to tell her that, like Scheherazade, her skin was 'yellow as oranges'. She ate the remains of the 'mandarin mountain' with her fingers and her eyes went dark with pleasure, the men admiring, and she scooped off the residual drops with her tongue.

The men looked on as we attempted to dance, the air around us peppered with tobacco, a light folded into a powdery glittering cloud blue as water, she in and out, white and blue as the metal of horns, a gentle-soft ignorant step, mouthing with the band:

> Embrace me, my sweet embraceable you
> My sweet embraceable you
>   embraceable you.

5

The room in the Hôtel de Cécile – our first shared domicile, a thalamus worthy of a bridal song – measured eighteen feet by twenty, an approximate cube, was relieved by a single french window opening on to a fanciful iron balcony and was unbearably cold in the early spring, smelling of flaking wood and turpentine. Here I undid her chignon with trembling fingers; undid her oily laces, her too-tight nacreous buttons, counting to her grandfather-wise *un-deux-trois*, from throat to navel; undid her dainty cuffs, the sliding locks of chains, the bows of ribbons, the secret clasps, until I had shed them around her. The 'parquet' curled underfoot. Her lip quivered with indignation. We heard, in the dark, the clandestine ripple of bathwater in the pipes, the nocturnal respiration of tramps, a hundredfold breathing through paper walls. Her nerves did not shiver with suffering under these blows, her eye was open and undisturbed and the cold grease of the floor did not make her lift her feet with uncomfortable surprise. The naked lamps in the street only slightly below the level of our balcony uncovered the cup of her abdomen, the hairless cylinder of one thigh and a knot of divided fingers over her breasts. I collected her jewellery with little jokes, scraping off a handful of weightless 'gold', glassy gems and Christmas-tree trinkets. Her body resisted this denudation though it did not move or betray, in any microscopic tremble, the fury that might have been growing . . . only the divided fingers shifted like a cuirass into place around her breasts.

6

We were driving, I recall, in the month of May along the winding, rolling road, the road that dips through glades and clusters of grey farm buildings to Senlis, whose spires and tower we could make out across the fields. We drove slowly, appreciating the blissful vertigo of the rustic bends, and she fell against my shoulder by a trick of gravity, her hand reached out and sought my thigh. Giant trees hung over the road – oak, elm, mulberry – and we sailed in their intervals of shadow. The great hunting forest of Chantilly, the lush geometries of Oise pasture, beds of milk and cheese. She sang on my shoulder, unobservant in a lullaby humour. The road was all green and dairy-gold. Over the tower a cloud moved in the shape of a conchoidal obsidian blade, blue and green in the heat of a summer atmosphere. I remember the grey mass of the tower tinted with lichen, its complex of crockets, carved gutters and sudden points like an opened multi-purpose knife. She sang, in the middle of our sailing motion:

> Avec la garde montante,
> Nous arrivons, nous voilà

and the confusion of the sun and shadow ran swiftly over her body like a silent film projected on to a sphere from which it perpetually slides off in disarray . . .

The events that led up to this excursion I also remember with exceptional clarity as I have dissolved and synthesized them an almost infinite number of times.

Dr Kessler arrived in Paris as he had promised at the end of April, having secured a position at a Parisian hospital. He moved in with a cousin near St Georges and sent me this odd invitation at the beginning of May:

My dearest Lovecraft,

Now that we are here together – in changed circumstances – I absolutely insist that you come with me to Senlis cathedral on Sunday in the absolutely spanking car (sic) I have just bought through Albert. We will make a *fête sur l'herbe* with salmon and a crate of wine just for ourselves, we will see the buildings and the parks, we shall go to the race-course on the way and have some splendid fun. I suggest that you ask also little Ania to come for a ride, she will be most happy (you must buy her a real summer hat). I will pick you up from your hotel at 9 a.m., if you agree? I look forward to seeing both of you at that time.

Yours affectionately
Wolfgang Kessler

He arrived in grey flannels, an antique driving-cap reminiscent of the earliest stage of the Motor Age, an expensive fresh-white cigarette slung from his lip with ugly suavity and his collar as pure as a rim of infant's fat. I bent through the window to grasp his hand and he shot up his smile – whetted on a grindstone – from the delicately shadowed interior of red leather and reflective mahogany. His elegance was warm, but hardened by a scientific flame and his streak of objective cruelty. His eye flashed over the façade of the hotel, providing material for a dry, innocent smile, perceiving the quaint touches of incipient poverty and our position in the world that they signified. He was effusive and gentle with me, touched the brim of Ania's new hat with an avuncular finger and thumb, and complimented us both on a variety of things as if we were his own well-turned-out offspring.

'Now we can take a spin with Uncle,' was his remark. 'This is a sort of treat, you understand.'

The Château d'Eau and the town of Chantilly are built on the river Nonette, which fills the system of stagnant canals that surround the château and lend it its fairyish name. The massive reconstruction of Condé's property rises over a lacework of dull aquatic reflections, the green segments of an obligatory *jardin anglais* and the quiet yellow façades of the town houses. We left our car in the rue de Connetable and went to stroll along the route de l'Aigle that traverses the park towards the château. It was hot and Ania and I fell behind Kessler's exact, over-energetic pace. His white shirt loomed before us, too full over narrow shoulders, the cuffs still tied to his wrists, an empty rhomboid of light. Ania turned her eyes away from him, fascinated instead by the giant stands of the race-course – regular and self-contained as magnified formations of crystals – by the comb of coloured flags and the sweeping curve of the barriers. But I could not remove my point of focus from the rhomboidal space, the shifting piece of cotton stretched between the blades of his shoulders, the black hair-line and the inch of pale flesh beneath. The peculiar language of his invitation came back to me in the wake of his silent feline step: 'spanking', 'splendid fun', 'dearest', 'fête sur l'herbe' . . . they did not cohere with this panther stride, the ripple of stale muscle. For a moment the memory of the words made me afraid of him. Behind the almost natural language and the correctness of the fabrics he wore – cotton, flannel, silk – the reserved Kessler-soul telescoped itself into abstractions, a rhomboid of light, a hexagon of shadow, a parallepiped of colour. The sunlight fell over his neck, touched from behind luminous coral ears, illuminated the soft luxurious materials. But I was afraid, I could not believe in him, his abstractedness made me nauseous. It was already an old suffering: fear of manipulation, ambition, the other's power. The glowing pieces of cartilage on either side of his head made me laugh, it is true, they were sure butcher's ears. But the gaunt and twisted body had a terrible hardness as it caught the light between the trees and parallels of grass; it was an instrument of incision and penetration, a repository of illimitable knowledge.

Finally he stopped and faced us in the glare, his eyes wincing in their sweat. He smiled broadly.

'You two are perfect there, beautiful. I wish I had brought my camera.'

We stopped also, frozen in his gaze. Ania avoided his eye, continuing to measure the shapes and light-effects of the race-course.

'Pretty flags,' he said, smiling in a thrill of irony that made him sway very slightly from side to side. I did not understand and turned to look at the flags. 'I wish I had brought my camera, old things,' he repeated.

Ania was now hatless. She turned to him and cupped her hand over her blinded eyes. A fresh sweat moved slowly over the wings of her nose.

'Must we see the castle?' she complained to me. I asked if she was too hot. She shrugged, still shading her eyes.

'The collection, the gardens . . . ' I muttered.

Kessler had turned and resumed his ruthless progress towards the carrefour des Lions, re-creating the white rhomboid. Ania watched it diminish.

'We could wait,' she whispered.

We could wait, but I had missed the meaning of the little scene. I persuaded her to move on.

'The interior, silly child, is wonderfully interesting and beautiful. Then we can see the canal, the Grand Canal behind the garden which is an extraordinary feat, as in Venice . . . '

When we arrived Kessler was already enlisting a guide and pushing banknotes into his pockets. He was master of the proceedings and we saw, as we were meant to, the crisp colour of his money.

In the car afterwards we were tired. Kessler drove us towards Senlis with the exuberance of a sarcastic and superior chauffeur, calling us 'his polemarchs', explaining with mock-servility the lunch he had prepared for us and bowing to us in the rear mirror. Ania laughed at times in delirium, rocking back against the red leather and gurgling in her throat under the powerful eye of the chauffeur. The mulberry trees left the outline of their leaves over her cotton dress with its folds of blue printed spots and puritanical white collar and cuffs. Her throat travelled in and out of their tracery, green, gold, green, gold.

Senlis was quiet and we could sit by the ramparts on the south side near the rue de Meaux and once more near to the Nonette. The chauffeur preceded us with obsequious charm: a white sheet under us, a parasol over us, the sheet smelling of steam and hygiene and the parasol admitting a rubescent shadow. He had bought some earthenware pots of *rillettes* and pâtés in jelly, the advertised salmon, toast wrapped in napkins and miniature jars of bitter cream, a covered dish of crudités, chicken pieces cooked in tarragon and two bottles of sweet wine in an ice-bucket. He, the genie, sat between us cross-legged dispensing his manna. His silk tie lay across his knees, a twist of emerald, and his plain brogues upturned, discarded in the sunlight. He reminded me of one of the female Hindu gods, elastic, fluent, sly. His arms reached all corners of our enchanted square. It was his obvious right to touch Ania's arms with the back of his hand, testing their texture, gleefully to discipline wandering strands of hair, to wipe off foaming clots of cream from her lips, fragments of pink fish and black toast crumbs. His hand was unsentimental and direct in these movements, but I could see an unsurgical pleasure in their agility. He was mincing and effete with her at the same time, as if every attention he paid her had to be noticed immediately. But Ania did not seem to be aware of him, never responding to his fingers. She pretended to fall asleep under the parasol and Kessler reclined in resignation, remaining motionless on one arm like an Etruscan on his way to the Underworld.

We walked into the town when it was cooler, unable to take much interest in its empty picturesque streets, its grey stone walls, the irregular undulations of cobbled surfaces and the cathedral, too big for its square, neglected and inadvertently romantic. Ania was still mouthing the same tune:

> Sonne trompette éclatante
> Ta ra ta ta ta
> Ra ta ta . . .

its martial energy lost in the droning heat and the slowly-gaining rhythm of boredom. I told her to sing something else, crossing to the other side of the street with rhetorical irritation. She was surprised.

'I sing for myself,' she shouted to me across the street, in an unwitting paraphrase of Carmen. 'Scowl as you like. Eh, Aubergine . . . ' (my nickname now, pertaining to the shape of my head) ' . . . ça t'embête? I sing.'

Kessler dropped behind to watch, much amused.

She shouted, 'In Italian, Aubergine . . .'

> Imini pimini
> Francesca da Rimini.

It was too hot to move. I was only amazed that she had used the nickname – originally tender and private – in front of Kessler. He had seen that it was possible for her to ascribe new essences to me: vegetable, mineral, animal, it did not matter. I could be abused, she was the loved one.

We went back, suffocating and furious. The prettiness of Senlis was almost disgusting. We decided that driving was more fun and exchanged ideas for destinations . . . the monastery at Jumièges, Compiègne, the valley of the saints at Fontenelle, Villers Cotterets and even Amiens. Ania objected to religious buildings and so we drove towards Compiègne, drinking the remains of the wine in silence and falling into cool amnesia in the flowing heat of the air through the open windows. As I half-slept I kept my eyes on the pale shaved nape of our chauffeur. I could see a familiar nerve vibrating at the junction of his jaw and neck with the flapping motion of a frog's gullet. Long ago, over a samovar of wartime tea, he had listed the qualities of his favourite children, the feet of A., the hands of B., the hair of C., and so on, and at the end of the eulogium the limp of Ania, the smashed body trying to make itself desired. What did he notice then, the limp being nearly invisible by that time? I was tired and fell against the vibrating window, I tried to remember the smell of the bitter tea, his life-story, Zurich giblets, shambles, limping lovers. What did he see? New buckles, poppers, clips, hooks. What pricked him in his bowels?

> Her lips two budded roses
> Her cheeks like blushing lilies
> Her eyes like orbs of heavenly flame
> Her neck a wondrous tower.

Perhaps the suggestive polymorphism of her name . . . Anne, Annie, Ania, Anya, Aniuszka, Anna? Did he think, like me, of two bobs of hair, a tropic fruit, a pineapple, a misshapen word of a baby? Was it the ankle-socks, the polka dots, the moles scattered in the shape of the Auriga constellation over a blonde arm, the light ornithic bones and the webs of young fat between? Her foot was against mine, in a torture of drunken sleep, and her head had rolled back into the sun that was behind us and her throat swelled and contracted in silence. We were passing over rivers and shingle beds, through refined and imperturbable provincial towns, through a rich mirage of chlorophyl. When my eye opened for a moment I saw the blue, bending flashes, the cubes of grey and the elms a shape of smoke. The nape began to sweat in the heat, and I saw with relieved gratification pimples of liquid grow out of the immaculate neck and stain the elegant collar. I felt I had scored a triumph, though I had gained nothing and nothing had happened. The rhomboid of light was at last stained by a secretion. I fell asleep again with a new feeling of peace.

When the car stopped we were in a forest, the forêt du Lion in the val de Seine, I heard him say before he tumbled out of the car. The door hung open and he was lost in the zigzags of shadow, relieving himself. The soft patter of his urine came back to us through silvan silence. I was still half-asleep, hearing the rustle of his water in the gloom, and could only see – through the glass of the rear window – trumpets of leaves above us glittering in the sky. I could tell, by the sudden stifling of light and the cessation of the motor, that we had arrived at a vital moment. He was sharpening his axe in the gloaming and would take her in this moment of forgetfulness . . . hatching in this nocturnal place plots of rapture. I had her in my foot-grasp, she was there, her nose upturned and snoring. She was dreaming and her hand twitched on my leg . . . the mass of past events was pouring through a private nightmare and I was not there to see. When she spoke I picked up the word 'Łazienki', the name of a park, but could not see what she was doing in the tulip beds she had told me about, or the colour of the water around the Łazienki Palace she had described, or the gyrations of the giant swans and our shadows over the steps of a fanciful amphitheatre. I had in my power only the fragments she had desired to make conscious in my presence. The missing time in Paris after the war, the house in Laon, did not appear. The past filtered through her snore, her limp foot and every cell bore its image closed up inside her. I could not touch, pilfer, learn. The sleep-words flew past me . . . 'ampoule', 'feu', 'creusé', and the name 'Piotr' . . . perhaps the face of a waving soldier in the opposite wing of the hospital, a face dismembered, smoking and cheery: he had written it backwards over the window-panes in steam or frost and I never saw, though he repeated it and she remembered it. A young doomed man hunting favours. Perhaps he reminded her of a childhood crush, the blond-haired cousin who used to take her swimming, to zoos, parades, ice-cream parlours. She says she does not remember her dreams, that she cannot make sense of the names and words I quote from them. The boy-cousin went to war:

> Ta ta ta ra ta
> Comme des petits soldats

the child dimly aware of the hopscotch rhythm of drums. Perhaps he went past her house, stiff-legged, gun-heavy, one eye upon her:

> . . . mon officier

blond in late summer, a good marcher, one leg of a centipede. Perhaps the blue gaze comes back to her in sleep, the solid slanting barrel and the stars of his buttons. Into a valley, into a fire . . . his destiny to be a popping combusting molecule in the great fire. She waved a handkerchief. In the dream I am sure he is there, the flower in her nightmare, waving and embracing. I cannot destroy him as he struts by, adored, and I feel the twitching hand on my thigh waving a flag for him.

Kessler slipped out from the shadows, zipping up, and wiped his hand on a fern. From the slit of an eye I saw him delay return, dither, twiddle, fumble, mumble, pry out twigs and roots with his foot, enjoying the fresh air. He thought we were asleep, and, seeing no cause to disturb, took time to meditate. I knew nothing of him. I began, however, to remember more pieces which I could put together.

He had made the cast for her leg and, being a good doctor, had examined her, touched and probed. He had brought her sweets at night, the new girl needed comfort. He brought her sweets for headaches, to stop her weeping and ease her solitude. He passed the bed at night – a regular surveillance – and paused, stooped, fumbled, inspected, took her pulse and listened to her heartbeat, measured her temperature, placed a Hippocratic hand over her brow gathering warm drops of nervous sweat, effected the calm intrusion of a stethoscope into her night-shirt. He was a sly fellow, he peeled off the top sheet, I could imagine, stripping her naked. At night, the babies were asleep. I remember the darkness of the ward with its taped windows. Anyone could have. The noise of the sirens was so distracting, absorbing the interior sound, that you thought of the bomb coming and not of the man nearby. It would have been easy, a sleight of the hand, a tickly-tick. I thought: Would I have? Cast no stones, you would have. You did, Hôtel de Cécile. More, kissed her feet and more. But she was no sleeping, crushed, tongueless captive. There was no medical varnish, no mountebank persuasion, no hunchback antics. 'Give me your body, I wish to take your pulse.' No, no, she liked me, she opened her eyes and stroked my hair. She was awake and alert, stroking my hair.

Kessler peered in at the window, curious at our slumber. Seeing my eyes flicker, he shook my shoulders lightly, with his indescribable gentleness.

'Wake up, Kamerad, it's crepuscule.'

'Evening,' I corrected him.

'Get up, come for a turn.'

'Where?'

'In the forest.

> Daß sind die liebchen Veilchen
> Die ich zum Strauss erkor.

Mother tongue. Most lovely.'

I agreed reluctantly, untwisting my foot. She turned over, still sleeping.

'Too much vin,' he whispered playfully, unlocking my door. 'Piano, piano.'

'I don't want to be long,' I whispered back.

'No, no . . . a turn. A poetic break, Kamerad.'

The car was tilted into a small hollow, lop-sided over green logs. He had driven carefully so that we should not be disturbed, in order to preserve our sleep. The doors hung open like the glossy wings of a beetle, in uneasy inertia as if the insect had been struck dead. We drew away, ambling into the forest. Kessler lit a cigarette and his momentary nature-worship disappeared. The combusting end flared up, as of old, and the exaggerated brows regained the macabre clownishness I remembered so well. He proffered the silver box engraved with violets – the artificial counterparts of those in Heine's poem – and we smoked for a while together without speaking. We walked in a slow distorted circle. He began.

'I wanted to ask you many things before, but I wanted to wait until we could be together . . . '

I could not meet his smile or the exaggerated softness of his voice.

' . . . being interested in my patient – you'll forgive the expression – and curious about you both, of course. It puzzles me . . . '

I thrust out my chest and began to exhale my smoke in a tough way through the nose. He looked up, almost amused, and I spat out at him, 'What's so funny? That I am not her doctor, that she is an infant Salome?'

'No, no, I'm not surprised at you.' He picked at his lips as they spread outwards in mirth. 'Nothing has struck me as being dangerous. Your cohabitation, if I may say, has taken her off the vagabond highways . . . I'm pleased with it all. The staff were afraid for her, and it has turned out in the best way.'

He plucked a handful of beech leaves and crushed out the juice slowly over his closed palm.

'You are all strung up,' he went on. 'You shouldn't mind it if I pay my respects in the form of enquiry. One has to know some things.'

I apologized. 'You're free to.'

'You see, I was thinking . . . you don't seem to have a position of any kind.' He paused, grinding the leaves into a green juice. '. . . an employment. I mean work, you know. Wages. You don't have such a thing, do you?'

'Why?' I gave a little start of fear. Here was the axe: not fit to support, insufficiency of funds – intervention for minor's sake.

'Don't excite yourself, Jamie. She's not within the reach of any law, of any institution. She's sixteen years of age, she's not a minor. Not really. No one can be bothered with them at that age. The world is in turmoil, in Germany the children are running tobacco, alcohol and their sisters. In this age little Ania is a grand dame.'

Yes, it was true. Why had I not thought of it before and absolved myself? Force of circumstance. The force of events had exercised a gravitational influence and I had not seen that it all, yes, depended on the events.

' . . . the standard of your own childhood does not at all apply. She is better armed. Think about her story – she is our contemporary, she has passed through the same circumstances. The notion of age that you have has temporarily disappeared, every difference has been telescoped down to a banal interval which the world now ignores. Your guilt . . . ' and here he smiled again and rolled up his eyes with the motion of sudden intuition ' . . . is preposterous. You seem to have dragged something with you from another world. It is not my business to examine what you feel. I am concerned only with the . . . the mechanics of things. With you it is all money, fantasy, promises and hope in the form of luxury. You know what the basic fuel is. When you descend in the pecking order of minor Parisian hotels, the mechanism is breaking down. We both know, don't we, that it is breaking down. And when it has broken down it will be the end and she will disappear.'

I watched him with a kind of childish disbelief: some have this genius for fine detail. I remained silent, fascinated by him. He continued.

'She, of course, is still unconscious. She knows nothing. You are Der Fliegende Holländer in her eyes . . . realize that she does not know or accept your secret. I don't mean that you have a "secret" exactly, you have a deficiency of a sort – not a moral stain. Nothing is your fault. But . . . ' another eye-roll, almost saint-like ' . . . you have wormed your way into a lie, that is all, a rather pretty one as it happens, a profoundly fruitful one. It couldn't be helped. Events acquired a certain velocity, difficult to master. You were inevitably complicit.'

I nodded, on the point of laughter, the kind produced by certain nerve gases. Through his passion for analysis he had actually sped on into the future, predicting the probable outcome of events with a vicious prophetic precision. He must be allowed to elaborate, Jamie must peek at his destiny.

'I am not judging you, old Kamerad. I think you understand what I mean. I have used a somewhat spurious professional pretext for involving myself: culpa mea, I admit, I apologize. But it has allowed me, you will not deny, to say the . . . ' he paused, wondering if he should dare ' . . . the truth.'

The truth had come, but it had not surprised me. Only the word had its purifying, detergent effect. There was a clearing of the air.

'Well said. You seem to understand.' There was the truth expertly propounded. I admired his squibs of eloquence. 'I am rich,' he seemed to say. 'Take my flesh if you will, it is yours.'

'It is not really a problem to lend you certain amounts,' he went on. 'You can take it without formality. It is green paper. We might share a servant for a while. You can ask any amount.' He paused again to smile, this time the sublimation of a little too much energy, not rooted in anything I recognized as humour, cunning or satisfaction. 'Of course, you must ask for it, you must make a proper decision. I am not a mechanical dispenser.'

I nodded, stupefied. I am not a mechanical dispenser. It was the dry end of a fond dream. He was admonishing me, cruel Figaro:

Non più andrai farfallone amoroso

burning my butterfly days. He had seized my gallant throat with irreproachable politeness and was wringing out the loose change. Scraps of string would fall out, a gummy handkerchief, sweaty bills, banknotes flaking into nothingness, a few coins with their goddesses and olive branches grained with grime, hairy folded lottery tickets and stubs of burnt cheques. He turned on his heel still crushing the leaves slowly and purposefully: he was searching out like a mathematician the equation of my commercial value, my past and future. When he had obtained it he would act more decisively. For now, I was still an unknown factor.

'There is no need for Ania to know this,' he resumed. 'It wouldn't make any sense to her. Poverty for her is a private world of her past. You made a mistake as it was taking her to the Cécile, it must have crushed her a bit considering the magnitude of your ambitions. She wrote me a letter last month – I asked her to – describing it all. I didn't believe any of it, to be honest. It smelt of promises. There you are, Kamerad, that is where you have put yourselves.'

He had begun retracing our path and I followed him at a distance of two yards. From close to, it seemed, the entire surface of his shirt was riddled with darker moisture. His composure burned energy. I followed in silence, constructing in my imagination the future his offer would make possible. The first move, I decided, would be to take her to Italy, to the Lago di Garda where we would begin again in simplicity and solitude.

I moved straight into his fantasy without considering the meaning of his proposal; it did not matter, I would have my lifetime of devotion. We would sail on Garda every morning as the mist rose, we would live in a pink and blue lake cottage among the eucalyptus trees, we would walk through the silent alleys of Salò with bread in our arms, we would compose letters at sunset over a purple beach and we would wear laundered cotton shirts and tennis shoes and only rise in order to walk to the boats which would take us over the lake.

When we arrived back at the car Ania was awake and feeding birds, absorbed in her benevolence. She reminded me for a moment of her mother feeding pigeons on a bench in St Denis. She turned only slightly and smiled for us.

'Salut, les gars,' she mumbled.

Kessler kneaded her cheek between two fingers, father-fond despite her chummy address.

'Salut, Ania. Bien dormie?' – his pidgin French was always affectionate. And perhaps the doctor was right, perhaps he had seen through her. We were indeed *les gars* coming out of the wood like mock-redskins, sweaty and boyish, and she seemed our equal with her undisturbed feeding manner.

'It's dark,' sighed Kessler. 'Let's go back to town.'

She appeared ecstatic at this suggestion. Brushing out her hair in an adjusted wing-mirror, she repainted her lips, coloured in her eyes, bobbed her hair with elastic and tuned in the car radio to the swooping descending arpeggios of a jazzing saxophone.

7

The final instalment of my father's money arrived on the last Saturday of May in a crumpled, sordid and somehow didactic brown package with the name and the address of the austere sender typed unnecessarily on the reverse side. The enclosed note was brilliant with indignation. Master Jamie was informed that:

1. He had severely disappointed the expectations of his generous progenitors and patient benefactors.
2. He had deceived these same guardians with false declarations as to his activities, ambitions, intentions and mode of life.
3. He had outgrown, at the age of twenty-eight, his automatic right to financial support at the expense of the said aggrieved parties, and this said means of assistance would cease irrevocably as from the date marking the letter (May 24).
4. He should, so as not to further aggravate his already considerable offence, return home immediately in order to explain his conduct in person to the said 'patient benefactors' as befitted a man of his 'station'.
5. He should take heed not to ignore the above injunctions, as he had done in the past, as the said aggrieved benefactors were at the end of their notorious tether, and their long elastic tempers were 'exasperated', extended to the point of inevitably destructive release, and their powers of foreseeing the consequences of their probable imminent action almost (sic) 'uncertain'.
6. The said patient benefactors were nevertheless still fond of him – wishing him a certain amount of indulgent love – and sent him exquisite kisses in the form of spontaneous inky crosses.

For me this was the most secret of letters. I burnt it while Ania was asleep: an *homme comme il faut* does not receive such things. My illusion was crumbling enough as it was and we had moved on to the avenue Trudaine, a prettier street but a shabbier accommodation, renting a single room in the apartment of Mr Hoeniger, a Swiss friend of Kessler. The avenue Trudaine was a wide, silent street unrelated in any way to its district, bushy with young maples that reached up to the elaborate ironwork balconies thick with ivy and pink flowers and the tall, aloof windows crowded with reflections of foliage, lace and symmetries of opposing façades like the sides of massive, ornamented machines. Inside, a voluminous bourgeois space was surrounded by servants' cubby-holes and miscellaneous storage areas. These latter were our domain. 'Temporary, it is understood,' I told confused and quivering Ania. 'It is necessary, you understand, that we wait. Everyone must wait, on occasion.'

She kept her wardrobe intact and became brighter than I. In my unmatched black suits – the plunder of that far-off trip to Zurich – of which the component parts (jackets, waistcoats, trousers) interchanged with horrible effect, in my brogues of weary sobriety, in my Satanic-grave ties and funereal collars, in my black socks dipped in the river Styx, in my chilly gold webs of chains and cuffs, in my crisp cotton vests modelled on ancient armour and my Persian pantoufles, I felt an old man. But she had absorbed the emphatic pattern of new dances and their syncopation and frenzy had worked their way into everything: her walk, her gestures of dressing and speaking and the mould of her body. The interior of the room in the avenue Trudaine, a box of unripe lemon yellow, maggot-eaten with reproductions of Greuze, was littered with the remains of American cigarettes, beached seaweed of stockings, craters of spilt aromatic dust and tubs of cream holding pink-stained swabs. Then came the phonograph and the medlies of songs accompanied by stilted routines executed in a reflecting window. She would draw me into this frieze, lifting my arms over her as she flicked under with a single revolution of the hips, trading off her mass against mine with uncertain skill and always tracing with her eye the movements in the glass, critical and exhilarated.

'How heavy you are,' she would say. 'It's your age.'

It was true, I could not go with her to the cafés and dance halls. If I did I would be obliged to procure my vermouth and consume it alone at one of the more secluded tables, hidden in shadow or absolved from participation by the cut of my suit. I was truly Monsieur Mourning, as I heard them say.

The bond I had laboured to weave between us was dissolved by each acceptance of a dance and the subsequent slipping of her hand into the alien grip of a lovely shepherd, the formalized intimacy of the double-dancing and the entering of a rare atmosphere together placed far beyond the functional electric haze through which I drank my limpid and prosaic Noilly Prat. And the absurd sessions in the window soon bore their fruit: she began to gyrate more gracefully than her shepherds.

During short summer nights she lay beside me under a small false chandelier which was transformed by a watery illumination from the street below into a vulgar cradle of prisms. The prisms would shiver in the currents of air, gloomy purple and phantom green. I would dream of Greuze's dove-girls, the haunting image of that painter's unfaithful adolescent wife, and her hair would knot around my wrist while a foot deep down in the sheets would beat:

tap tap tapa tap

in her dream, the drumbeat of a happy hour. Her powder could still be removed from her face with the tongue, and I found in it a velvet, bitter kiss unique in texture. Under her eyelids I could feel with my lips the trembling burr of a hundred instruments and the heat of other bodies.

She would bring young men to my table, startled creatures from underwater – I have forgotten names and faces – and make them sit with us in a comfortable group. She patted their hands when she laughed and my-little-peached them with her painted fingers, leaving the violent colour of her mouth over ears, chins, jaws and noses. I was sullen and jealous over my impeccably superior drink. Glossy and gossamered ephebes picked her up in distant secrecy by the zinc bar or by the doors opening on to the street or by the ice-cream counter, by empty tables, by fire exits signified by glow-worm letters or by my own stern and helpless presence. They smoked in her face, fawned and frolicked. When she whispered in their ear they would look over at me, rolling the butt in a naive snarl, and draw away with ludicrous indifference. She would curtsy, regard me archly and smile with the ecstasy of regained freedom.

Once when she was slow-dancing near the ice-creams with a tender and muscular sailor I left my place and slipped through the drifts of bitter smoke to intercept a warming embrace. I was impaired by drink and my slurred words tumbled out noisily.

'Il est tray, tray tard, vous savez,' I said to the sailor. 'Elle a besoin de dodo.'

But they did not hear. Her eye had seen through me with bland analytic power. The sailor – his shaved blond hair bristling in a blue light and his mouth half-open in a kind of clumsy bliss – turned to examine me as I touched his shoulder with fearful respect. He did not understand: could I be serious, what was I? Was I some copepod . . . he screwed up his eyes to see me better . . . was I imaginary, a scratch on the interior of his cornea? They continued to dance, shuffling away from me and dreaming of Hawaiian beaches. His arms tightened around her and he scraped her brow with his grey jowl. I interrupted again: 'Il me semble que . . . ' but the unconscious duo swirled away, a cocoon of whispers.

I left a note at our table and walked home northward up the long hill. I waited in bars on the way hoping that the sea-going character would pass by holding her on his arm (unexpected gentleman) or that she would pass by alone with her remorse. I drank in an empty space, measuring the nocturnal-aquatic forms brushing against the outer tables of the *terrasse* with my memory of her figure. But, recalling the handsome muscular arms with their tattooed designs of imaginary fish and palm trees, the suave heavy machinery of the neck and shoulders and his bliss-parted mouth, I began to doubt. After all, yes, a sailor (I sang to myself):

Bright and breezy
Free and easy,
Well y' know what sailors are.

I saw him bent upon his desire. A flash of lightning had fallen and split me away from her and I had no role to play. But she would read the wounded, epigrammatic note I had left on the table, would leave the seaman with protestations and appear in front of the glass in her red shoes and white dress covered with tiny red apples. The sailor had been happy and she had hung on his neck, they had smoked cigars together. She would come only at dawn, which is when they say farewell to sailors. They take their fancy, merry men. I could only wait and eat with deliberation a jar of maraschino cherries, dipping each one in a shallow dish of whisky and not bothering to wipe the juice from my chin. The summer night being short, I walked to the avenue Trudaine in near-light after the mournful consumption of the cherries. I waited in the street and listened under the window, thinking that she had slipped into the building before me and was disrobing in confusion before our bed. Her feet would be blue already, their habitual dawn colour, and her hand would hold a slumbering clock . . . I would have to make breakfast without waking her and read the newspaper by the window until she came out enveloped in her fastidious odour.

But when I climbed up to the room I found that it was empty. The sailor had held her, had he? I slept for an hour in a chair. When I woke, a horse came over the cobbles of the street below me, a balloon rose up in the condensation of the window and I heard the crowd in the street. The sea rolled in the dawn and the girls were waving handkerchiefs:

Ship ahoy
Sailor boy.

They were lowering waxy throats into the morning air, offering an orange apiece, demanding two pretty doubloons and a pair of silver dollars. They sold their plackets, they hoisted their buckled shoes, acrobatic, above the shoulder; their lovers in the crow's nest had not tasted an orange on the high seas. Engines were ticking over in the avenue of maples, I heard a chauffeur speaking on the pavement, talking of an airport and an early appointment. The first combustion engine, a mist over bricks and a sweet aubade: the car leaving, the ship arriving. They would sell their handsome oranges and lemons, shouting:

Silor boiy!

doubloon apiece. A whole dancing crowd massed along the wharf, Ania in her dress coloured with red apples. All the nice girls waved their handkerchiefs, sailor-boy blew a kiss. How long should I slumber in semi-sleep? The dawn would shovel her up smelling of brine, girdled with seaweed. The love-struck mermaid. The sea would sing in her ear and in the cavern of her throat, pining for a mortal man. She came with him up the neat and orderly avenue Trudaine with the mist behind them, his arm of fish and palm trees around her, around a snow-white bodice laced up behind, his massive hand on her tick-tock hip. She waved from below and I waved back to them, to Ania and the sailor with his boyish innocent smile. They were off for a spin together.

I woke up in the chair and went to the window to scan an empty street. The mist was rolling down it, as in the mountains and the sea-towns. There was no one alive. Only an old man, loaded down with plates of glass strapped to his back, called into the doorways, 'Vit-ri-eeer!' and the dawn receded before him. But as I had crossed to the window a wave of perfume had broken over me. The door was indeed open, a slender half-inch. I crept to the bedroom. The bed was humped and disordered. I could see the feet thrust out to breathe, down-turned and pale: she had slipped past me and was asleep. When I came closer I saw that she was still clothed and a tiny ripple of fruit lay over the sheet where her arm had fallen. I bent down – her neck smelt of tobacco. Where his hand had been. My hands smell only of talc and old paper. On her throat was an oval thumbprint, the mauve of a bruise. I bent down further, listening and examining. Her breath was regular. She was unconscious, numb with alcohol, fragrant with bitter rye and liquorice. I kissed her behind the ear and the flap of cartilage was cold and brittle. She could not be roused or troubled. Whereas before I would have raged at her and held her throat for ransom, delivered hysterical blows against her arms, here she was inviolable in a morning sleep, rolled up like an aquatic organism – a trilobite or shrimp – frail and ancient in her shell. I returned to the window, perspiring with relief. Animal functions were the safest . . . sleeping, feeding, mating. Each function held her down and dissolved her dangerous independence. They were the surest states – unconscious, eternal, impersonal. From them came no infidelity or individual pleasure. I had her bound, imprisoned, castigated and innocent. I rejoiced in her sleep.

8

That year it was a shadowy and sentimental summer, hot and watery, heavy with cloud and shot through with celestial electricity. Her passions were jazz and dancing. She arranged her hair in high bizarre tufts, stiff in sphincters of coloured elastic like Aztec plumes, like the blond metal of ceremonial helmets. The oval bruise faded from her neck. She continued to dance with other men in the bars and at night she lay beside me under the ghostly prisms.

One evening late in the summer we moved into two small rooms in the Hôtel du Brésil, in the second *arrondissement.* From the street, the vestibule was endless, like the corridor of a penitentiary . . . the window boxes were crowded with withered cacti and geraniums, a smell of fried *boudin* and burnt apples shrouded our first night. I had explained to her the strategic necessity of moving to the Brésil, the advantages it offered, but there were tears in her eyes as we poured out cold water into a tin basin and made our ablutions in a silence insulted by the furtive circulation of tap-water elsewhere and the tense footfalls of strangers in the tiny rue d'Aboukir. Looking out into the night street I saw for the first time the gaslit menagerie, the blue and silver of gourmandise and the pyramids of cauliflowers and earthy carrots. I saw Verron haggling with an Arab, his fingers cutting through the dark with a passionate merchant's violence, and the blubbery wife in a hair-net parting the lace of the first-floor window in order to watch his progress. I caught it all in one glance, with a cynical eye, and I knew that the scene was the perfect embodiment of our condition. I knew that this hotel was closer to our true state than all others.

Immediately, she found the Bar St Tropez with its juke-box and priestly bar-stools that turn clockwise in a full circle, and a willing bar-boy who would make her cream cocktails – 'on account of the lady's charm' – and she sat there a whole day celebrating her freedom as one creases greedily a rediscovered banknote. She was drunk when I found her and resisted furiously as I pulled her out of the St Tropez to a chorus of hoots and whistles.

'Go suck your own!'

'Whore-monger!'

In the street, she turned on me herself.

'A la gare, Aubergine. I'm not yours . . . '

I followed her at a distance of four paces, an executioner's shadow, watching the oscillation of her path.

'You're mad, Aubergine!' she muttered.

The abuse continued in the vestibule. I took her past the reception desk, twisting her arm. In our room, the coloured gaslight filtered upward through the balcony and brightened the ceiling red and blue. She collapsed on the bed and curled up in her coat.

'You have no right,' she sobbed. 'You have no right.'

I did not have the right and I sat overlooking the glare of the street's monstrous equine heads moulded in fire and smoked a pack of cigarettes until she fell asleep. When the fruit stalls closed up I went down into the street and wandered from one end to the other until my soles smelt of the orange skins ground into the cobbles. I knew that she would escape if I left her to herself. Jamie was no longer Monsieur le Prince, he was an arm-twister whose breath smelt of rasping tobacco, whose fingers smelt of jolted vermouth, whose muscles felt like mindless stone.

When I returned she was awake and we talked for ten minutes before she fell asleep again. While we talked her eyes were fixed on the ever-present images of *Vogue* and I was back at the window overlooking the now unlit and pestilential street. She snapped over the pages of tall American models with hatred while I persuaded her that it was futile for her to return to Poland in search of her mother.

'You say all this,' she answered, 'but you know nothing, you kartoffel English.' It was her fondest jab to assimilate in savage metaphors races and dull vegetables. 'Why not follow her? I could, Mr James.'

'How would you find her? Poland is in chaos, Warsaw is empty. Everything has been destroyed, where would she be?'

'My grandmother has the address, of course. And you forget, it is my country, what should be so very difficult?'

'Besides,' I went on, ignoring her and becoming more sly and ashen-faced, 'you need money to go. I've told you we have to be careful, we're waiting for money to arrive. Now you want to go off? You want to find your mama? I understand. But you need money and we have to eat.'

'Before, you told me . . . ' her voice quivered on the furthest edge of its control, 'you told me to forget everything and let you deal with things. Now you say (she stopped and nervously poured herself a glass of water) I cannot go anywhere or be with my mother. You said we would live in a nice house and have nice friends. You said we would eat in big cafés . . . we would have a nice car . . . '

I was frightened by the beginning of this sudden confession, though I knew already its probable outcome. I went to the bed and took her arm.

'I would give you the money to find your mother, but, as I have explained, now is not the time. Maybe later, in the spring, if you still want to go. But now is impossible. I don't mean to be cruel. My estate (I winced at the fabrication) is somewhat strained now and you cannot have the money. But listen. (I leant back into the bolster and drew her closer with one arm, tipping her head against my shoulder.) We'll write to Mama and we'll write to Sylvia. We'll send our address out on a special card to all the governments:

L'HÔTEL DU BRÉSIL

PARIS

The government will tell us where they are, the government knows all about people. After all, they don't disappear without trace.'

She sank against my shoulder and closed the magazine. She had given up, her mouth tasted of alcoholic peppermint and the smell was making her sleepy. On the verge of tears she rolled up to sleep.

'It's not my fault,' she whimpered. 'It's not my fault. . .'

I hurried on this sleep, stroking her hair.

'We'll write to Auriol, we'll send a special message – we will, tomorrow – we'll send notices everywhere. I'll give you the money, I'll give it to you, tomorrow we'll go to the police, the post office, the mayor.'

When she had fallen asleep a second time, I wrote a short letter to Kessler asking if he might lend us a certain amount of money. He would be expecting the request, so I did not waste my time on formalities – it was a commercial letter cloaked in the brief terms of a doubtful friendship. I asked him to meet me the following week and at the same time told him we would not be in Paris for very much longer. I had decided to take a small holiday with Ania, a tour of the south, a short voyage to 'aid her full recovery', and we would be leaving at the end of the summer. When I wrote the word 'recovery' – I explained to him – I meant to refer to the 'disturbance' in her caused by the events of the war as Kessler had described it to me. Almost unconsciously I had succumbed to the suggestion that she was sick, perhaps only in a small way, but certainly sick, undernourished, suffering. I did not think of it as I wrote; I had assumed it in the course of thinking. Kessler's hint – never stated as a bald admission – had entered my conception of her. He had not used the word 'sick', he had merely made known his private thoughts as a man commanding a large amount of medical and personal information relevant to her case. But the fact that she was a 'case' (his case) had not seemed unusual to me. I had acquiesced: she was a case, she was sick, Kessler had told me that she was sick, and between Kessler and myself she was referred to as a kind of patient. I was too slow then to realize that he had invented the terms and obliged me to accept them. He had turned the woman I loved into a bearer of illness, a slowly closing wound.

9

Down the cool corridor in early autumn the slap-slap of elderly pantoufles – the rubbery flippers of a heavy walrus – would make me start thinking she had at last returned. I would run to the window, a patter of naked feet. The slippers would approach, return, approach, pause, return, and the breath of the cleaner who wore them would come and go with them, the sound of a plane shaving hard wood, or the whine of a distant saw. Aubade: the motors bursting in the cold and the bell of St Eustache. I laid the table for breakfast each morning in the same way, with the crockery decorated with gold stencils of plum blossom and bamboo bridges that I had bought a year before, when I had been wealthy. I would buy the bread at six o'clock and it was hot, emitting a sweet wheat-flavoured steam. Opposite the window, the yellow walls returned slowly to their daytime splendour, bubbling with age, stained by gutter-fluid. Through a dark glass . . . Verron the grocer, smelling of moist dawn kisses, the neat Pythagorean shapes of piled fruit, silver swirls of water carrying off tragic cabbage leaves into voracious drains. My cheek was smooth after the slow, joyful shaving, but the thyroid would be nicked and smudged with blood. I would count the pigeons on window-hoods . . . *eins, zwei, drei, uno, due, tre, yi, er, san,* in all the languages I knew, to pass the time. Still she would not come, even after the amphibian slippers had faded away into the depths of the furthest uncleaned rooms. The smell of disinfecting apples was absent, only the odour of boiling coffee enshrouded the breakfast, and I would have to wait for another footfall, hard and youthful, before I could wave to fat old Verron with a free heart.

When she did come she would walk quickly down the exotic little alley, keeping to the middle of the road with her head tucked down into her scarf, sly and precise. Just before entering the Brésil she would half-turn and look over her shoulder – to left and right – with the speed of a small reptile. The steps would come at last, rushing up the spiralling stairs. She would run in, eating an orange, flushed from the walk in the cold, her mouth wet and sugary, and kiss me on the cheek without a word. She would light a cigarette and sit down for her coffee and I would serve her, not daring to ask her where she had been or whom she had seen. At seven she would retire to bed and sleep alone far into the afternoon. While she slept, I would gather up the pseudo-oriental cups, the fragmented loaf, the soiled plates and the butter-rimmed knives and leave the table bare and pitiful. After a few hours I would hear the tinkle of jewellery and sound of a strong brush sifting through and drawing back thick hair. She would be singing:

Dis-moi tout bas des jolis mots d'amour

and mumbling the words, a hairpin pressed between her lips.

I would not accompany her at night unless she did not want to dance. I would only take her to drink at sedate cafés and half-silent bars where she would sip her creamy drinks quickly and contentedly, and hum to herself until she became bored. It had become a sad affair, I marooned by my greater age, she dreaming of greater possibilities. If I could take her away from the dance halls and the young men in black suits, if I could enforce solitude upon us . . . I asked her again about our 'holiday' (I had already asked her to come with me and she had sneered at the idea), this time folding out before her a soiled, improbable map of Italy traced over with Hannibalian routes.

'Oh, but yes, yes,' she whispered wearily on seeing the itineraries of red ink. 'If it makes you happy, yes, I will come.'

I crumpled up the map triumphantly.

'We will take the train to Milan next month,' I announced. She stared out of the bar window at the objects flashing out of a watery darkness with the pale splendour of lamp-fish and bathyspheres.

'I don't mind at all,' she said, vacant and resigned. 'Where is Milan?'

I unfolded the map once more and showed her.

'Oh,' she sighed, placing her finger on the space where Turin should have been, 'Mi-lan.'

'Are you sure?' I took her hand in a sentimental, confiding way. 'Will you come?'

'Why not?' she hummed, sucking in the foam of a milk Kahlúa from her upper lip. 'Why not, if it will be fun?'

'It will be fun,' I assured her. She did not have to be persuaded as before. She asked to be shown my planned itineraries in detail and began to ask questions about the cities through which they passed.

'But what is this?' She bent over the map, examining with a peal of laughter an elephant drawn in soft pencil on the road to Rome . . . a doodle in honour of the Carthaginian who had gone before us and who was my first hero. I almost said 'Elephantopolis', for a city which did not exist, except as an accidental emblem, seemed then the most perfect symbol of our elopement-escape . . .

I met Kessler on the boulevard Raspail and we ate together during an autumn rainfall, he frugal and delicate, I hungry and obscene. He watched my fingers, somehow doused with mayonnaise, with a premonition of disgust in his eyes. For the first time, I was dirty, my hands grey above the mayonnaise and my shirt grey above my hands. He pushed his *pommes frites* around his plate in aimless indignation, and we attempted to converse:

K: If, on the other hand, you feel that it would be too much, a burden . . .
J: No, it seems the right amount. I've worked out the expenses.
K: I want what is best for you two. Well, if you're sure . . .
J: I'm sure it's the right amount, it's very kind of you.
K: (waving) Oh, how laborious.
J: I just wish to . . .
K: You are always thanking and if-you-pleasing. Superfluous, and idle.
J: In fact, I would like you to come, maybe later.
K: Later, later, always later. Take the gift and go.
J: Well, if you're sure . . .
K: Yes, yes. I am sure.
J: We owe you . . .

And so on until the early evening, when the café chose to close and we were gently ushered out into the street, I stoop-shouldered and still apologizing. Despite his rhetorical irritation, he was clearly enjoying my humility.

'Well, when do you little birds go?' he asked as we lit cigarettes at the entrance of the Montparnasse cemetery, in which could be seen long avenues of black trees curved over impeccable gravel.

'Maybe next month. Is it too soon?'

He stopped and considered.

'Not at all. Next month, next week . . . what difference? I approve.'

'You understand,' I kept apologizing, 'it's a loan. We'll pay you back next year. We have no choice and I don't like to, but . . . '

He held up his hand again like a medieval king carved into the façade of a cathedral.

'Balderdashing, Kamerad, absolute balderdashing. I give it to you. I absolutely give it to you.'

He took my hand and shook it with almost shocking spontaneity. I began to feel the old laughter rising in my gorge . . . 'balderdashing' . . . ! He then passed his arm through mine, creating between us a stilted male intimacy as we strolled on. Our berets made us look like two French veterans returning from the cemetery. Kessler went on.

'To my mind this place is no good for you. You have been unhappy and poor. This auberge existence will destroy you in the end, as you know. Bohemia is inverted prosperity, and now there is no prosperity to live from. At your age – you are twenty-nine? – it is becoming dangerous for you to give up everything for a woman who is twelve years younger than yourself, who has only recently emerged from childhood. While you are away, I will look for a job for you. I told you before: without money you are doomed with her. Now, buy your tickets and please sort yourselves out . . . '

I nodded at his sound sense. I was collapsing into a state of degraded dependence barely disguised by my old gold studs.

'I am fond of Ania,' I said, relaxing my arm deeper into his grip and allowing his father's softness to penetrate me.

'Yes, yes,' he whispered, my confessor.

'I must try to persuade her . . . perhaps she will . . . ' I could not cohere and he nodded his head as if dismissing the attempt.

'You are quite right,' he concluded. 'I will give you everything you need.'

We had reached the station dedicated to Edgar Quinet and his step had slowed to indicate that I must soon abdicate my position on his arm. Finally he turned to face me and placed his hand on my arm.

'I will send you the gift by post. You need not feel grateful, as I have said. And please do not tell Ania. You would be lost if you did.' He said he had a dinner engagement and that he would have to go by metro to Pyramides. A purplish rain was thickening in the spaces between lighted restaurant windows and the elaborate glass propylaea of the luxurious cafés. He smiled in the downpour, shaking his shoulders like a cold cat.

'Before you go,' he added, 'I think Ania and yourself should come with me to the sea – to Honfleur – another little outing with Uncle before it gets too cold. We could go next Saturday and spend a day picking mussels – ha! ha! Rock pools and all that. I'd like to see the little one before you carry her off to the other end of the world. What d'you say?'

I nodded again, giving in.

'Prima! I'll come at eight and interrupt your cosy breakfast.'

And he skipped off, impish and exquisite (though somehow brooding) down the rue de la Gaîté, dodging with a puritan's art the extravagant advances of the prostitutes and turning at the other end and waving to me – faintly puzzled that I was still there – with a glistening open umbrella.

10

We did not stay long in Honfleur . . . only the time needed for Ania to eat an ice-cream soda on a deserted sea front. We drove southward instead into a region of low cliffs and flat, empty beaches. At the point where we descended on to the shingle a group of schoolgirls were busy plucking crabs and anemones from small pockets of sea-water. Ania was drawn into the group and the wind blew up her white dress against their fluttering black.

'Les jeunes filles en fleur,' remarked Kessler, deeply delighted by this sudden scene of marine beauty. She left them with a shellfish hanging from between two fingers, gleaming wet and smelling of brine. She took off her sandals and went towards the waves while we sat on a breakwater and smoked. She hobbled over the cracking shells and tiny pebbles, leaving small eddies and swirls behind her legs.

'Not cold!' she called back to us, and Kessler laughed.

'Not cold, ha, ha! She's white as a coconut.'

She waded further out, edging forward in a sideways movement, her head thrust towards the horizon. A few sails slanted leftward over the distant rim of water, caught in an invisible motion, the motion of stars.

'. . . tickly, the shells . . . ' her fragmented voice shouted back, laughing. Her head turned and we saw for a moment the twist of a smile. She was up to her knees.

'Is she going to swim to England?' asked Kessler, grinning hugely.

Is she going to swim, I thought?

' . . . used to it, not so bad,' the voice floated back. She had stopped and was looking out over the ocean. Her hand was raised to cover her eyes. I imagined her standing on the furthest extremity of a continent, peering over the edge into a blue aquatic emptiness, where the nations end. She would stare at it for hours, hypnotized.

'Catch a fishy!' shouted Kessler.

The gulls swooped down near her head and collapsed into grey swells of water. She turned again and considered him blankly. Birds, fish, crustaceans . . . they did not exist in her universe. She touched lightly the tips of the sluggish waves, drawing the colourless water through her fingers. She was alone in the ocean and the gulls did not matter.

'How beautiful she is,' said Kessler gleefully, lowering his voice.

I looked: yes, mermaid, blonde for him. She began to walk parallel to the beach, casting only momentary sidelong glances at our breakwater. She looked pale and hungry, her body thin under the white dress gathered in before her thighs by one hand. The water foamed around her knees, her hair slipping backward. I thought: yes, I see his vision, Venus in her shell, a tourist attraction, or Chloris spewing flowers from her mouth, a vomit of periwinkles, cornflowers and roses. And I would be her Boreas, her winged captor.

'Look at her wincing,' said Kessler, still jolly. 'All those crabbies!'

She was wobbling along an underwater hair-line, pricked and buffeted. The sea-creatures were after her toes.

'They're snipping!' she cooed, mock-frightened.

The gulls rose from the rocking water and flew off inland, leaving her alone in the waste. She was moving away from our part of the beach towards the next breakwater down, ambling slowly in her sea-kingdom.

'Ania!' Kessler cried. 'Smile for us!'

She did not hear and stumbled on, scooping the waves in her hands. The black-robed schoolgirls went past us again and she waved to them . . . the shellfish was still between her fingers.

'Salut!' she wailed. 'Salut!'

Sea-maids, nereids, crunching shells.

'Salut!'

In the Beginning, the sea and its organic dust. Then mermaids, coral polyps, cowries, lampreys, dolphins. She waved again, splashing. Behind us a single red flag blew inland, obeying the first cool north wind. Kessler began to feel cold, burying his hands between his thighs.

'She must be dying, the little one,' he laughed.

I waved for her to come back in. She saw me and waded towards us, downcast.

'You'll die!' I shouted. 'Hurry up.'

'I'm hurrying,' came the rebellious reply, lifted on the wind. Her wet naked feet scraped the shingle and the powder of ground shells, her shins were filmed with black crystals.

'At last,' sighed Kessler, relieved. 'Home from the sea!'

She ignored him and sat near me to dry her feet. A glazed melancholy had come over her, as if melancholy smelt of salt and sea-wrack . . . the melancholy of seas, departures and drownings. She had heard the sea-bells that knell for the sailors:

Ding dong dell

and the knocking frames of coral. She was singing a Polish song:

Already a month has passed
The dogs are sleeping . . .

the song about Laura who waits for her Filon – the ancient love song.

Kessler and I began to walk alone over the shallow grass hillocks to the car, because she would not come with us. We could hear the clatter of pebbles thrown towards the sea and the lonely moaning of the song, its incomprehensible words. When I turned back after half an hour, she was still there, crouching against the wooden breakwater. She was dreaming of home and the mythological bison in the forests of firs.

Aprica, Aprica

I

The sun had not risen when we arrived at the lakes. The train had descended from the mountains along the last tail of Switzerland, shedding a grey moonlit smoke. She was asleep when I made out the orange trees and the blue rim of the lake below, the white houses with their green shutters, and the mist over the water. As the train descended the air was warm on my face, I leant out far into the night and swallowed it with a dumb, ecstatic gurgle. By the lake I saw palms motionless in shadow like the majestic vegetation of the Nile. A hotel still glittered in the tropic water, revealing a jetty of boats, and a triangle of waves shimmered in the same light, moving yet not moving. When the train stopped she was still asleep. I kissed her as the whistles blew, shaking her shoulder.

During the night I had had this dream about her, which only the lanterns of the officials at the Italian border had disturbed:

We were walking arm in arm through the streets of a modern city, ordinary city streets, straight, wide and lined with automobiles. The pavements were shaded by slender orange trees planted within circular iron grates and the strips of sunlight dividing the roads were often traversed by the giant shadows of aeroplanes. As we walked along the streets, I noticed large yellow circles painted over the paving-stones at regular intervals of thirty yards, in which groups of people were standing as if about to be collected like dustbins.

'For those', explained citizen Ania, 'who wish to dispose of themselves.'

After walking several blocks, she herself entered one of the yellow circles and told me to follow her.

'This is foolery,' I said.

'No,' she retorted. 'We'll meet afterwards.'

I would not go into the circle.

'You're fooling me,' I said.

'If you don't come in now', she admonished, 'it will be too late.'

I would not step in, and the other people standing in the circle began to glare at me.

'Get in!' they shouted.

Ania pleaded with me. I would not go in.

'Very well,' she concluded, 'Mr James may die alone if he wishes.'

'Get in!' shouted the others.

I waved goodbye to Ania and walked on down the street. Behind me a dog-catcher's van was drawing up by the yellow ring. It was a bright sunny morning, and I wanted to buy a good cigar to smoke after lunch. After a while I found the right shop and went in without looking back at the pavement where I had left her.

I remembered the dream as we dropped from the train into the warm air, our faces slightly flushed, and ambled slowly the length of the *quai* to greet the holiday town of Como. The station was empty, and the sight of the orange trees in the gardens nearby suddenly made me uneasy.

We walked to the hotel by the lake and I felt the drowsy smell of lake-water and unripe fruit. I had reserved and the night-porter was expecting us. He ran down the humble steps and took our bags into a vestibule of plastic bixa trees and orange electric light.

When we were alone I went on to the balcony to watch the dawn. Ania had fallen on to the bed and was asleep in her black coat. Through the tall half-closed shutters I saw her breasts in the dark rise and fall without sound. The hotel I had seen from the train was even brighter from the balcony, the strings of pleasure-boats rolled in the breeze, some flying thin elegant pennants, and knocked together with the crisp sound of demonstration skeletons.

2

I found her in a cube of clouded sunlight – her breath smelling of marmalade and her hair loose and a breakfast of flaky sweet rolls and butter curls between us – saying, 'Get up, get up, there are boats.'

She slipped back to the sleek panes of glass secluding the balcony and pulled them apart to admit the wind I had smelt the night before, and the distant sound of motor-boats. She was wrapped in a sheet and went back and forth between the window and the bed in olive-green slippers. Already I could see the curd yellow and pale blue of the lake.

'Look at the boats,' she said, 'how pretty they are.'

As the glass panes turned in her hand I could see the reflections of white houses far below. I called her over.

'My wadna Aniuszka.'

I kissed her in her odour of lemon marmalade.

'My kartoffel English.'

She was yellow and blue with the lake. I fed her sops of brioche soaked in coffee.

'My little whale . . . '

But she wanted to see the boats.

'They will go away for lunch. Don't stay in bed. Take me.'

The aroma of ovens, the buttery grease. I did not want to. Later, would she?

'No.' She shook her head. 'It's not kind of you.'

I rose and the water was below me, fringed with ash trees, ilexes and cypresses. She was dressed before me in a summer hat, now an early autumn extravagance. She was excited and flushed.

'Oh, Aubergine. So slow.'

I was intoxicated by the warmth and could not be rushed.

An unused road led out of the town, darkened on one side by a file of high cypresses. The interval of light falling from the east between each tree was exactly regular, but I found that I had to shorten my step every six paces in order to touch the light every time with my left foot. The road was long and the cypresses stretched its entire length. I played this banal game with myself until I was convinced that, as in the paradox of Zeno, I would never reach the other end since I was obliged to subdivide my trajectory again and again to infinity. I noticed that Ania was pulling ahead of me, the bars of shade falling over her shoulders with precise regularity. My hands were still pale and vein-ridden – phantasmal in this world of dark green and impermeable blue. But she already seemed swifter and more solid.

'Escargot!' she taunted, six yards ahead. 'What's wrong?'

I stopped and looked at her, amazed at my exhaustion. Something was draining away from my heel like the chemical from the heel of Talos.

'I need to rest – the heat,' I replied.

I was not hot, only autumn-warm. The lakeside was even cooler than the town and my temperature was low. My hands were ghastly in the sunlight, covered with tiny faded freckles like a thrush's egg, the freckles of an old man. An interminable distance curved behind Ania which she did not notice, an eternity of sun-shadow alternations. A light dust was rising from the road, a jaundiced dust which made the last trees seem even more distant. She rested her weight on one leg and watched me with curiosity. It did not make sense to her. The paralysis of fatigue had never touched her. The premonition of age was a mystery even to me.

'Ill?'

I shook my head, resuming the walk. She took my hand.

'Poor Escargot. We'll go slower.'

I shook my head once more.

'It is only the heat,' I explained. 'It's gone.'

'Sure? I'm glad.'

We walked for half a mile further along the cypress road, and it was difficult to believe this tenderness. The grain of her voice itself had changed.

Higher up, gravel tracks led to untended villas closed off by rusting gates too high to climb. From here we could see the whole lake below and the mountains to the north touched with snow. I told her about the invasions that had poured over the mountains: Brennus, Alaric, Attila and the tragic Conradin. I told the story of the latter's decapitation in Naples at the age of sixteen, and of the military tactics of the Huns. We were lying under pine trees and the needles were falling in our hair, as if sent down by tiny armies of invading barbarians. In turn she told me of her grandfather's estate in Mazury, where she had ridden the horses he bred. In the far east, she said, were the most savage forests in Europe, where the last bison of the Ice Age lived, and the snow foxes from which her grandfather made hats for his grandchildren. The lakes there, she said, were *lakes* – unlike the pretty Italian imitations – bigger than seas and deep as lunar craters. If you sailed for three days, she said in a strange fit of pride, you could cross over the narrowest of them . . . and the ice in winter was 'thicker than a whale's fat' – a phrase of the old man's.

We came back down through the empty villas, the walls enclosing the twisting roads tipped with lemon trees, and here we sat down.

'What is your name again?'

'Lovecraft.'

She shrugged.

'Skilled in amorous arts.'

'Oh.'

'And what does "Malina" mean?'

She paused and pursed her lips with painful guilt.

'Raspberry. You don't like it?'

'We should be married. Amoroso and Raspberry announce their . . . I will think of you differently from now on . . . (the idea of the sub-acid drupes arranged on a conical receptacle would always shadow her). I will think of that fruit.'

She went on to tell me that her sister shortened her name to An-An in honour of the international word *ananas*, because she had been a plump and milky infant, with coarse hair.

'Pineapple-Raspberry, then.'

'Yes, it's absurd.'

We lay on our backs until our arms and legs were covered by the yellow sow-thistle and star-like chicory. The lake sparkled at the bottom of the hill, pale in the noon-sun, stabbed with bright slanting sails.

'What were you like, in your childhood?' she asked. Suddenly she was curious and I had prepared no narrative.

'I was undersized and ignored. I have an older sister named Mary – a dull Catholic name which I convert to "Maria" for private use – who is bigger than me, and I was eclipsed.'

' "Mary" is not dull. Were you really jealous?'

She had not understood and I nodded, mock-afflicted.

'It's sad,' she said, wide-eyed and pitying.

I smiled to see her ruthful.

'Now, Ania,' I told her, 'you tell me.'

She put her hands over her chest.

'I tell?'

'You know I am interested.'

When she did so I found that hers was a longer story, decorated with troikas, wooden chapels, baroque villas and the Gothic fantasies of Wawel Hill. The black spires of the Kraków cathedral were ringed with haloes of golden spheres like models of the solar system. The Venetian loggia was filled with gypsies and their monkeys. The blue trams went snaking under gaslights between ochre houses. At the centre of this incunabula floated the mirage of her grandfather's farm and the apartment of her aunt in Kraków, a large apartment on a street called Wierzyniewska with a dark spiralling staircase leading up from a vestibule from which one could see the street and the rumbling trams through an open door. She described this apartment with loving exactitude: velvet divans, carved mirrors and wallpaper bearing designs of interlacing vines and ivy . . . and a gramophone with a manual crank from the flourishing horn of which she heard the song 'Le Temps des Lilas'. Or – she was confused – did it come from a musical box with a panel of concave mirrors before which a miniature ballerina in a lilac tutu rose up and pirouetted in stiff jerks, her arms an arabesque? Over the carpets rested a skin of dry petals from crumbling house-plants, its smell never departing from the rugs. From the window she watched children mounting the trams through folding doors, young women in the park on the other side of Wierzyniewska reading on their backs.

'And Papa?'

She turned over clockwise, away from me, sensing my fascination.

'The Frenchman? There is no French family. They are all dead. Papa was sometimes in Poland, but not much.'

'With the aunt?'

'No, in the country. When not working, he came down to the country.'

She then twisted the conversation away from her family.

'If I cannot go back there, I have no home. So I am here with you. I am roasting under the lemons.'

She lay on her back and held her hands like blinds over her face, filtering through parted fingers the small green puffs of rind clustered over the rim of the wall. They were there to confirm her desire for silence.

As we were walking down towards the lake through the long mimicries of cypresses burnt over the road by the sun, she stopped and clapped her hand to her mouth. She then reverted to rapid French.

'I remember something else, though. Basia (the aunt) used to go out at night and take the last tram from Wierzyniewska Street. I saw her from my room when I was not asleep. She would cross the street quickly and wait for the tram under the trees lining the edge of the park so that no one would see her. Sometimes the tram would not come for fifteen minutes and I could see her fretting across the street, terrified that someone would come. She wore a black veil and a ball of false berries near her ear. I never asked her why she waited for the tram, I knew it was her all-important secret. The light inside the car always showed her face tense and frightened. She would be alone and the driver would look back over his shoulder and examine her for a minute in her solitude, delaying for a fraction of a second the closing of the doors as he looked up and down, up and down. Poor Basia.'

3

By Lake Garda it began to rain and we stayed in our room writing letters and smoking cigarettes. The room was garnished with dirty wooden furniture and a brown quilt under which we ate grapes and pears. On the table a fruit bowl of the same dreary pine-wood held a mound of rotting figs that the manageress had forgotten to remove, and the sweet exotic odour remained in the room for the three days we lived in it. From the window we saw an oval of grey water sunk into a ring of hills, terminating in the lush promontary of Sirmione.

She had cut her hair short and now brushed it back smoothly from the hair-line and over her ears. Having used a heavy, blunt pair of scissors, the lines were jagged and abrupt, clean and slightly brutal. She told me that this was the way they cut the boys' hair in the summer in the Polish countryside. With her old military knapsack she was like an adolescent commissar inspecting with detached vitality the poor streets of provincial cities. And since her face still bore the faint remains of tiny cuts, the men who stared at her in the street might have found something intangibly sinister in her, a buried evidence of subjection and cruelty. The ear that Kessler had noticed as being savagely wounded still, in a strange way, did not cohere properly with her face, as if its position had been subtly changed without inflicting visible damage. I noticed that she pulled on it and fingered it unconsciously, twisting the lobe between her thumb and forefinger for minutes on end. I also found the ancient and withered doll he had mentioned, carefully hidden at the bottom of her trunk, and I saw that its golden hair was studded with particles of dried blood, black as tiny olives, and that the eyes had been torn out by hand . . . a filament of nail was wedged into one socket. I had never seen her touch or display this doll: it remained, simply, a solid fragment of the past.

When it rained, we lay under the quilt and took in the odour of the figs, exchanging stories until we fell asleep. Through a paper wall we heard a guest playing a guitar and singing. Over and over he repeated a quick obscene song extemporized around a ballad of a woman with three castles:

> Voi non la conoscete,
> Ha tre castelli,
> Eulalia Torricelli da Forlì!
>
> Un castello per mangiare,
> Un castello per dormire,
> Un castello per . . .

but above us all a woman with heavy feet shouted down for him to leave out the smut. We could hear a pyramid of voices and behind them the rain crackling on the distant water of the lake. When the guitar ceased playing and the singer – I imagined him a hunchback in Mezzetino's costume – sighed with disgust and sudden melancholy and trailed off into silence, the murmur of this water drowned out the world.

We took a train south, descended at Nogara and wandered off the low platform into a field of sugar-beet to sleep. As we lay at noon under trees dividing the fields, the juke-box in the station café hurled out wartime hits. Ania woke in mid-afternoon and walked back to the café to drink a lemonade. When she returned, she rolled me over to wake me.

'Always asleep, Aubergine.'

Her skin was now freckled and spotted with tan. Her breasts fell downward into her shirt and her apple-odour tumbled from them. The road at this point swung near the railway line and we could hear farmers and their families marching along it on their way to the fields or to the town . . . they hallooed her as she ran back across the field and jumped over the rusty tracks in her bare feet: 'Olà-a, vagabonda!'

Three men in the cafeteria came to the windows and pressed their faces against the glass: a gangster was lying low in the sugar-beet, his girl was keeping him informed. But they shrugged – it would be weeks before the military came to fetch him. I lay in the sun and did not move.

'Always asleep,' she repeated.

I thought: if the farmers do not come, we will remain here and, cursing, she will shake my shoulders and her breasts will brush low against ribs and sternum, reaching my throat, and I will be happy. In the eventuality of this purposeless journey continuing, I would make her sleep in the afternoon in every beet-field in the flat valley and she would skip naked over railway lines and drink lemonade in bars under outraged noses suspecting the presence of a hood and his whore. In this way, I thought, as I watched her under the guise of sleep gyrating softly and lazily among the tall plants, I shall invent a pastime and concoct a circle of happy days.

4

Of Verona, nothing but a morning's play in the arena of pink stone and its interrupted discoloured arcades. I expected a tragic sand in the pit, like the sand of bullrings, but found instead an operatic proscenium and orchestra built of flimsy planks and covered with electric cables.

We climbed St Peter's Hill after taking photographs on the Roman bridge at the point where the river Adige falls over shallow stones and becomes a series of decorative miniature rapids. The steps ran around the fragmented amphitheatre between small houses and cypresses, creating sudden platforms looking over the city of pink cupolae and matted roof-tops. Again I fell behind in the ascent and often lost sight of her at the sharp angles of the path. I had to stop and sit under trees, hearing her sandals rattle above me. I thought, it is my heart, it will not move the blood, it will not bear it. I heard the sandals stop and pause, recommence walking and pause. When I could move again I found her lying under a wall of unripe hips, reading *Cities of the South – a Guide.*

'You are really ill,' she said solemnly, taking my hand.

Again I felt exhausted in the heat, I could feel my sweat passing into the dry grip of her fingers. When we had reached the castle at the summit of the hill I had to rest on one of the outer walls, falling sheer to the slope of cedars and funeral cypresses, and I slept until the bells of Sant' Anastasia came rolling over the river at the hour of vespers. She had wandered over to the other side of the forecourt and the shadows of the trees covered her. She was talking to a man with a pipe and I could identify them in the shade by the puffs of smoke. With one eye, as I woke, I saw them rocking with silent laughter and the triangle of her dress near the smoke. I called her name and sat upright. She did not hear, though we were alone in the great forecourt, and I waved extravagantly. She did not see, they were laughing. I got up and began to walk.

Over the suburbs gas-clouds sparkled in the sun at a low red angle; the empty castle with its glassless windows sent out an odour of burnt wood across the open space and into the corner of warm shadow where they were laughing. As I came near them I knew it was my heart, pounding and convulsing in its cradle of fat. The face of the man, I swore, was the face of the sailor, the sailor with his blissful smile. I searched the skin of his arms . . . no anchors, certainly, but I could swear that it was him, that he had found her again after so many months. When they saw me they drew apart and their smiles fell: my face must have been ghastly. The man smoothed down his hair and picked up a bag that had been lying on the ground between his feet. I looked at him madly . . . no, not the sailor, but he showed the same confused disdain. Ania held me gently by the lapel of my jacket.

'Niccolò,' she said, demonstrating with her hand.

'I see.'

'Niccolò has been trying to sell me some cosmetics.'

Niccolò smiled, opening the bag.

'Shampoos,' he murmured. Out of the bag came label-less glass bottles filled with amber detergent.

The face of the sailor had been thick with battered muscle, handsomely regular and cruel. Now I saw the wasted bird-like eagerness of the vendor with his smell of bad tobacco and bartered perfume. We were both thin, weak men . . . he with his poverty, I with my stuttering heart. We were relieved by the sight of each other.

'It is true, what he says,' continued Ania, 'we have nothing to wash our hair with. I am so dirty.'

The man nodded, proffering the orange bottles.

'Please, please Jamie, buy just one.'

Now that I saw how grotesque the salesman was I reached into my pocket, into the damp roll of banknotes curled like a snail at the bottom. I peeled one off secretly and drew it out calmly. Drops of moisture had appeared over my face and she leant over to touch my chest, a little frightened at the heat under the shirt, for she said quickly, 'You're ill, I know,' and I could not reply.

When the salesman had taken the note I pulled her away down the steps and towards the town. The river was dark and violent under the bridge, the small rapids roaring in the echo of the vaults. A single electric light shone over the gate-house, and the via Alessio and the Lungadige Re Teodorico were plunged in darkness over the water. Her hand went back to my chest, searching out the pulsations of the heart.

'One . . . two . . . three . . . ' she counted.

'I'm not sick,' I said. 'You forget, I am young.'

'You!' she laughed. 'You! You are prehistoric. You are an ancient ruin. You are my funny old man, you can't pretend. You can't hide your oldness from Ania.'

In Bologna we lay once more under the rain and talked into the night. We were making our way south in small, random steps, and as we progressed Ania became increasingly withdrawn from the events of the journey and the passing scenery. The sightseeing began to become meaningless and she confessed to me that it did not matter at all to her where she was. On arriving at a new town, we would simply walk into the nearest hotel, whatever it was like. From there it would be easy to catch the next train . . . At night she wanted to talk about her childhood, as if she were piecing it together for the first time. Her descriptions became more obsessively detailed. In our Bolognese bed she told me more about Kraków and the summers she spent there with the pathetic Basia, and the visits to members of her family both in Kraków and in Katowice. She listed with joyful ceremony all the houses they had called at and all the scenery they had seen.

'Basia's sister Elżbieta – my other aunt – owned the house near Zakopane in the mountains . . . like a log cabin, with verandas and wooden porches. From the roof you could see the mountain called Rysy hanging over the lake called Morskie Oko. Elżbieta's house was on the edge of the town, her garden was divided by a river that came down from the hills, and my uncle built a bridge over it from which we caught fish and dangled our feet in the water. All the rooms of these houses smell of wood, the pine-sap. The shutters have small hearts carved into them, through which we could see at night the moon on the hats of the mountains and people walking on the mud paths under the conifers. And my grandfather came for his holidays and sat on the veranda showing the women the stars, repeating: Den-eb, Ve-ga, Al-gol, Arc-tu-rus, and laughing because they could not say them.

'Sometimes we had to go to sleep when it was light and Mama and Papa were in the garden speaking French – we could hear them walking over the bridge of logs and Papa pulling her dress playfully and Mama pushing him away and throwing his hat in the river to make him howl. Yes, and they came to sit by the convolvulus near the window and Sylvia made me be quiet so that we could listen, and we heard them talking among the white flowers like little trumpets, and Papa saying to her in French, "You are happy with your pranks," and she saying, "You are happy with apologies," and he laughing and breathing softly over her hair. They were near the window and we heard them kiss, because at night it is so silent in the mountains you can hear an insect walking on the wall and the rubbing of its wings. Through the heart we saw his arm around her, intruding through the bellbind, and the white cuffs with shining studs, and the shape of her shoulders in the middle of the trumpets. And we could hear the words and the crackle of his shirt and the sound of her hands adjusting her hair, touching his collar. He was thin and delicate, she was heavier but weaker. She spoke a rambling, broken French and he nodded slowly when listening to her, his hand resting on her shoulder with a solitary gold ring on the annular finger. They were alone for hours, escaping from my aunts and my grandfather, and Papa picked off the bell-flowers nervously one by one and I would find them in the morning in a ring around the seat. He would hold me, when we went riding, and call me *petit ananas* after the witticism of my sister, and take me to eat mountaineer's soup made of butter-beans in the skiers' relay stations.

'But I only saw him for one summer . . . normally it was Basia who took me to the relay stations and the cemeteries around the wooden churches. Mama, you know, was always sick, she could not bear the cold in the mountains and would not go out with me. She was always taking *tilleul* in her room when Papa was not there, with her body against the heat of the fire, her eyes immobile and colourless and her legs covered with steaming damp towels. Basia would brush her hair and sing to her, but she always had to sit like this as if paralysed by her vulnerability. She came in to say prayers with us, making us kneel down all together and holding our hands. Her own were always damp and hot, smelling of plain unperfumed soap and lime-tea. She saw the heart in the shutter, its proximity to the beds, and told us not to look through it . . . if we did, she said, a troll would be there waiting with his eye against the heart and we would be turned to wood. It is strange, but this threat – which only amused my sister, as perhaps it was meant to do – terrified me and turned the wonderful carved heart into a supernatural aperture about to reveal the eye of a demon made, like an electric bulb, out of pure fire. It has always been curious to me, the cruelty of this ruse. Mama knew I was terrified and she said nothing. She was glad I would not look at her among the convolvulus.'

5

One morning, the bells were ringing in a tower of pink and green marble. Under the window I heard an engine running, reminding me of the avenue Trudaine. She was asleep, curled up at the edge of the bed; a new city had appeared under the sunlight but I could not move from the bed, or from the room where sculpted garlands of plaster fruit bulged from the ceiling and needles of dry blue light played over them, the reflections in a Neapolitan cave. I waited and smoked a cigarette, the smoke turned grey and purple, washing the plaster fruit, then settled like a weightless mist over the ceiling. For an hour it lay there in the breathless morning. The bells ceased, rang again, ceased. I heard the pigeons settling on the hood of the window and the sound of worshippers drawing near to the cathedral. The needles of light turned slowly, describing a section of a circle over the ceiling. She slept without moving and did not yawn or murmur.

Towards midday I rocked her shoulders back and forth, but still she did not stir. I went to the window and drew open the curtains to wake her, but she did not open her eyes. The bells of a more distant church, a church on the other side of the city, tumbled in on the sunlight; the newspaper boys were shouting under the saplings along the boulevard. I sat down on the bed by her feet and massaged them slowly until she rolled over with a weak cry, pushing the wad of sheets away from her. Her hair was sticking in something, adhering to the pillow in dark, thickened strands. I sat nearer her head and pulled off the sheets. She was still unconscious and her throat was wet. I wanted to roll her back towards me but dared not, for she was shivering in her sleep. Her hair stuck to the sheet too and her hand was moist. A small quantity of blood had fallen over the pillow and sunk into the sheet. Her hair was trapped and entangled in it, the light hairs of her arm near the elbow were matted together. The blood had come from her mouth during the night, a dark, mortal blood that was still damp and warm. The doctor had not told me, he had said nothing about blood. I could not wake her, though she was breathing normally. The blood was drying slowly and she was not in convulsions. When she finally woke, she complained of a slight nausea but was otherwise normal. She did not mention the ejaculation of blood and felt no pain. I wrote a long letter to Kessler full of terror and helplessness, alarmed by my ignorance. As I described to him the quantity and colour of the blood, I began to tremble so that the words scattered themselves over the page and crumbled into disorder.

6

Near Volterra Kessler had arranged a house for us. I had not asked him to, though I had mentioned to him that I would need a more permanent residence for November and December: I had told him that I was sick of dragging her around hotels. The house was empty while the owners – a Swiss doctor and his family – spent the winter in Interlaken. We were free to occupy the whole house and even to 'eat their grapes' . . . We arrived on November 5 when the moon was on the wax, the volcanic hills were still orange and hazed, and the cicadas were still alive in the trees.

The rough, cubic farmhouse controlled a small hectare of vines and fig trees displayed over regular terraces unfolding downward into the valley where a river and a dust road fenced in by poplars crossed the flat bottom. Set within a fantasy of lattices bearing grapes and dog-roses were small wells and a sundial bearing the Venetian inscription *Horas non numero nisi serenas*.

As we opened out the shutters of the top bedrooms overlooking the valley, a volley of rifle shots echoed over the clear space separating us from the mountains opposite, and a pack of dogs broke over the road far below, followed by the flashing reflections on the barrels of the guns and a squad of green rubber capes. Square houses set into the hill flashed grey and white, as clouds passed over the slopes, the dogs ran on under the vines and filtered through peach orchards and plots of quince trees, and fragments of smoke floated up over the ilexes and firs. The acierated surfaces of leaves, the tiny blue river, the clear edges of stone walls, the old rifles, the spherical olive trees and conical hills fixed the light trapped between them into a solid aerial mass with the brilliance of a plaster wall pigmented with blue Mediterranean dye. Through this concentrated air, larval and heavy, we saw the new world, the hunting and forest world, with its commotion of gunfire and falling water and its solemnly violent shades: dark orange, green and black, the heraldic colours of a nightmarish and mystic natural tournament.

The house was stripped of furniture and we slept in a bare room on a metal camp-bed, with an oil-lamp by us on the floor and a china wash bowl that reminded me of the Hôtel du Brésil. The floor was wooden and we would come to bed with our feet torn by splinters and stained with the blood of beetles. In the dark the giant moths attracted by the oil-lamp ricocheted from our bodies and fluttered in the sheets, their death-dances tickling our backs. The cicadas hanging in the orange trees just outside the house made Ania get up and go to the window, and I saw her against the globular trees leaning out to hear them, her eyes closed and her outline bristling with moths, gnats and mosquitoes.

The Swiss family employed a widow and her two sons to work the farm and a woman – a bright rose birthmark in the shape of North America extending across her face from her left ear to her nose – came often to our kitchen to deposit eggs and milk. The sons, returning from the olive orchards, had to walk around the house and we could hear their boots linger on the gravel under our windows every night. I became convinced that they had seen Ania one night, sniffing the cicadas in the orange trees, and that they knew she would come naked again to hear the insects. After a week, I told her not to go near the window at night. I added then that she should not greet them in the plantations. I told her that if they took off their hats or held out their hands or simply spoke, she should ignore them and come back to the house. I told her that she could speak to the old woman but that the sons were not her business. I gave her instructions for answering the door – if it was the old woman she could deal with the matter herself, paying for the eggs and weighing the olives on a pair of bathroom scales. But if a man called, she had to close the door behind her and call me to see him. I told her that this was politeness, that here it had to be done in this way. Strangely, she acquiesced: I did not have to persuade her. I told her, furthermore, that she should not go into the town in the evening . . . that she should only go with me during the day and that she should not tell anyone her name or where she lived. The remoteness and solitude made it easy to watch and control her. If she opened the front door and stepped on to the gravel, I heard; if she ambled too far alone through the wild grass leading up to the wood, I heard her steps falling in the weeds; if she went down into the valley through the peach trees and the olives, I heard her jumping down from terrace to terrace; and if she spoke to the old woman on the dust road I could still hear the voices and decipher every sentence. I could hear every movement in every room of the house and could identify the exact weight of her step, so that if anyone else entered the house I would run downstairs immediately in a high temperature, ready to release an ugly, preposterous rage.

Ania began to sleep longer, sometimes remaining unconscious for two-thirds of the daylight hours. These sleeps were impenetrable, fixed in a dizzying stillness that amplified the silence outside and turned faint gunshots and the cries of the dogs winding through the hills into anguished sounds enacted over a supernatural peace. When I could not wake her I would remain in the room beneath hers, waiting for the first yawn and the creak of the boards as she began to walk. If she woke coughing, I would have to rush up to see if there was any blood. Nearly always the coughing was dry, but violent. She would struggle for breath and lie helplessly on her side doubled over, waiting for the convulsions to pass. The coughing came from deep in her lungs and surfaced in a hoarse, almost silent, croak that stretched her mouth and seized up the muscles of her throat, throwing up webs of saliva over her pillow and causing her eyes to fill with water. The water I forced on her would be overturned and she would thrust me away with indescribable force. Sometimes she slept after the coughing and woke only towards evening, weak and incoherent. Then she would eat and lie in my arms and I would coax her back to sleep with Grimm's tales and thimbles of *vinsanto* and hot milk.

She began to write a kind of diary on loose leaves tied together in a cardboard folder, writing only with a red crayon and marking her entries with the date and the exact time of day. Eventually, her system of writing became more elaborate and methodical, riddled with solipsistic symbolism: she would write in blue crayon before noon, in red crayon between noon and five o'clock and in green up to midnight. Each day of the week was marked by a different symbol at the head of the page: a stylized fly for Monday, a circle enclosing a bird for Tuesday, a blue heart for Wednesday, and so on. She invented different names for herself, to correspond with each day and its symbol, which she used to sign herself off with at the conclusion of each entry: *petite mouche* for Monday, *petit oiseau* for Tuesday, *un coeur percé* for Wednesday . . . I know this because I would read through parts of this secret file when she was paralysed in one of her deep sleeps. The diary was entitled simply 'Ania Malina', her real and baby name put together to create a writer different from herself, a woman still merged with, drowned in, her childhood. The fragments I read (illegally and guiltily) were a reconstruction of that infancy. I read the description I had already heard of Elżbieta's mountain house and Basia's nocturnal escapes, the two memories that had come back to her first and which clung to forgotten facts which she could not bring forth. In this book she began to rewrite the part of her life that had vanished, with its crushed, intangible figures: the father, the younger mother, the cousins, the grandfather, the aunts and the older sister. I soon noticed that each of these figures appeared in the text in a separate colour detaching them from the stream of remembered events and places. The father, Baba, was often written in pink and the mother in buttercup yellow. There were drawings of them in the same colours on the facing pages, warmed by radiant suns and placed in swards of blazing flowers. Baba always wore a formal shirt and at the end of his sleeves hung giant cuff-links coloured in orange to denote an impossible gold. And in between the written page and the coloured drawings I often found pressed rosemary- and thistle-flowers, like mummified re-creations of those that had ringed the window and shutters with the heart-shaped apertures through which her father's arm had passed around the naked shoulders of Maria Januszewska.

7

A road of loose rubble led up from the house to Volterra with its Etruscan gates, joining a wide modern boulevard a kilometre from the principal gate, a hygienic boulevard that offered space for a promenade darkened by cypresses and that looked over the volcanic mountains and the sloping enclosures of crops. We laboured up the spinning road and the slanting boulevard in the early morning, through tangles of jeeps and idle soldiers, and spent whole mornings in the quiet bars while I fed her like a child with sops of brioche and milky coffee. While I read the newspapers she would go into the streets or stand at the bar near my table in her cotton dress, raising her eyebrows at soldiers or making the barman tell her stories which she did not understand and which filled her boredom. She hated the town, its austere fortifications, the unmoving shadow in its streets. When I saw her leaning listlessly against the glass doors, her cheek and breath smudging their surface, counting to herself the passing citizens who moved nearer – deviating almost imperceptibly from their path – to see her a little better, examining the same triangle of mauve flagstones, I knew that she was bitter and lonely.

One evening we did not leave the town until an hour before sunset, having passed many hours over newspapers and glasses of liqueur, and the boulevard was invisible in its envelope of trees as we descended, the valleys below bare and solar brown, and the olive trees sparkling from afternoon rain. The pavements were wet and her tattered sandals riddled with moisture. When we reached the country road she began to walk more reluctantly, with soft resistance, until we could hear the weakened cicadas rattling in the trees at the level of our shoulders, louder than our steps. She leant up and brushed the trees weighted with pomegranates and quinces with the backs of her fingers.

'You', she said suddenly, 'have been writing letters. Thick and secret letters.'

I covered my eyes to look down at her, because the low brown light was bouncing from the puddles in dull flashes. I did not answer.

'Yes,' she went on, 'I saw you go out to the post with the latest one last night. You were very quiet, but I was watching. You post your letters on tiptoe. You go alone and you make no noise. Last night you went up there very late. Are you surprised I saw you?'

When I could make out her form I saw that she had a pockmarked quince in her hand and was contemplating its inedible freshness. I smiled sweetly.

'Yes, I'm surprised you noticed.'

'You creep up in your black hat with your latest letters. I see that you are writing to Dr K. in Paris. Have you told him about the peach trees and the vines and the funny little Italian town? He must be curious about us. Is he?'

'I don't know. I suppose so.' I stole the ugly quince and rolled it over my palm. 'You know, you cannot eat these raw.'

She pressed my hand and smirked.

'Yes, I know. We ate them when I was small . . . stewed.'

We sat on a wall of uncemented boulders overlooking a quadrangle of apple trees and waited for the sun to disappear. The blue star Vega and the wings of the constellation Aquila descended eastward and the bow of Cassiopeia whirled overhead, dragging the sharp point of the great star Capella. When it was dark the stars of the bears shifted in a giant circle over the north, around the drab hub of Polaris, enfolded in the faint twists of Draco and fading into the almost invisible string of the Lynx. We sat in silence. The moon was already there, burning over the metallic olives. The water continued to fall and we heard it dripping in the fields. She reclaimed the quince and threw it over the wall into the apple orchard.

'I understand,' she said. 'They are your letters. Why should you not post them in a black hat on tiptoe at midnight? Though I would like to know what you say.'

I was not prepared for this and could not answer.

'I know that Kessler has written to you . . . why should you not write back to him? There is a lot to say: Ania and her sickness, Ania and the hospital, Ania and her misbehaviour.'

I began to shake my head.

'No, nothing like that.'

'Nothing? Nothing about little Malina's illness and her strange sleeps? You should be more observant.'

I remained silent and she went on.

'If you think nothing, that is surprising. Don't you think I *am* a little sick, Jamie? The good Swiss medicine man looked me over and he has his opinions at least.'

I lay back and began eating a rotten apple from the grass slope beneath us. She observed contemptuously the brown bitter cavities in the fruit.

'Do you think I am sick? They made reports. Kessler has read them and has his opinion . . . did you ever read them? No? You must, they would explain away your worries, you would learn. Only . . . ' her voice subsided into a whisper ' . . . we aren't sure about it, we can't say what kind of sickness it is. But I asked you: you must have an opinion because you write to Kessler and tell him what you think. You tell him, I suppose, what time I go to the lavatory, what time I wake up, go to sleep, what I say in my sleep?'

'No. I tell him nothing. I tell him things in passing.'

'But you do tell him. You tell him and you send him your ideas in secret. You must think . . . '

'I think nothing.'

'You think nothing in your letters and you send them in secret? I know you think something. You notice everything.'

'What do I notice?'

She paused and rubbed her eyes as if they were irritated and then plucked her lips. It was cold and her breath smoked in the moonlight.

'You notice when I am ill. You write it down carefully in your letters. I have read some interesting parts. You notice my "unaccountable sleeps", my "unaccountable discharges of blood", my "unaccountable moods". You mark down the times at which these occur as if it is valuable information. And then you tell him that you "do not understand", and would he be so kind as to tell you more about the past? It all "leads back to that". So I ask again: do you truly think . . . '

'I think nothing,' I repeated. 'I am not a doctor with opinions.'

'Who is the doctor? The man in Paris . . . the greedy Swiss man. Shall I tell you . . . ?' She frowned, humorously, and lobbed the useless apple which I had not finished back into the orchard.

The moon tilted over the trees, displaying a leering *Mare Tranquillitatis.*

'I have not organised it in my mind,' she went on. 'There was a pretty hospital full of children and a doctor was there to see to my leg. He was not good-looking and I didn't like his hands, the odour they had – antiseptic chemicals. You could feel the bones in his hands, there was not enough flesh on them. There was, however, something nice in them, as an afterthought. He was greedy, despite his clean smell – you remember him at Senlis? Well, he was reluctant to let me go . . . to go from St Lazare. He had a queer idea of me.'

'He was probably concerned for you.'

'Yes, he was, I know.'

'So he would not let you go immediately?'

'He did not say so. I guessed, because I could walk and there was no reason to stay there. You know, one does not argue.'

'He did not think you were sick. He wanted to be sure.'

She fell on to her side along the wall and expelled a lungful of air with a bored moan.

'Yes, to be sure . . . to be sure.'

'But he said nothing?'

'Why should he have? I wouldn't have understood his reasons. I only want to know that *you* do not think I am ill.'

'I never said so.'

'Then promise: no more letters to that man in Paris.'

I was slightly amazed at this skill, but could not dismantle the logic.

'I promise.'

I saw that she was persuaded of her own sickness, with unconfessed strength of conviction.

'You have to admit,' she went on, 'that it's impossible to go on with a sick woman. You would go mad.'

'That would make two lunatics, two lunatics could get on.'

'But'–she visibly relaxed–'you don't think anything bad of me, I shouldn't ask things like this. You're bored and cold.'

She got up and stood in the road, struck by the lunar beam.

'You see,' she said, 'I am lunatique.'

I stood in the road also and took her arm. The surface of the road was drier as we walked down towards the farms, and the tiled square roofs were visible from far up, the anchors of high motionless ropes of fire-smoke. The red spark of Betelgeuse had risen in the south over Procyon and Sirius, the winter stars, glaring over the stark geometric farmhouses and their whirls of husbandry. The seas were scrambled over the moon's face – Imbrium, Nubium, the Sea of Fecundity – their phosphorescence dabbled in plots of vines, and the pond by our house threw up a plate of water that held them together, divided by bars of cypress-green. The hundred fields rolled away down into the valley, blue and silver, a Roman fountain.

> Nous arrivons, nous voilà,
> Avec la garde montante.

I sang back, 'like little soldiers':

> Sonne trompette éclatante
> Ta ta ta ra ta.

She stepped down the terraces with their edges of stone, and ducked under the squatting olive trees, running. It was still warm and I remembered a Latin lesson of my childhood in which a fat and morbid master had knelt down before the class and kissed a fragment of dirty parquet to imitate the Roman legionaries returning over the Alps after twenty years of service against the Germans and, says Tacitus, kissing the earth when they saw the valleys of Italy and weeping 'Aprica! Aprica!' – the South, the South.

8

Ania's repertoire of songs extended only to fragments of four melodies, none of which she could recite in its entirety. They were: the 'Choeur des Gamins' from Carmen, which she had seen on the stage as an infant, the Polish national anthem 'Jeszcze Polska Nie Zginęła', the French national anthem (though only the lines 'Aux armes, citoyens!' etc.) and Ernest Chausson's romantic song 'Le Temps des Lilas', which her aunt Basia had played on a manual gramophone and which the observant child had associated with that woman's melancholy pining, seeing perhaps her taut and suffering face, withdrawn into its own world, every time the record was played. It was this song, which she knew best, that woke me as the windows were opened and the glare of the sea, a perfect, still parallelogram of blue water, and a wind smelling of sand and hot stone fell into the room:

Le temps des lilas
Ne reviendra plus . . .

This time the water was bare and vast. The light was immense, reflected from a flat ocean to blocks of white stone. There were no boats with tilting sails, no cypress trees and no lemon residences buried in the obscure luxury of pines. This sea was hard and ringed with stone. She opened the shutters and the shrill light burst in. A sterile wing of brown rock infringed, far away, upon the horizon.

What seemed the remnants of a town, the dregs of a volcanic disaster, clung to the curving desert coast and raised a stubble of cracked and frail white plaster against the onslaught of the sea. A line of palm trees marked an ocean boulevard and a string of rusting lamps on a looping cable. The shore was violated by a faint green scum and the strip of sand remained empty and colourless. On our first walk there we could not hear the sea above the dull clatter of a sea-front café which was, in any case, deserted: the suction of limp wavelets went unnoticed. Above peeling bunches of houses we could see the crisp perimeter of an amphitheatre, an incomplete shell of arches, and a fragment of a marble head on a pillar – a Julian emperor – staring seaward, empty-eyed. From the café we could see the sweep of the ocean, the brownish headlands – now tipped with solitary fires – and the oval motion of the bay. It was smothered by an artificial silence, the silence of the decaying, helpless town which imposed itself upon a whole sea. We drank on a concrete terrace, caught up in grey gusts of litter, and the lamps on the precariously festive cable wobbled in the wind, throwing sinister zones of illumination over the road. The palms stretched in the breezes, hissing along the boulevard, and their sprays of fronds overlapped above the gloomy pavements.

'It's the holidays,' Ania said, brushing her glass with great civility against mine and kissing me when the gesture of a celebratory sip was completed. 'The sea is nice,' she whispered, at a loss for truthful words.

Further into the town we found a smell of drains, a constant rim of waste paper. Children followed us, holding our hands, wiping Greek noses. The bars were quiet and her eyes darted, disappointed, among the old men collected under bare bulbs. In a cowardly way I displayed her as an adolescent wife, acquired for reasonable and practical purposes: procreation, companionship, *le ménage*. Otherwise, how would she appear to them . . . an abducted Venus, a childish-fresh Jezebel, an incestuous sister? She was soon known as *la moglina* and in this context they forgivingly explained away her too-adult cosmetic excesses, her languid cigarettes and her brash alcoholic tastes.

The xenophobic hotel, a rough monument suffering under violent red print (the words 'Albergo Cesare', after the fractured bust) held sway over a portion of the ocean boulevard, a dirty section of beach and a frigid slice of sea. The summer tables, normally littered over the beach, even though separated from the parent hotel by the silent road, had been gathered in and laid in nostalgic stacks in a locked dining-room. Winter cacti, froths of curling red flowers, had been posted along our sill. A jug of fresh water – a crystal jug on a tin plate – was deposited by the bridal bed, left as an accidental seal of approval, an epithalamic offering. The sheets were starched and virgin, tinged with healthy blue, folded back at one corner and miraculously warmed on the night of our arrival by a copper bedpan. On every landing a plastic *Opsiandra* palm flourished in sordid shadow, and the smooth ruby of the velveteen carpet – bright and smooth as the inside of a lung – faded away up stairways and under doors. A black-robed maid brought hot water in a deep china bowl early in the morning and a towel draped over one arm. She knocked and entered, without regard to marital functions . . . sanctified concupiscence erasing itself from the tables of sin. So the water would steam on the small cabinet by our bed, a cloud of rose-petals, and arrive after several minutes in the form of warm droplets on the ceiling above us. And the sea was always there, a Greek, Roman, Arabic sea, a depository of forgotten names . . . Ortygia, Thapsus, Helorus . . . a lake of triremes riddled with dolphins and the wakes of vagabond nations.

During the second night, she began to cough once more and I found flowers of blood on her pillow, as I had done before. She seemed unconscious during the coughing and showed no fear, no mild distaste, at the sight of her own blood – a dark, rich lung-blood. But the effort of long spasms of expectoration left her exhausted and sluggish. Then a word of fear would come, instinctively and crudely, she would wake up, twisting in the bed as the seizure came and went, and move near me saying, 'What is it?', feeling the blood dribbling over her chin downward into the sheet with the soft tick-tack of a leaking tap. I had sworn not to write to Kessler. She would not listen if I talked of hospitals. The black-clad maid squinted at the blood when she collected the sheets, and said nothing. Ania forgot about the stains, or pretended they did not exist. But she had said it: 'What is it?' and sometimes in Polish 'Matko Boska, Matko Boska' (Mother of God), revealing her fear. The blood did not wash out and I found the pink marks on the returned sheets and pillow-cases. The next discharge she effected secretly into the basin and I saw only the unwashed remains speckling the bowl. If I asked her why she hid the blood from me, she would become silently furious. She would say that I had promised not to write, that I had no reason to observe and analyse. If a true fury came over her in the course of one of these tirades, she would hurl the glass cups that were stacked over the basin against the walls, and they would shatter against the plaster surface stained with roach blood and fall into a million pieces with a sickening singing sound.

A mile from the town, following the monotonous boulevard, the sand became cleaner and the curve of the shore sharpened then broke up into rocky indentations, creating tiny coves with cusps of white sand and punctured with deep pools. No rubbish fell here from the town; the occasional automobiles moved silently along the highway, screened by walls of rock. We could swim far out, seeing nothing in the water or on the shore but the enamelled bodies of automobiles moving along the road, flickering in and out of the palms, the dust hanging over the town and the stained ruins of the Roman buildings.

It was from here, swimming out into the cold currents and drifting into the deeper water, that we first saw the gypsies in a too-new car racing along the ocean road. Ania noticed them and touched my foot under the water.

'Gypsies!'

At the same level as the water the black car slipped past under the trees, the dismantled roof revealing a long turquoise scarf unfurling in the wind and a red cowl huddled over the wheel. An irregular ball of colour flashed in and out of the sunlight, leaving loops of smoke in the air behind it, and a radio echoed out over the ocean, a song jangling with trumpets. The car pulled a small wooden trailer painted blue and yellow, and the hubs of the wheels were coloured in with savage patterns. The body of the car in front was new, a glittering black, bristling with fairy-bright chrome. A sleeve of malachite green was laid along the rim of one window and a naked woman's shoulder against the edge of the rear door. There was distant shouting, the sound of a tambourine and its ring of cheap cymbals. Ania waved, treading water, and the malachite arm fluttered in response. The rise of a wave covered the road and when it had subsided the sleek automobile had disappeared into the town, dragging its cacophony of trumpets into the streets.

And on the same road, as we returned barefooted from the beach with our towels over our shoulders despite the cold, Ania found pieces of orange peel scattered over the smooth tarmac in dismembered chaos.

'Yes,' she held them up with pride, 'gitans!'

9

We spent Christmas alone, locked up in our room. Despite her pleas we never went in search of amusements. But during the first days of January the gypsies we had seen on the coast road appeared in the town square where I took Ania to drink in the afternoons, and we finally saw them, dressed in the colour of tulips, holding small monkeys in their arms and playing guitars. We watched through the glass doors of the café, and the babyish North African macaques climbed over their shoulders and turned shrill blue eyes upon the audience.

'Please,' Ania said, 'I want to give them an apple.'

I gave her the money and she ran off to buy apples. When she returned, the macaques were still on the musicians' shoulders and she hung back, embarrassed. One of the men beckoned her forward and took the apple, allowing in return the monkey to swing on her arm. Macabre in a pin-stripe suit stained with oil and straw, a wide tie encrusted with brooches holding false stones and a pair of military boots, he bent down and scooped off the macaque from her arm. Knowing that I was watching, she recoiled. He offered her the end of the monkey's leash and she stepped back further.

I read her lips: 'No, no, I don't want it . . . '

Her cowardice amused him. He curtsied by plucking out his trousers. On his shoulder, the little monkey bit savagely into the apple and he stroked one of its legs.

' . . . no, I don't want it.'

'A cute little cupid, a lady-killer . . . ' (I read his lips too.)

'It's looking at me!'

The prosecution of his laughter changed her mind. Suddenly she went forward. She took up the leash and drew off the monkey from his arm. The audience stirred with pleasure.

'If the little one wants to dance,' he said gently, following her. 'Ha ha, tango, capriola . . . '

The men behind me clapped and I felt my hand shaking. He

was walking round behind her, his dark hands on her shoulders, imitating the strut of the macaque.

'Ecco una ballerina!' he shouted.

I could not move, I could only watch the muscular hands filled with orderly veins blue as anemones balanced on her shoulders, and the shuffle of the boots taken from a slaughtered giant in a roadside ditch moving in time to Ania's skip, co-ordinated with the rhythm of the song the group were now playing. Particles of snow began to fall slowly on to their heads.

The song finished and the gypsies went into a performance of circus tricks. Ania released the monkey with a small start – as if she had remembered in that instant the presence of my supervision – and the man in the oily suit bent down to speak to her. She came back to the café and pushed open the glass doors.

'Must we sit here?' she asked. 'I want to be near.'

I said it was cold, would she mind closing the doors and sitting inside? I said I would get her some chocolate as a recompense. She sat down, leaving the glass door to fold back into place.

'I prefer monkeys to chocolate,' she whispered.

We watched the circus arrange itself in the square, haloed by the lights reflected in the glass, the snow falling over their hair and coating the fur of the monkeys. One of the men had stripped down to the waist and was swilling mouthfuls of petrol, flexing the muscles of his stomach and the pectorals luminous with brown grease.

'Il mangiatore di fuoco!'

'Hercule da Caltagirone!'

A drum rolled and the shivering white athlete stepped on to a carpet and inflated his lungs. An arc of orange flame, a leap of monstrous saliva shot up from his lips, dissolving with a faint hiss into the snow and illuminating with its crack of fire the soft and wondering oval of Ania's face.

As we watched in silence the acts and antics unfold I remained alert, ready to pick out the face of an abductor. The features of the man with the false brooches had pierced me with the horrible swiftness of light transmitted over vast distances by mirrors. I waited for another moment when they would stand revealed once more by the concentration of desire. At this point I almost insisted on leaving. I was held back only by Ania's visible pleasure. She was fascinated by the women . . . by their cropped hair, red and yellow bathing-suits, their muscular legs bloodless in the cold, and a white paste covering their faces. For the audience they were obviously grotesque, inhuman *pagliacchi*, shaved, aborted women. Their eyes were formed into huge abnormal hazels by rings of black paint, and the napes were shaved high up to the base of the scalps, so that the violent black of the hair was a clumsy shock, a sudden twist of ugliness that made the white shoulders, the white faces and the white arms artificially attractive. And she was fascinated by their powerful feet, the ability to stand effortlessly on the ends of the toes.

'They're lovely,' she said, a little dismally.

The women had taken to their hands and were moving with magical speed around the perimeter of the square, causing the women watching to sneer slightly with instinctive disgust. The players applauded, cracking jokes which the old men could not pick out from the warmth of the café. They began to mutter, suddenly disappointed.

At the end of four songs, the monkey-handler who had danced with Ania emerged in a brilliant white coat, his face painted white and red – red nose, orbits, ears and lips – and wearing a hat speared with a parrot's feather. He was introduced as 'Pietro Arlequino da Niscemi', a fantastical title for the children. And I saw that he was a kind of half-dressed Harlequin, a mime-artist as in the English theatre, carrying a lath as a wand and theatrically invisible to the players around him. Underneath the coat a gymnastic hose tapered down to nimble and elegant legs. The coat was spangled with hideous brooches, the same as those that had covered his tie. Now there were gold rings in his ears and paper buckles on his military boots. His eyes rolled in their red apertures, performing heroic expressions. It was going to be a mime about a thief.

'Look.' Ania smiled. 'It's Dario.'

'No,' I corrected. 'Pietro Arlequino da . . . '

But he had evidently given her another name as they were playing with the macaque.

'I know,' she went on, 'but that's for the audience.'

'Did he speak to you then?'

'A little.'

'Did he now? Was there a reason to?'

She shrugged and looked away.

'I don't know. He liked my apple.'

The harlequin had ordered a song and the mime went on with

the singing and the squealing of the monkeys in the background. I paid no attention to the plot. The face of the harlequin had acquired again the peculiar tension that had drawn me to it before. Detached from the machinations of its body, it remained a fixed point above everything else, charged with its own electricity, expressionless, larvate and devoid of muscular subtlety. I ceased to notice the movements around him. The mask, now seemingly made of ivory or porcelain, made me think of my father's house. The labyrinth of corridors, the stagnant pools with a skin of lilies, the bedroom with the high windows and the scarecrows gaunt and weirdly elastic in the turnip fields. I had seen it there and heard its breathing behind the glass in the bedroom.

Jack Frost, Jack Frost,
When he gets in
All is lost.

A sudden recognition startles the nerves. I looked down at Ania but she was laughing. It was necessary to leave, to evade the agility of the spirit in the mask, but I could not pull her away without a scene. Unaware of the peril, she was biting her nails with glee. With every twist in the plot of the mime, the mask came nearer. In this way they creep up, serpentine, until it is too late and they are ready to lash out. I had made the first muscular preparation for the act of standing and grasping Ania's arm when the mime abruptly came to an end.

Ania was amused and rose to her feet to applaud. I had found it tedious and hysterical, but did not want to cross her. I agreed that it had been funny.

'The clown is good, better than Hercule.'

'What about the bit about the egg . . . ' she shrieked, ' . . . the egg and the chicken?'

'The egg . . . yes, certainly.'

'They are real experts. Another apple.'

'Just one, then.'

I took out the necessary coin and she ran off again. When she returned to the square, the players, having displayed a cardboard box with which to receive their wage of tossed vegetables, were preparing to leave. She threw the apple into the box. As I had foreseen, the harlequin spotted her and bowed, the macaque, now returned to his shoulder, bowing with him, with a blue gaze.

'We are indebted,' said the bow.

She returned elated.

'What experts they are,' she said.

Despite the urgency of escaping, I wanted to watch them for a while. The sudden collapse of the illusion and play of unworldly antics had surprised me. For some time I had been convinced, while watching the mime, that the players were beings set apart from the cruel definitions of gravity, temperature, hunger, etc. Now they were counting cabbages in a damp corner of the square. The shutters of the upper storeys of the houses facing on to the theatre of events were closing with mournful claps, the snow was appearing in sinister lines along the cracks between the paving stones, and the old men were drifting soundlessly out of the café into the world of ice and shadow . . . the supper-hour. We waited at the table until the café lights could be seen clearly in the snow beyond the glass doors. The players disappeared gradually. The mask had undone itself, wiped itself away, and the brown face re-emerged slyly into reality.

As we walked back to the Albergo Cesare we saw them ahead of us, turning off into the bare fields with the monkeys chattering in their cages. The high, powerfully built frame of Pietro Arlequino, thrust between the women, floated under the lamps ahead, and the parrot's emerald feather still stuck into his hat quivered a little madly in the gusts of snow.

'Don Giovanni,' they were shouting at him in mockery, because he was between the women, 'Don Giovanni, "La cì darem", ha ha!'

10

One night I woke from a dream and found that she was not there. The bed was smooth but empty, and the door of the hotel room had been left open two inches . . . the red light of the corridor carpet glowed in the space. We had gone to bed together, we had fallen asleep together telling stories, but she had left the bed and opened the door without waking me. The room was cold and her dresses lay melted over the chairs and racks, the shoes littered over the floor betraying a struggle to choose quickly in conditions of secrecy and urgency. In the basin lay a stick of rouge, and smudged red fingerprints smeared the rim of cracked china. I searched through her bag, which she had not taken . . . she had removed only a pack of cigarettes and a comb.

All through my life I have suffered from the myths of abduction. Lifting me suddenly into the air in her arms, my mother demonstrated, to terrify me, the power of the Erl-King. At the invisible end of the labyrinth of corridors the Stair-Man lived crouched in a crack between the floorboards. If it was not the Stair-Man it was the scarecrows in the turnip field who come to life at night animated by the light of the stars, the Rumbletum in the larder, the Angel in the moon, the Druids in the drains, the Stick-Man under the lily-pads, the fairies in the roots of the trees and Jack Frost who opens the windows of children's rooms with icicle fingers and enters with the silence of a bird. The stealers of children come from another world, they enter our nights with the secrecy proper to the misformed. Their bodies only suggest our own, related to them by a sleight of the mind . . . in reality they are the images of animals, vegetables, landscapes, trees, rooms and the shape of certain well-known shadows that accompany the habitudes of sleep. I had begun to see them following Ania, watching her steps at twilight, shadowing her movements in the darkness which is their natural element; I heard their soft whistles of enticement and while she slept I waited for their fingers to scratch the glass of the windows and for the siren-voices to rise up. The child who is carried away is transported to another dimension, she is lost to the senses, the common language is stripped away: ascending to queendom, descending to nightmarish slavery, she becomes an alien. The intruder effects an irreversible transformation. The child stares back at her parent with the uncomprehending gaze of a stranger.

At the same time, the abductor who shadowed her began to acquire a definite physiognomy. He would be equipped with the same features that appeared before me in a mirror, though arranged in various ways that would make him seem, for a while, an unknown figure. My dreams secreted this face as naturally as they would a memory from my past, coloured by an indescribable significance somehow attached to the mechanisms of hysteria. I saw it at the window, peeping in through the half-opened shutters; I saw it once in the crowd of a bus – a rigid, purple hand fixing it to a hanging strap among the swaying faces; I saw it in the vineyards, lit up clearly in the sun but unnoticed by others; I saw it among the crowd open-eyed in the haze of candelabra – the gaze turned towards us, a chip of turquoise in a pagan mosaic, seeming to alight upon her neck; I saw it between the trees along the nocturnal streets and zigzagging like an Adonis butterfly in our shadow, a light, transparent object, crafty, insectile, unstable and airborne with vicious gaiety. Everywhere it followed us, hovered over our decisions, flickered between our fingers, circled our routes, imitated our gestures. Like the face of the Stair-Man, it could not be dispelled. I could not speak to it or command it to vanish, I could not call Ania's attention to it or order any other person to pursue it; and above all I could give it no name . . . this hybrid spirit – half-animal, half-plant – on the perimeter of my vision, who never leaves my side, prepared always to snatch up the trinket of a child which catches its eye and promises it the reward of the magpie.

The night-porter was asleep and I did not wake him. In the street, a finger-breadth of snow had fallen and frozen, revealing a single track of small footprints departing from the hotel door. A burnt match lay on top of the hard snow, uncovered by any fresh fall. The snow had stopped and the tracks remained clear: it was easy to follow them to the town centre. In the square where we had watched the travelling players the footprints were replaced by grooves made by a car's wheels and it would be impossible to follow these if they left the town. I went over to the café and peered at the clock over the bar: 3.30 a.m. It was not possible. She had disappeared; it was like the nightmare summer in Paris. She had made no promises, but now she was older: we had come to an understanding. She had not done this once in Italy, she had been stable and content. It was possible the police had picked her up in the square while she was . . . taking a walk? But I knew that she had made a rendezvous with the gypsies and that she had met them there. She knew, of course, that I would have forbidden this. She had learnt by now the uselessness of confrontation, the infinite value of discretion and evasion. The feet met the grooves in the snow and they vanished together in a complicit furrow that swung round the square and pursued a side-street which I knew led to the highway by the sea. In an hour I could reach the place where we used to swim, but I did not know where the encampment was along that road . . . only that the camping field was off the highway, though hidden by the hills.

I turned back and returned to the hotel. By the door I picked up the match: I was going to ask her, in absurd fury, if it were hers (it was the only evidence I had). I did not think that 'evidence' was necessary, but I wanted to throw this little burnt match in her face and cry 'Is this your match?' . . . a gesture powerful enough to crush her. I forgot that Ania would laugh, sneer and throw it back at me, calling me 'Aubergine le Policier'.

I returned to the room and sifted through the chaotic shoes that she had left. I deduced that she had taken a red pair, the best she had. I threw the remainder against the door in handfuls and shouted inventive obscenities in French so loudly that I was soon hoarse and perspiring. Someone began to knock with the heel of a shoe against the ceiling and I heard the Italian cognates of the same words bawling and grating in the silence. What did I, Son of a Whore, think I was doing? I threw the glass jug against the wall and it smashed in a livid bubble of water. My face was wild and red in the mirror, bloated with hot blood, and webs of sweat had formed under my eyes. The man above was, it seemed, going to descend and kill me. I locked the door and lay on the bed with the light on, listening to his heavy, angry steps – the heaviness of a bear, a boxer, a pasta-eater. I waited and he did not come. After a while his lurid snoring resumed: I had listened to it night after night, and recognized its rhythm and tone. I had a sudden desire to run up while he was asleep and sever his nose with a razor . . . no more snoring, no more threats! I would give the nose to Ania and frighten her out of her mind: 'You cannot manipulate me, you cannot run out . . . look what I have done!'

At dawn I was still awake and I ran down to the maid, who was boiling water for the guests in the kitchen. I asked her where the *camminenti* were and she gave me instructions. I stole a knife from the table in the gloomy dining-room and ran out into the town.

The hills near the sea were still sprinkled with light snow and the road was iced and deserted: the tracks leading off from the lamplit highway were dark between walls of loose stones and colonnades of cypresses. When I had found the right track I could hardly see the fields beyond the funeral-trees and the ledges of stone brimming with cacti. The track of rough boulders and formless sand led up into the hills, through a lemon orchard, through blasted vineyards, through tracts of white rock and grazing goats. The sea lit up behind me in the sun (silently and slyly, a mound of grey between the dark trees) as the farmers began radiating slowly out over the fields.

A road curved over the nearest hill and dipped sharply into a cold and stony valley, winding between fig trees and black, crooked almond trees. I could see a fire far down the side of the valley, flickering behind bushes and partly hidden by the course of a stone wall. There were no farmers here, and I remembered that this was the edge of a farm, the wall was the perimeter and the gypsies must be beyond the wall. I left the track and cut across the sloping fields over fragile packs of ice, under the stripped olive trees and moving mist. The black car was tilted over on the uneven ground, reflecting the camp fire. They were awake and I could hear their voices. But when I emerged over the stone wall into the light of the fire, only one was there to greet me, the harlequin who had taken Ania's apple. The others were gathering firewood in the valley and he did not call them back.

The clown was still dressed in his stained black suit, now riddled with grass. He was boiling a can of coffee over the fire, suspending it by a long metal stick above the flames. His military boots were undone, revealing the white flesh of wasted feet. He did not move as he watched me climb down from the wall. There was a moment of haggard gazing between us and he held out the metal stick with the can of coffee dangling from it, a dumb gesture of guarded welcome. A brown liquid was foaming over the rim of the can and I could smell the harsh coffee, burnt, tasteless, thick. He withdrew the stick, raising his eyebrows.

'No?'

He laid the can aside and covered it with a plate, then squatted by the fire. There was no reason he should know the purpose of my visit . . . he had probably never seen me with Ania. I came close to the fire and let him look at me (squinting, racing through his memory, his gallery of hostile faces). I examined the camp while he waited: a small tent nailed to the hillside, flapping in the wind, boxes laid around the fire and animal cages rocking gently from side to side in the shade of an olive tree several yards away, sheltered by the wall. In the darkness I could see the eyes of the monkeys shining in the light of the fire, blue and orange disks. The others were calling to each other in the wood, but Ania's voice was not among them. Nor was there any sign of her in the camp. The harlequin had decided that he did not know me and appeared amused. I was cold and nervous and had to bring forth the question: I asked him in Italian if he had seen Ania. The smile widened and he sat back on his haunches. I repeated the name.

'A girl?'

I nodded, searching through the scattered boxes with my eyes for traces of clothing.

'Here, no.'

He shook his head and uncovered the coffee. The foam had subsided and he picked up the can to drink. His eyes did not move from me as he did so. There was nothing to do but go back. The camp was empty and the growing light revealed nothing around me. I could not search the car without pushing him aside . . . and the other voices were now approaching, struggling up the hill. I stayed by the fire and we looked at each other in silence. There was dancing mockery in the harlequin's eyes and his face looked older in the dawn, stripped of colour, narrow and sharp as a tooled stone, an arrow-head or hand-axe. The coffee stained his lips a sickly orange and made the inflexible, theatrical smile darker and more artificial. We waited and the voices grew louder. There was no food, perhaps the savagery in him was hunger. I noticed that there were no signs of sorcery on his body, only a slender gold ring inserted into the lobe of one ear, a thick purple stain covering the cuticle of the index finger of his right hand and a small scratch on one temple that did not bleed but seemed inflamed a livid pink, an old infected wound. There was nothing to say and the visit was becoming farcical. Ania was not there and I had come into the hills for nothing. The harlequin must have been laughing . . . I could see his laugh hidden behind the coffee-stained lips and howling deep in his throat, making the muscles quiver along the length of his neck and causing his eyes to concentrate with malignant curiosity.

I thanked him and went back up through the field of olives, not turning in case I met the mocking eyes. Just before leaving, I had seen the other four black and emaciated figures trudging uphill out of the wood with huge fragments of wood – whole branches with leaves – on their shoulders. For no reason, I thought that if they had all been there together they would have killed me . . . they could have fed my white and tender flesh – the flesh of a citizen – to their little macaques. When I reached the top of the hill I at last turned back and saw the fire glowing under the wall, now pouring out a greenish smoke, the smoke of smouldering, freshly picked wet wood.

The thought of returning to the town filled me with dread and disgust. It was light as I walked by the sea and fishing boats had reached the horizon, putting out melancholy white sails. I passed the point where Ania had picked up the orange peel from the road and I could see the head of the Julian emperor erected above a forest of flowering cacti and eucalyptus. The amphitheatre was indistinguishable from the sky, the colour of functional bone, and a light snow was again falling over the sea. The road was empty and I could not hitch a lift.

But a hundred yards from the first buildings of the town I found her on the sand a few inches from the water. Her red shoes lay in the sand nearer the road and she lay curled on her side, breathing slowly in her sleep. She did not hear me approaching, but when I touched her arm to wake her the flesh unconsciously shrivelled away from me . . . the arm was cold, heavy and inorganic. I struck her face lightly with my palm. She was haggard and ashen in sleep, her features sagging into the sand. I forced open her lips – cracked and lateritious – and her teeth were stained with blood, as if her gums had been bleeding. I had not noticed before how thin she was, her ribs bursting under her shirt and the flesh on her neck pulled tightly over a rope of muscle I had never seen. I lifted her up by her shoulders and shook her awake. The coughing began immediately and she doubled up to vomit. I held her upright and wiped the pink saliva from her chin and neck. She was conscious and stared at the sea as I pulled her on to her feet.

'It's light,' she said, taking my hand. 'All the boats . . . '

I carried her to the road and we sat and waited. I told her to put her shoes on. She was weak and I could not ask her questions . . . I straightened her hair, wiped her mouth, put her shoes on for her.

'I came out,' she said, paying no attention. 'I was coughing, it upsets you.'

I did not believe her, but perhaps the harlequin had not seen her after all; his hatred might have had another cause. I could not help asking, 'Where did you go, then?'

She pointed to the beach.

'Here.'

'Why did you stay here? It's almost freezing.'

She shook her head.

'I fell asleep, I was tired.'

I could not forget the face of the gypsy and the stain on his yellow nail. I had to ask her.

'Did you see the players when you went out last night?'

She looked at me in silence, her eyes tired, empty and bewildered.

' . . . the players we saw in the square, with the monkeys.'

She made no sign and continued to stare at me. We began to walk back into the town. Snow clouds had massed over the hills since dawn and the first white gusts were falling now over the road, the suspended lamps and the eyeless emperor. She shivered violently on my arm, wobbling in her fanciful shoes. She was gasping softly to get her breath and when we reached the hotel she was asleep. I carried her up to the disordered room. A gale was rising up in the street under our room and by the window, with its view of semi-frozen slippery flagstones and roaring litter, I wrote my last letter to the good doctor Kessler.

11

rue St Georges
Paris

Dear Lovecraft,

I cannot explain everything to you now, you would probably fail to see the necessity of obeying me, but you and Ania must return here as soon as you can. Ania's mother has come to me . . . as the man responsible for Ania. She says she doesn't remember you, that you have no right, that she will take action etc., etc. I really would advise you to come back immediately and sort this out. If you have any problems with money, I will pay all expenses.

Kessler

The train was moving in its asymptotic line, approaching the curve of the sea but never touching it, and Ania was asleep while I read. She had a book, *Plants and Trees of the Mediterranean*, spread out over her legs and glazed images of orchids, roses and peach blossom were tumbled into the ruffled blue polka dots of her skirt. Her foot was posed on my knee for support, a naked, faintly-veined foot with tiny, dirty pink toes. I read the letter and wondered whether I should tear it up and claim that I had not received it at all. Its destruction would set me free for perhaps two more months, eight weeks with Ania in a hidden place. I would not obey Kessler yet. There was still a chance that she would heal and open up to me . . .

The sea was now cold and I did not want Ania to swim, but she would slip out before dinner, as it was growing dark, and swim a hundred yards out and lie on her back for quarter of an hour. I began increasingly to see her floating in the sea at twilight, *pour être solitaire*, as she confessed. This solemn bathe made her gay for the duration of dinner, after which she would go up to sleep and would not talk to me until the next day.

'I go to talk,' she told me resentfully, 'with my mama and papa in the sea. It is stupid, you think, mais c'est comme ça.'

I took her instead for crepuscular promenades, to keep her away from this ritual. She dressed carefully for these walks, with melancholy precision . . . a long raincoat reaching down to the middle of her shins, belted and buttoned, a triangular scarf with printed clusters of cherries, sun-glasses, gloves, a pair of tennis shoes over bobby-socks, stained with the salt of old water: a bizarre uniform of ironic protest.

'The sea here, you know, reminds me of my family.' She flung sand and pebbles into the water and her voice was cracked. 'There are wonderful lakes where my grandfather lived. The ice in winter was as thick as a whale's blubber. If you sailed for three days you could get to the other side . . . the old man used to hunt in a fur coat, like a cave-man. Fir trees, ducks, eels and carp and so on. That is why I liked it. Did you not go to the sea for holidays?'

I nodded and smiled without nostalgia: British stone promenades unfurled under sunny flags, the flags of the nations and the flags of the hotels. My feet burned on the tarmac and crowded, pricking shingle.

'But,' she went on, 'not like here. My sea was bluer and full of people.'

No one passed us in the narrow streets leading down to the shore, and the ocean lay in wild emptiness. I realized that she did not think it pleasant, that the lack of parasols and ice-cream was painful to her. Only the distant volcano interested her: a cone of snow on the horizon and the fine black ash that sometimes drifted through the air and settled, a macabre dust, over the sill of our window. She often wanted to take buses up into the hills, or to Taormina, simply to look at the volcano, *pour voir les éruptions!* But the coastal towns filled her with contempt.

'Always the same hotels. Rotting old men.'

'Shall we go then? I thought you liked the sea.'

She stopped on the beach and selected pebbles for skimming, deciding on her answer, and did not reply until she had hurled several small aerodynamic stones far out to sea in graceful, bouncing parabolas.

'I do. But here it is different. I am trapped.'

I expressed artificial surprise, but she did not turn to me, instead throwing the pebbles skilfully.

'You can take me where you want,' she continued. 'I cannot decide it.'

I drew her away from the game and held her arm: it was shaking and expressed no strength.

'If you want,' I said, 'we can go back. If you want to find your mother. Maybe you will have more luck now.'

'Why do you think so?'

I began to walk a little faster, a panic developing.

'No reason. But you may have luck. If you want, we will go back.'

She stopped still again and removed her sun-glasses, revealing vacant, hunted eyes. We walked on and tears came into them. A mist from the sea covered the beach and shuttered off the lush volcanic mountains overhead. I could not tell her about the letter. I hoped she would feel differently when we were in another city.

'We will go tomorrow,' I announced, and we finished the promenade in silence. We trailed back through the village with its single electric light over the central square and I could see the water dripping over her face and sinking into the edge of the absurd raincoat, leaving a rim of moisture in the material. Tomorrow, I thought, she will have forgotten, she will be healed, she will wear her red shoes . . .

We travelled on the same train, clinging to the same coast, until the volcano vanished and the hills were barer. The sea-world and the Greek theatres were slipping away, the experiment had failed. The aquatic romance had collapsed, the names under which it had been played – Siracusa, Acireale, Riposto, Augusta – had become an agglomeration of visions linked up to each other by the metallic gristly sea, the grinning sclerotic eye of the clown, the burned shores of smooth pebbles and marmoreal fragments, all carved on hard translucent stones, a glyptic dream.

During the night I prayed for sun on the following day, so that the sea would be blue. If the sea were blue, I thought, if the sun were to warm the water and heat up the shingle and sand and make the cicadas return, she would begin to heal and open up to me.

The Eye of the Sea

I

The girl came down the garden path, over the lawns and between the rhododendrons and the Holy Sisters in white hats came after her, fussing, and she sang:

The dogs are sleeping
The dogs are sleeping

the ancient love song, and plucked up buttercups, and they pursued her with little twitters into the summer-house.

'Come back, come back you naughty.'

But she had dressed up and would not.

'Father Tadeusz says. Come out, now.'

The girl threw her buttercups at them and ran on.

'He can see you, little one, Father Tadeusz is shaking his head.'

The girl ran down to the river, slipping between them, and they twittered.

'What a wisp, a feu follet! Come on now, you must.'

She would not and they played tag. The girl was quick and they all laughed. Her ribbons flew behind her, glittering in the sun, and the Sisters could not catch them. Her feet were bare and she was too quick for them, so they played. In the distance a road was smoking near a wood, a bicycle was crumpled up on its surface emitting a faint steam.

The house lay in a hollow, its walls made of white planks, and convolvulus grew up to the roof. The roof was made of candy and the doors were made of icing, the windows were pink and filled with gypsophila. The trees were covered with smilax and guns were popping in the forest, red and white dogs rushed through the bracken. The house was shaped like a cube and hearts were carved into its flaking shutters; the glass was shadowed with lace. A coil of smoke rose into the sky above the roof like the wake of an aeroplane.

I was happy and lay back on the lawn, it was a blue day. The summer-house was made of bone and pierced by fanciful windows, quaint edges and decorated lancets. The Sisters had pursued the disobedient girl across the road where the soldiers were examining the remains of the smoking bicycle. The fields in which they were playing were coloured by mustard and poppies and grey patches of rotting machinery and discarded uniforms. The girl in ribbons and the Sisters danced through them kicking up the mustard flowers.

'Father is watching, be a good girl!'

'It's time for your sandwiches.'

They did not see the men in shirt-sleeves polishing their guns, or the naked men bathing by the road, pouring buckets of brown water over themselves and drying in the sun, stretched out in the rusty sorrel.

'Mistress Raspberry will not obey. She needs a lesson.'

'She will be sent to bed.'

The girl pulled out her ribbons and let her blonde hair fall down her back.

'Tie your hair up!' the Sisters wailed. 'The Father will see.'

But the girl ran ahead of them, back to the bridge. I could see her smiling and throwing the ribbons away.

A man had stepped on to the lawn and I could hear his shoes crackling in the grass, moving towards me. It was Father Tadeusz coming to rouse me and shake my hand. He was benevolently round, his white suit bulged at the equator and revealed a golden watch-chain. It was hot and his thick face sparkled with a subdued perspiration. He bent and showered me with drops.

'Mr . . . ?'

'James. I am Jamie.'

He smiled and dabbed his brow.

'Welcome.'

The girl was running around the summer-house and the Sisters squealed after her, gathering up the scandalous ribbons. The Father leant back on his heels, hanging his hands in the pockets of his waistcoat, and smiled.

'These girls,' he murmured.

He wore white medical shoes, an antiseptic frock-coat and a leisurely straw hat. He held his pipe in one hand and knocked out the burnt tobacco with the flat of the other. Now the Holy Sisters had seen him as they ran around the summer-house and were filled with mild terror.

'Raspberry!' they shouted. 'The Father!'

The white gentleman waved and the girl saw him as she ran. A slight darkness flickered over her face and she slowed her pace. The Sisters caught up with her and grabbed her hair.

'The ribbons, do up your hair . . . '

The Father chuckled and rocked back on his heels. The sunlight struck him from behind, lighting up his butcher's ears, illuminating the bristle under his hat and the aggressive hooked features of his face. He was not angry and waved his hand carelessly over the struggling women.

'Let her,' he said quietly.

The girl was now neat once more, her hair tied up in the white ribbons and her knees wiped clean of soil by the immaculate handkerchiefs of the Sisters. She did not twist their arms as they brought her to the Father to pay her respects. She curtsied and smiled for him.

'Good afternoon, Raspberry.'

'Good afternoon, Father.'

The Father took out his watch and studied it with pleasure. There was, he said, time to play before the 'curfew'. The Sisters curtsied and gathered behind him and the girl drew away triumphantly.

'A little time,' he went on, 'half an hour. But do keep your ribbons in and be clean when you come in.'

He plucked her cheek gently and patted her head. He seemed to be haloed with the white light reflected from his frock-coat. There was no crucifix on his chest and I knew that he was a doctor. His hands were pappy and smelt of coal-tar soap – medicinal hands. He turned to go and the Sisters bowed out of his way.

'Remember,' they cooed to the girl as they followed the Father, 'half an hour.'

It was late in the afternoon but it was still a sunny day. The candy was dripping from the roof and the jambs of the chocolate doors were smelling like burnt sugar. The girl waited until the Father had disappeared before she removed her shoes with a wicked wink and ran back to the river. I was cooler now, so I put on my jacket and followed her to the oriental bridge made of bare slender legs, overlooking the neck of an oblong pond covered with water-flowers. As I walked down I could see the bicycle steaming in the heat and the spokes spinning slowly in the wind, and flashing in the sun.

'I'm not swimming,' the girl called back suspiciously.

The road was covered with flowers, racemes, cymes and umbels. Beyond the road was the wood, quivering in the heat rising from the tarmac. The body under the bicycle was twitching in this shimmer and the head of golden hair was fixed in a pool of oil. The steam thickened and swirled upward over the trees . . . he was burning.

'I will not go in naked,' she protested, hoisting up her skirt and creeping to the edge of the pool. 'I shall go for a . . . wade.'

The waters parted and her little feet went in, provoking a viscous slime of algae that stuck to her shin. She grimaced and stepped further in. The lily-pads knocked against her and she plucked them up, fingering the rubbery drops under the leaves and stalks. Only the centre of the pool offered inviting waters, a triangle of pure, lifeless liquid free of lilies. She looked at it longingly and licked her lips.

As it became darker the group of washing soldiers rose from the verges and towelled themselves in the red light. Their bodies were muscular and white, the bodies of troglodytes. The girl did not notice them and they sauntered back into the woods still naked, their backs pitted with scars and their flesh drained of colour. I recognized them by their muscles and the shape of their naked legs and shoulders. I knew the names and identity numbers of each one, and the names came into my mouth as I watched them. I wanted to shout them out and make the dead bodies turn to see me. But if I called I would have to see their eyes in turn, the empty orbits cleaned out like oyster shells. I let them go and they filtered into the wood which was now glowing red from a distant fire . . . a village burning. The Milky Way was blotted out over the trees and the sky was traced over with shining bullets. The sun had fallen quickly and the girl was now a little frightened by the pool.

'The Father is waiting,' she whimpered, 'the Sisters are waiting. We should go back in. Father Tadeusz is not gentle after dark!'

She sat down and wiped her feet against the grass. I saw that the skin was freckled with tiny red spots, the imprints of leeches.

I opened my mouth to tell her to hurry, but no voice appeared. She saw me gaping and sniggered.

'Yes, I know, Father is waiting.'

We walked back over the lawn. The windows of the house were lit up with soft light and the door stood open. She was late and her mouth was quivering with apprehension. I wanted to go with her into the house but she pushed me back from the door.

'No, no, you cannot. If you wish, you may kiss me here.'

She waited by the door and leant timidly against the jamb.

'Just one kiss, before Father comes.'

I leant over her and rested my hand against the sticky icing . . . my foot did not trespass over the threshold into the fairy-house. Inside was a different world.

'Go on,' she whispered, tugging my lapels downwards, 'go on. Now.'

I leant down further and smelt the warm sugar in the door, the apple-odour of her throat and the mud she had drawn up from the pond.

'Go on, go on.'

I stooped and kissed her and the sugar came off her lips, a bitter, caramelized sugar. Her tongue was made of liquorice, her gums tasted of mint. Her skin glittered with crystals that dissolved into a sweet juice under my tongue. I could crush her fingers slightly so that they crumbled like cake. She was made of the same material as the house . . . the house would not endure flesh. She slipped away and faced me over the threshold.

'Dinner and curfew,' she said simply. 'Now we must say goodbye.'

Behind her the walls of coloured bricks shone out of the gloom. That was all I saw of the house. As I waved she stepped forward and closed the door. There was a sound of feet and female voices, and the bolts rattled behind the door. When I turned to look once more at the wood and the artificial road I saw that the river had been swallowed up in forest and that the house was in a primeval clearing littered with timber, axes, pools of white shavings and a simple wagon made of beech-wood.

★ ★ ★

A year after this dream I walked up to the sanatorium in the mountains on a burning July day, along a rubble road that ran through forests and fields of blueberries. Ania had told me in her letters about the trees struck by lightning and uprooted over the road, the reindeer in the valleys, eremitic log-cabins built into precipices and the cable-cars flying to the ski-stations founded in the permanent snow. The road could be abbreviated, where it was tortuous, by staircases made of boulders cutting through the forest . . . on the bare foothills it was crowded with tourists making their way to the holiday lodges and the nature trails. Ania had drawn the reindeer and the pine trees on her letters, so that each had been a quaint alpine postcard in the middle of which her large coloured scrawl (she wrote with red, yellow and blue wax crayons) evoked a contrary landscape of grey corridors, recreation rooms with radio-sets, narrow sanitized beds and half-hearted decorations of paper flowers, political portraits and bright agrarian paintings. In the paintings hung along the corridor and over the beds, she wrote, she found stooks and the gables of timber barns, the same terrifying mountains and the apple-faced peasants – the *górale* – in goat-leather breeches and green hats. The real landscapes were for her the reverse images of the paintings, their corrupted shadows. She did not walk in the hills with the others and concoct bouquets with the nurses . . . she had seen the pretty reindeer in a book, she had seen the mountains from a disinfected bed in the post-operation ward.

I had risen at eight and gone out with hiking-boots and a felt hat. I could see the sanatorium from my hotel room, a sprawl of white wooden buildings, but it disappeared as I walked up into the hills and only when I was close to the gates did it reappear, its windows blinded by the sun and its garden roses lit up behind the graceful fence of carved wooden spears. I was early for my appointment and decided not to go in yet. I sat down opposite the gates – on the open grass at the base of a ski-run – took off the hiking-boots and socks and watched the sweat slide off my feet into the grass.

At the end of a pink gravel drive a clock made of blue metal was set into the white tower of the hospital and dominated the entrance with its golden numbers and luminous hands in the form of arabesques. The blue of the clock was deliberately serene – the Eye of Time – darker than the sky and of greater importance. I had seen it from my room, a stud of dream-like blue and gold in the white tower tipped with a slender onion dome. Ania had never mentioned it, she had never seen it. She had not described to me the avenue of pink gravel and birch trees, the fences, the beds of roses or the swinging gates of rusty scrollwork. The doors under the tower – the main entrance – were open and the swinging glass doors behind them reflected the sunlight, unmoving and opaque. The doors did not move and no one arrived at the gate after me. The windows (four tiers of plain white frames fringed by dark red shutters with slats) were vacant and silent. Some were half-opened, some were masked from within by canvas blinds pulled down half-way, and over others the shutters had been closed, revealing tiny smears of rust around the external hinges. I could see gardens rolling down the hillside, lawns enclosed by yew hedges, small fir trees and the same elegant fence. The sanatorium was like a summer villa – it had not been built as a hospital – or a rambling baroque Polish town hall, a Warsaw palace. It controlled a little empire of cultivation, plots of flowers, regular lawns and concise pathways. Birds sang in its trees, peasant gardeners preened its corners, worms worked its earth. It had been carved out of the mountains and watered with vigilance . . . its modest rectangular shape could be seen even from a short distance, and the jagged Tatra surrounding intensified its air of reasonableness: it had grown into an enchanted circle of order in a wilderness.

I presented myself at midday. The clock of lapis lazuli boomed over me as I disturbed the serene glass doors and entered a cool corridor hung with pictures of cornfields. I was expected and the receptionist took me to the third floor herself. The stairways were deserted and the corridors of the first and second floors plunged in shadow. But the third floor – the sanctuary of the young – was sunlit and loud with voices. I was left near the door and told to wait. The ward consisted of a single vertebral corridor flanked on either side by rooms partially walled against the corridor by lattices of celadon-coloured glass. Faces were already up against the glass, flattening their noses against it and peering around the shabby, peeling jambs. The word circulated: 'Cudzoziemiec!' (stranger) – something in my dress separating me from an entire nation. The eyes were female, as were the naked feet running over the wooden floors.

An exterior heat seeped in from the cubicle-dormitories, the heat of sunlight pouring through clear windows. I was still pricked with sweat and blades of grass were printed over my palms and legs. The girls whistled and tapped on the glass. They smelt of soap like the nurses of St Lazare: soap, gravy and iodine. A feminine heat flowed into the corridor and they began to run from room to room to see me, 'Ania's friend', as they already knew. I waited as the heat increased almost imperceptibly and the girls in blue dresses skipped across the corridor and whispered. This was her home, her resting place. Her mother had picked it out from hundreds of identical institutions, choosing it for its mountain views and pure fresh air, for its rose gardens and its pretty tower. She had inspected it four times – Kessler told me – and had chosen it with intense satisfaction. ('My daughter will find herself in that place.') I had come in July because I knew that the mother would be on the Baltic beaches and that I would be alone with Ania. And as I sat with the rumour of voices and fingers tapping against the lattice of glass and the odorous heat rolling from the open doors, I felt fear at the thought that I would see Ania in a grey shirt, holding dirty cubes of sugar in her hands and limping with an old fracture. The memory of the battered throat in its collar of bruises tormented me during the half-hour that I waited for her.

The nurse returned and took me to Ania's room. As we disappeared down the corridor the girls massed behind us and giggled. The nurse told me in French not to mind them, and then, not to speak too long to Ania, not to encourage her to leave the room, not to open the shutters of her windows too wide, not to give her bonbons, not to excite her by talking of the past. She then asked, looking round at me quickly, 'Mais, vous êtes le mari, monsieur?'

I expressed amazement and she fell sulkily silent. They had been convinced the 'jolie Aniuszka' had a husband, and there were rumours – I later found out – that she had aborted his premature child. When we reached the shuttered room I saw that the nurse was flushed slightly and that her lips were locked in a peculiar disgust. She waited in the frame of the door as I crept to the bed with my mountain flowers. Ania had just been woken and did not sit up for me. Her eyes were open and she was smiling, her fists clenching the rim of the sheets. I sat on the bed and waved the flowers over her head . . . She picked out the white ones and laid them under her chin, then closed her eyes again. Her voice was flat and superficial as she repeated the word 'Aubergine'.

2

I was permitted to visit only every two days, but went every morning to the scrollwork gates and the impeccable fence and the avenue of pink gravel and beech trees. If it was not a visiting day I would observe the hands of the blue clock and the patient ramblings of the gardeners as I lay on the ski-run. Her window faced on to the front garden and its shutters were always closed. On visiting days I took handkerchiefs filled with blueberries and the customary flowers. No food was permitted, but I smuggled the blueberries in and she ate them until her fingers were purple. And the first time I brought them, she horrified me . . . she kissed my hands with gratitude. I was still a saviour and now her illness had accelerated.

A visa for three months would enable me to become familiar with the staff at the sanatorium, they would allow me to take Ania out, and perhaps to walk with her on the hills. I knew no one in Zakopane and the nearby cities were alien to me: no relatives would speak to me. Once I tried to find the Januszewski country house near Nowy Sącz but it had disappeared, I could not find the river and the bridge or the house with its shutters punctured by decorative hearts. The taxi driver I hired was mystified by my descriptions and by the address that Ania had given me. We went from farm to farm with no success. I mentioned the wealth of the family, the size of the gardens, the motor cars and the stables, but with no effect. The driver told me in German that the little girl must have been dreaming, that there was no Januszewski manor around Nowy Sącz. I asked whether the Germans had requisitioned the house and later burnt it during their withdrawal. No, he said decisively, there is no house and never was . . . the little girl had to be mad (his gentle word was *bekloppt*).

'Such a place, she has to be dreaming.'

I asked him about the name 'Januszewski'. He had never heard of it, he could only say that it was 'not a peasant name'. If I wanted to find them, he advised, I should go to Kraków and ask the police or the government people.

'It is possible, you see, that they were meant to disappear.'

But I had already searched through Kraków for the apartment of Basia . . . it did not exist on Wierzyniewska Street though I had located the right building, the park and the bus stop on the other side of the road. The vestibule had been exactly as Ania had described it to me by the Italian lake. The trams ran past the door, the spiralling staircase rose up in iron darkness. In the park the chestnut trees covered the benches, a street lamp leant over the tram stop. But there was no trace of the aunt; perhaps Ania had been taken to the apartment in Wierzyniewska Street as a child and had since become confused. The populations of the cities had changed during the war and therefore it was possible that the Januszewskis had moved and that the new people simply did not know them. The street was now quiet and dusty and many of the apartments were still empty. It was possible that the family in Kraków had migrated to another city – Katowice, where an uncle of Ania's lived, Wrocław or Łódź . . . but the child's eye had picked out the objects in Wierzyniewska Street with extraordinary accuracy, she had reason to remember it. On the third floor – the floor Ania insisted had been her aunt's – the name Warszewski was printed under the bell. There was no reply to my call. Through the keyhole I could see a bare room, unvarnished boards, full daylight and wooden chairs. The room must have changed, the previous decor ruthlessly purged, or Ania had mistaken the number of the street, the floor, or even the street itself. On the fourth floor an old woman told me in broken French that the Warszewskis had been living in the apartment below since the end of the war, and that no Januszewska had ever lived there before that time. An adolescent boy on the first floor told me that the Warszewskis had been there since before he had been born, that they had been there as long as anyone could remember. He said that he knew all the children in Wierzyniewska Street and that none of them was related to any Januszewska. Ania had mentioned no other street in Kraków and if I could not find the Januszewskis here they would be lost to me for ever. I went to the bottom of the street and called into all the apartments whose number contained 7 or 9, but the combinations yielded nothing. An elaborate and deeply rooted family had disappeared without trace. Everything had been erased behind Ania: the house in Laon, the soldier-papa, the house in Nowy Sącz and the world of the apartment in Kraków. She was alone and sealed off from the world. The sanatorium was her refuge and her home. It was possible even that she had dreamed up her family, its country houses and its comforting hierarchy of grandpapa, sad aunts and innocent children. She had created a world of ornamental bridges, cottages buried in bellbind, honeysuckle, and buttercups, papas and mamas, forests and mountains, verandas smelling of resin, lakes and blueberries and stars with inhuman names: Mirfak, Vega and Aldebaran. She had put together her own childhood.

On the first Saturday morning I arrived early at the sanatorium and insisted that the shutters be opened on this one occasion. The nurses explained to me that Ania had been tranquillized during fits of violence and that they had sequestered her by order of the doctors and sedated her regularly over a period of three weeks. It was necessary to remove her from external stimuli, as if simulating preparation for sleep, to keep her room dark and her mind closed in upon itself. But, seeing that the sunlight and the small sounds of the mountains through an open window produced no effect upon her, they allowed me to open the shutters and the windows and wheel her bed nearer to the light. The doses of tranquillizer had been reduced and now she could sit up to speak. I saw in the stronger light for the first time that her eyes were darker, as if tinged like carnations with ink. Her teeth were discoloured – a smoker's yellow, though not the effect of nicotine – her facial bones protruded under a nightmare paleness and her eyes had sunk slightly into the orbits as if deflated from within. One arm was peppered with mosquito bites of syringes and the carelessness of a violent moment had stained several of the pricks with mauve and yellow bruises. She was not aware of them except as insect bites that made her scratch. Her wrists were also marked with red rings, the trace of straps that had tied her down. The nurses were nervous and uncertain as they took me to her room, as it had perhaps occurred to them that Ania did not belong in so mild an institution. There was only one sequestered room, and only one room in darkness on the floor belonging to the adolescent girls. Her mother's money had bought her a place and they would wait for a short time before deciding what to do with her. I began to realize that they welcomed me with some relief. Perhaps I was the husband after all, the husband home from the sea, the man to carry her off . . .

At first she could not believe that I had come. Instead of speaking she wrote down single words on a small slate with a piece of chalk and the first word was 'Witam' – Welcome. She wanted me to talk to her, so that each word she wrote down was meant to suggest a speech on my part. Thus she wrote the word 'Paris' and I told her in picturesque terms what I had done there since her departure, how the river looked in winter, how the apple trees around Notre-Dame looked in spring, how melancholy the great cemeteries were in summer, how the pavements turned colour with every season; she wrote the word 'train' and I told her about my journey, its list of scenes. When she wrote the word 'Kessler', I told her that the doctor was anxious about her, had only reluctantly agreed to her mother's request, was looking forward to her return to Paris, if it could be arranged, and was communicating with the doctors at the sanatorium. This last was a lie, but I was convinced she would welcome an attachment – however remote and abstract – to her own past, even the past history of her illness. Other random words followed and she held my hand with delight, though not quite seeing me, as if my voice were the only thing that she could seize.

There followed pictures on the slate, ideas too vivid to be explained by her own voice – the zigzag of the mountain-tops, the rectangles of the window frames, the rounded tubes of the bedstead, the shapes of bottles and needles, the outlines of the nurses in their starched hats, the corollas of flowers and the chaotic forms of clouds. And after these came a series of numbers, one at a time, and the shape of a wall-clock in one corner of the slate. She could hear the chime of the blue clock under the tower, she must have listened to it for weeks, counting down each group of fifteen minutes as a game to make the passing of time in some way real. I told her that the clock was blue with golden numerals and she arched her eyebrows in surprise, writing the word 'red' on the slate under the clock. I shook my head. 'No, blue!' She considered the fact and her expression completely altered. The discovery that the clock was blue was significant to her and I watched, uncomprehending, as her eyes wandered out of the room and stiffened in abstraction as she tried to imagine the clock. It was important for her to see the clock, to possess an image of it, as if it had appeared again and again in her dreams as the author of incessant, inevitable numbers and as the arbiter of her helplessness. Perhaps the colour blue made the clock more inanimate and inflexible, a Plutonic figure of supernatural judgment. It was the clock that pinned her down on her bed during the night when its sound was the only principle of organization in the middle of endless silence. She wrote the words 'Tac-toc' – the mechanism pushing the seconds back and forth, as if she could hear the cogs and chain, the belt mechanism gathering breath on the hour and the ghostly shifting of the minute-hand over golden numbers. She repeated:

Tac-toc
Tac-toc
Tac-toc

and redrew the inevitable figures gracefully with elaborate flourishes. But when I questioned her – I asked her, tentatively, if she knew how long she had been in the same bed in the isolated room – she could not see beyond the simple twelve numbers, she could not string them together to form hours and days. She was adrift to the definitions of a blue tin clock . . .

During my third visit she began to talk without the slate, her voice deeper and slightly harsh, and she told me about the violent episodes of the previous month. She had thrown a glass tumbler at a nurse, which had smashed against a wall and showered the nurse with fragments of glass that cut her near the eyes and over the neck. Another time she had thrown a wooden clog at a fellow patient and on several occasions she had used nail-files, clips and brooch-pins as weapons against staff. She said that the nurses had been shocked and afraid of her and had asked for her forcible seclusion. She did not remember the specific reason for each outburst.

On the fifth visit I found the shutters of her window already opened on my arrival. Ania was on her feet, dressed in a butter-coloured dressing-gown, her hair controlled in a coil of tight plaits, her eyes alert and blue, her hands red with the exercise of cleaning the floor with a scrubbing brush. As I approached the room from the corridor I heard her singing the German song about a little rose, which a nurse called Ewa had taught her:

Röslein, Röslein, Röslein rot
Röslein auf der Heiden . . .

This one time she was transformed. The room stank with disinfectant, and suds whispered in the cracks of the floorboards, still stained with warm water. The windows were wide open and the mountains shimmered behind in the oblong spaces, capped with snow. Closer to, I saw her throat displayed by the open collar of a thick cotton hospital shirt – emaciated and immaculate, pure of the scars I had first seen there. She had been given permission – apparently – to entertain, and the open windows were the testament of her confidence. A warm wind came through them. She went to sit on the bed and made me stand by the window furthest from her, where the sun was most intense.

'I am going to draw you,' she said, holding up a folder of paper that the nurses had granted her. The papers were slashed with colours . . . she had been describing the unavoidable mountains with garish child's crayons, memorizing the nurses, colouring the ski-run and the path of pink gravel. 'Now, don't move.'

I leant against the frame of the window, dipping into the sun, and watched her work with the crayons.

'Do not blink,' she commanded, 'I am beginning with the eyes.'

She remained bent over the paper for half an hour and, each time she looked up to examine me, her eyes were superficial and single-minded. Through the bars of the bedstead I could see a red and violet face appearing under her hands . . . a black mouth, vermilion eyes and yellow cheeks . . . the face of a clown or a travelling player.

'You are handsome today,' she said slyly. 'The walks are good for your health.'

I felt myself blushing. Perhaps the violent caricature I could see taking shape was a truthful picture for her. I could only say, 'You also look better today,' and she bowed to accept the silly tribute.

'We can walk together, if you like,' she continued. 'You have only to ask Madame Niedzwiecka for permission to take me down to the village. If it is sunny and dry, she will agree.'

'I will ask.'

'Or you can take me to Morskie Oko in a carriage . . . the peasants will lend you one . . . or a car, a taxi.'

'We'll go there if you want.'

'Yes, yes, it's so frightening!'

The lake was called the Eye of the Sea and she demonstrated its ocular shape with her arms – a subtle elliptical circle. And the colour of the water . . .

'If you were the colour of the water you would be like this.' She held up my portrait like a captured shrivelled head and pointed to the hair, a deep cobalt blue. 'The water is like this.' She laughed and rolled up the drawing. 'I have made a mess,' she confessed. 'I have to hide it.'

I went over to the bed and sat down, undoing my collar to ease the heat.

'If I ask Niedzwiecka, will she let you come to the lake?'

'I think she'll be happy.'

'Then I'll ask her now.'

Ania slipped back between the sheets without removing the dressing-gown and lay on her back with her arms crossed over her abdomen. The room was now clean and dry, the suds having dried into the wood. We could hear the gardeners prying into the bushes below the window and the clicking of their shears. A bee was trapped in the lattice-work and flew against the glass again and again, buzzing softly over the sound of Ania's breath as she deeply inhaled her moment of peace. Her feet were warm and slippery with detergent as I picked them up and laid them on the bed.

'You must go,' she said, 'your hour is up.'

The nurse tapped on the door as she said it. I promised, 'We will go to the lake at the weekend. I will ask.'

Quietly I undid the scroll as her eyes were closed, unrolling the portrait. The clownish gargoyle was there, as I had expected, as violently coloured as a tropical fruit. The hair was cobalt, the colour of the eye-like lake, and the edge of the flesh was a diabolic red. It was the face of a tormentor or a god of war. With a swift and simple green line she had etched in the mountains behind me: I was there in her world once more. The nurse opened the door timidly as I was rolling up the portrait again and standing as if to leave. Ania was almost asleep and the nurse motioned to me from the door . . . it was a sudden, unnatural sleep overcoming her with ease and provoking no struggle. The nurse crept past me and closed the shutters so that the bed was secluded in darkness. She took me almost threateningly by the arm to draw me away. But as we were moving towards the door I thought that Ania had turned her head on to its side and that her eyes were open – they were visible by a subdued glitter – watching us steal over the wooden floor and open the door on to the sunlit corridor. A bar of light created by the slats of the shutter had fallen over her head and perhaps I had seen the bitter open eye caught for a moment in this accidental illumination.

3

After spending the afternoon by a stream at the ski-station at Kasprowy I walked back to the town at nightfall, along unlit gravel footpaths and then wide streets bordered by conifers and log farmhouses on the outskirts of Zakopane. The pavements were full of silent couples ascending the gentle hill to reach the low forests. No one was descending with me. I stepped into the road to avoid the couples – the shadows under the trees made them invisible but for the white shapes of their summer shirts and dresses. The farms were lit up and I could see their sloping fields, crude enclosures and carved gables. Lower down the farms gave way to summer-houses in the middle of gardens sealed off with low wooden fences, the same houses that Ania had described. Some were crossed by streams and small rivers vaulted with home-made bridges, the houses sunk with age below the level of the road and cherry trees stooped over the pavements. She had not invented this memory, its scenery lay all around me; but during the day as I walked past the same gardens on my way to the sanatorium, I did not notice the relationship between the dream gardens and those smelling of earth and roses. There were also children playing on the verandas and families drinking tea outside; paraffin lamps were hung over porches, and the dogs and children were lit up by their sallow, oily flame as they ran around the lawns.

I turned off the main road and began to wander through the network of houses, struck by the sudden hope that, after all, she had meant these houses in Zakopane itself and that she had remembered her childhood vividly and accurately. Several of the houses had hearts carved into the shutters, honeysuckle growing on trellises over the walls, and were divided from the paths of soft black mud by fir trees. But in the darkness they were nearly invisible and I could not pick one out. I spent an hour on this adventure and only retreated back to the road when the dogs tied to the porches became deafening in their alarm.

The hotel was nearly closed when I returned, and the reception hall was a deserted museum of stags' heads, polished panoplies and crossed Tartar sabres. I unhooked my key without making a sound and climbed up to the grey, unheated room that overlooked the highest portion of the Tatra peaks to the east and the sanatorium itself, a glimpse of white roofs, settled at the base of the grass ski-run. I had not chosen this view deliberately; I had noticed the sanatorium only on the second day. (While trying to sleep I had heard the bell of the clock and, on going to the window, saw its blue face immediately, suspended over the trees. I had realized then that for the first time in several months we could hear the same sound at the same time; that whenever I heard the bell, she would also be listening to it in her bed.) I opened the window and watched the lights from the houses, the lights in the windows and the haloes of the paraffin lamps disappear one by one. From the allotments behind the hotel rose a smell of cabbage and turned earth, a warm night smell, and the ubiquitous pine scent. I lay immobile on the bed and waited for the moths to float in from the night and whirl around the electric bulb. I smoked as the room became colder, lying on my back, my chest bared to the naked light. I remembered smoking in this way in my room at the hospital and thinking of Ania's distinctive bluish toes.

It was nearly quiet now, the porter's feet echoed briefly on the stairs, circled the landing and faded downstairs with suspicious hesitations: he had noticed the missing key and had come up to examine the light under my door. In the vacant stillness left by his departing footsteps the clock began to chime three times for the quarter hour before ten.

★ ★ ★

In the hospital the corridors were tiled with squares of wood-coloured linoleum, fitted together like a puzzle and scrubbed and polished soon after dawn every morning by an army of cleaners dressed in black uniforms and bearing the Red Cross on their armbands. They regulated their work by the sound of the chiming bell, covering each stretch of corridor between twenty-five rooms in fifteen minutes. In every room they planted a bunch of freesias in a glass jug and a small mat of coarse lace on every bedside table. They opened the shutters and let the doors of the cubicles stand open for a few minutes to air the patients, then closed them silently and, picking up their buckets, left the corridor like a babble of ghosts, leaving behind them a scent of cleansing lemon. Each room was the same size, the same colour, with the same windows ventilating the same amount of space with the same quantity of light. Panes of glass were set into some of the doors, some of the cubicle walls were brightened with photographic posters: onion domes of Kraków, peasant euphoria, craftwork . . . and some of the bare floors were made gay with local rugs. At seven o'clock the nurses brought tea, ladling it out of a mobile samovar into bowls decorated with bamboo bridges and plum blossom. The girls sat up in the morning light and drank slowly, with dazed eyes. The doctors came at eight o'clock and saw each girl individually, sometimes closing the door firmly behind them in order to be alone with the patient. Walking the length of the corridor, one could see their white heads floating in the panes of glass and the glint of their instruments as they waved them about in the sunlight. The nurses wheeled aluminium trolleys up and down the corridor, untidy carts of bottles, trays, instruments and sheets. They stopped by each door and read through the lists clipped to a hard board. Their faces were alert and rosy, morning-faces, strands of blonde hair falling from under their ceremonial cotton hats and tangling over their cheeks: I had seen each one before and although they did not look at me directly face to face, I could recognize the features of each one and the mannerisms of their walk.

Before entering the room each nurse would tap softly on the door, waiting in methodical silence, stooping slightly like listening deer, until a small cry admitted her. They talked among themselves in the corridor in hushed voices so that the girls should not hear them, but in the rooms they were almost silent in the performance of their duties – administering syringes, taking temperatures, arranging bolsters and making beds. Only at this hour, when the doors of the cubicles stood inadvertently open, could I catch a glimpse of the patients. Nearly always, the girls would be sitting upright against the bolsters, sipping their tea. Their eyes followed me as I peered through the open doors. Every door would be ajar, to the left and to the right, except the last one on the left – a door of peeling, creamish paint with no panes, only a pin-head of glass, an observation point, bored through its centre – a door which was always locked. I would attempt to open it when the nurses were elsewhere, but it stood firm: it was locked deliberately and on no occasion did I see the nurses bringing tea and sheets to the last room on the left, which was marked by the tin numeral 22. Yet it was possible to look in through the tiny channel of glass set into the door. Unlike this part of the corridor, the room itself was brightly lit, the shutters permanently folded back, and the table, cupboards, chairs, blankets and vases were in perfect order. Even the freesias flowered under the window. The bed was untouched and empty, the edges of the sheets and blankets always tucked in and the pillow never dimpled. I could never be sure that the room was empty; I thought that the girl in the room must be hiding somewhere where the eye in the door could not penetrate, perhaps pressed flat against the door itself, or against the adjacent wall. She could have hidden under the bed and watched my eye flickering in the glass. She must have heard my footsteps in the corridor as I was approaching, giving the alarm. Alternatively, the room was truly empty . . . it was locked for no reason except to keep out the mice and the other inquisitive patients; yet I never saw the girls in the other rooms walking up and down the corridor, or visiting other rooms.

By mid-afternoon the ward would be almost soundless. The doors closed, the nurses resting, the girls sleeping. Then the clock would be heard most clearly, as could the breathing of the slumbering patients. On a hot afternoon I could pace up and down the corridor and examine each room – that is, by listening and by peering through the glass in the doors. These hours were monotonous normally; but one day something happened in relation to door 22. As I was straining to gaze through a keyhole – it was the door marked 7 – I noticed a shadow falling over the floor at the other end of the corridor. The door had not opened and I saw that the shadow was growing from under the door, squeezing through the crack and rolling slowly over to the opposite side of the corridor. As I walked down towards number 22, I saw that it was liquid, as thin as ink, pouring from under the door and forming a creeping pool that was inflating like a balloon. When I realized that it was fluid I began to retreat and the dark puddle extended towards me, staining the linoleum and its artificial yellow grain. I backed away, feeling the walls with my hands, unable to run or warn the children. When I had reached the middle of the corridor I closed my eyes and heard the nurses running to the door, fumbling with keys, calling out to an imaginary occupant. Even where I stood, I did not escape: I could feel the warm liquid in my socks, permeating my soles and the broken tips of my shoes.

* * *

The porter's footsteps returned at midnight, as the clock chimed once more, this time the sinister twelve strokes, and paused by my door. He had seen my light from the ground floor and was suspicious, knowing that I was an outsider. He did not knock but waited like the nurses in my dream and listened. When I was fully conscious I could hear his breath brushing the door near the keyhole, through which he was attempting to see my bed. I did not move and finally he shuffled off, muttering, and left me to silence. The moths had burnt themselves out, resting motionless on the walls, overturned on the floor or hovering in the mouth of the open window. As the last stroke rang from the clock, I leant out of the window into darkness, breathing in the cabbage fumes. The sky had brightened – the effect of the moon or the scattering of clouds – and the mountains were visibly mauve. I turned off the light and lay down on the bed fully dressed, leaving the window open. I wanted to sleep with the smell of allotments, the smell of the rue d'Aboukir, and the moths stirring around me. But I had already slept too much and could not fall unconscious again. I went out on to the landing in my shirt-sleeves. The porter had disappeared into his back room and the stairways were plunged in obscurity – I could walk out of the hotel without being noticed (it was the porter's duty to report such 'movements' to the police). I decided to go out as I was, since it was warm, and to stroll about the streets. There would be no one there to question me or to demand my papers. From my window I could see the emptiness of the town and the secrecy of its alleys. The hotel room, with its naked walls, its transitory conveniences and desolate memories, had filled me with a sudden nausea.

4

When I called at the hospital to take Ania to the lake, I found that the vehicle I had requisitioned was unnecessary: a doctor had offered to take us there himself in his own car. He would leave us half a mile from the lake and would return after an hour to the same place to collect us. In the meantime – it was agreed – I should take her to lunch at an isolated lodge overlooking the lake. Before leaving, I was interviewed by two doctors who gave me instructions: Ania was not to eat too much, drink too much, climb or walk uphill to excess. In short, I was not to 'exacerbate' her condition.

The half-mile walk was easy, a gentle gradient and a hard-surfaced road through thin forest. The doctor remained in his car saying that he might join us later for lunch, so that we were alone when we reached the lake. Ania had not spoken during the drive, her hands locked together, white, in her lap and her face turned away to watch the spectacular gorges and peaks. She was still dressed in the hospital's grey cloth and her hair was carefully ordered under a mountaineer's woollen cap. It seemed darker and its colour dulled. The cap was gay – decorated with yellow geometrical stags – and made her face look paler than it had been during my previous visits. (Before we had left the hospital that morning, the doctor had made a strange gesture: as we were waiting on the pink gravel path for the car to be driven to the gate, he plucked Ania's cheek and said, 'She hasn't had her exercise lately.' The skin was so pale that his fingers left a bright glow of flushed blood on her cheek. She had turned away and covered the brief mark with her hand.) She walked without difficulty, pointing out to me the black head of Mount Rysy, marbled with snow, and the line of the Czech border formed by the crenellation of peaks. When we arrived at the lodge overlooking the lake, Ania shrieked to make echoes around the giant crater.

'It *is* like an eye, no?'

The lake was an eye, not by virtue of its shape but of its colour, the same blue she had showed me. But if it was an eye, it was Cyclopean, the eye of a punished god lying on his back and gazing upward out of its prison, dreaming of revenge.

'Listen,' Ania said, leaving the echoes to fade. 'The waterfall.'

The water fell from the side of Rysy, a hole puncturing the rock half-way between the lake and the clouds. After a hundred feet, the underground river dissolved into a falling spray and struck the still water without foam or ripple. It punctured the surface of the eye and passed underground again, leaving only a haze of floating spray in the air. We watched it for some minutes and the sound grew louder, running around the empty funnel of rock. The clouds were slipping downward slowly, a few inches at a time, and it began to rain. Ania was cold and I tugged her gently towards the lodge.

'Are you hungry?'

She shook her head but accepted the invitation.

'No, but let's go in.'

The dining-room was empty and only two tables were laid with cloth and cutlery, pewter bowls of alpine flowers and flasks of water. The fire had been lit and the room was warm. We waited for the doctor but he did not come. There was one other visitor to the lake, a man in a blue cape, ambling almost imperceptibly around the lakeside path, moving small boulders tentatively with his stick, throwing pebbles into the lake and making echoes as Ania had done. Far up on the slopes above him a grey dog ran from bush to bush, and he called its name again and again . . . 'Szarik! Szarik!' . . . perhaps simply to make an echo. By the time he had reached the furthest rim of the lake it had begun to rain heavily and the water was transformed into a grey, battered surface of tiny indentations. We sat in silence and watched the dog-walker circumnavigate the perimeter of the lake, his cape billowing in the wind, and the dog running among the rocks. Her hands were still locked together on the table, a knot of white and tortured knuckles, her face turned away towards the window and greyly immovable under the picturesque cap.

I asked her when her mother had last visited her and she began to count laboriously on her fingers in French.

'I don't know. In April? She came before her holiday in Gdańsk. She came with our cousins from Katowice, they all came together to see me. I didn't know my cousins had grown up.'

'When will she come again?'

'When her holiday is finished, of course. She's gone to the sea near Gdańsk for her health . . . but she was beautiful when she came here; she wore a black hat and a veil and red berries in her lapel. A veil! And she smelt lovely, like cloves, she wore lipstick and perfume. Everyone was jealous, you should have seen. The nurses had to wipe the lipstick off my face when she had gone. She had some things for me . . . eggs, chocolate, cake and some cherry *compote*, from my cousins' farm – they make it in summer and I put it in my tea. See, I smell of it now.'

She leant across and breathed over me a warm, damp odour of cherries.

'The eggs were hard and I painted them, I'll show you. She also gave me some hair clips and a comb. I'm sure I looked messy to her. My cousins said the room was too dark, that I should do more walking. The nurses only allowed the shutters to be half-opened then – I must have seemed a ghost to them. They stayed for an hour and I played chess with my cousin Tomasz. His hands had become so big! Mama walked around the ward and criticized everything, changing the flowers, moving the beds, petitioning the nurses to change the curtains – it's strange they let her – saying, "Ania doesn't like red, red will make her weak." I was proud of her for being like that. The doctors were amazed; I think she impressed them. When she was leaving they made little bows from the hips up, holding her hand gently and almost kissing it, and the nurses spoke in hushed voices . . . they saw that she was grander than they had thought, that she was very elegant. It was a surprise for me too, she was so poor during the war.'

I thought for a moment of the sugar-bearing ghost of old, and the bitter tramp. 'When will the holiday be over?'

Ania turned to me for the first time. 'You have always been so full of questions. She will come away when the sea is cold, most probably. She has her brother or brother-in-law . . . I can't remember . . . in Warsaw, and she will go there in September. She said she would write before that, and maybe I will go with her if I am well. But really, I don't know. You could write to her if you want – if it's really important to you.'

'No, I can only stay another four weeks. Visa.'

She nodded and turned back to the lake. The grey dog had now arrived back at the lodge, leaving the blue cape stranded on the far side of the lake, and was barking in the forecourt. A waiter came out in mild astonishment – a sound! a sound! – ready to silence the animal, and accidentally saw us in the corner. I ordered tea and bread rolls and *naleśniki* for Ania. When these came we ate in silence and waited for the man in the blue cape to come around the lake. There was nothing else to do.

'He must be mad,' she muttered several times. 'Look at the rain.'

We could see him struggling under the shower, in which there now appeared particles of ice and half-formed snow.

'Snow in summer!' I pointed, knowing that it was being blown down from the caps. We sat in silence for a further quarter-hour. The tea vanished and the desiccated pancakes, filled with cheese and vermilion preserve, shrivelled into cold tastelessness. I wanted to walk, but had been told not to take Ania out in the event of rain. The doctor would soon return and we were forced to linger over our half-meal.

'You said that you might be leaving the sanatorium in September? Is there a chance?'

'I was told by Dr Nowakowski in person. He said it was possible. He said there is no reason I should stay longer. He knows more about me than anyone else and I can't see why he should have been lying when he said it. I'm sure he's telling the truth.'

I would have to leave before that hypothetical discharge, unless it could be changed to an earlier date.

'If the date could be brought forward, I could be here when you come out.'

She turned back to the lake and said nothing. The sudden thought of an unexpected renewal of past pleasure had made me say it too directly. Her mouth was quivering with scorn and her fingers unlocked and drew apart in sudden confusion.

'No, it cannot be changed; you should not ask the doctors anything. But I will come out soon, I know. You can come and see me then.'

I looked at my watch: the doctor would arrive in ten minutes.

'When I am released,' she went on, 'I will go to Warsaw and live with my mother, at least for a while. I can get a job in the films, acting and modelling. They're making films there now and I can work with them. They can make the best of anyone and make a big thing out of it, you'll be amazed. They will make something of me, I know, something perfect and untouchable. One day you will see it in its perfection, I will be more perfect than a painting – you won't recognize me as a lady with flowers in her hair. They'll change the shape of my body and the colour of my hair; they'll give me clothes to be filmed in. My mother won't believe it. Malina will be a woman, a different being, and there will be a reason to remember her. You will see her everywhere, in the magazines, in the cinemas. That will be a shock for you all to see me in the magazines.' The rain had ceased now and the surface of the lake had smoothed itself out into its former eye-like metallic blue. The dog-keeper in the cape was starting back towards the lodge, still calling the grey dog. 'Even him,' she said cruelly, 'he will see me, whoever he is.'

Before the doctor arrived, we went out and down to the lakeside. The water was waveless and its colour preserved up to the shore, unchanged by the altered depth of the pale shingle of the beach, a thick, untransparent solution seeming to hold a solid blue mass suspended a few inches beneath the surface. Into this brilliant mass nothing could penetrate – the pebbles thrown at it vanished as if they had been consumed by an electric current. There were no animals around the water; the sound of birds had been expunged by the disinfecting silence of a vacuum. A world had been created by the stillness of the crater, the grotesque barrier of the mountains, the violent depth of black stone and blue liquid, the lunar brutality of its forms – mountain horns, dry trees – and the dumb clarity of its light, bounced back and forth between twisted pillars of rock, the blue disk and the dazzling cones of snow until it was unbearably thin and bright, reproducing the extreme images of a dead world with the distorting luminosity of a lens. I recoiled from this brilliance after a few seconds, but Ania crouched down on the shingle and remained to enjoy it, at ease in the presence of its sterility. She tried to make images in the water with her face, but the surface threw nothing back; the mountains created no reflections, the sky did not colour it and it could not mirror any circumambient colour. Its blue came from within itself, the pigmented jelly of an eye absorbing and subduing the world, and hence the perfection of its name. She told me that it was one of the deepest lakes in Europe, and that its name properly referred to its sea-like depth. The currents flowing through its water may have run vertically, leaving a still, lithic surface layer without expression and without motion, with only the appearance of a gigantic imprisoned gaze. In this mortified field of vision her face would have emerged momentarily as a speck of dust at the edge, a floating particle. Perhaps that is how she imagined it – the blue giant's eye, taking note of her in spite of her microscopic size. She lay on her belly and stared into the water from a ledge, paddling with her hands, and waited for the reflection to form out of the solid cobalt blue. I heard then the sound of the car's motor approaching from the valley, increasing and fading in turns as it wound in and out of the rising bends in the mountain road. The dog-keeper had suddenly come near, glistening in his wet cape, and the waiter had come out on to the crude perron before the front entrance of the lodge to watch the coming commotion. The motor grew louder and Ania heard it also, turning her head away from the dim aquatic image and drawing herself up on to her knees.

'He's back,' she said dully. 'Am I dirty?' She displayed her knees and her hands.

'No, not at all.'

'Then they will not complain.'

She stood up and shook out small stones and loose earth from her crumpled dress. And then the red and black automobile appeared from behind the lodge, its horn braying, its windows rolled down and the doctor waving at us humourlessly, only a half-smile breaking up the formality of his face. Ania walked up to the car and the perspiring doctor in a stiff attitude of welcome, curtsying before the open door and saying in an actress's voice, 'I am ready, Herr Doktor.'

5

Throughout August I visited the sanatorium every afternoon, so that I was soon a familiar, lonely figure with my handkerchiefs filled with cherries and my handfuls of flowers. I was admitted respectfully, with bows and discreet formal greetings, and shown straight to Ania's room without ceremony. For some reason the nurses now assumed that I was German and ceased speaking to me in French: I was greeted at the front door with 'Guten Morgen, Herr Luffkrass' and told ritually to be 'sanft und freundlich' to the young girl. The nurses no longer waited by Ania's door and my visiting time was extended to two hours. I was soon permitted to take lunch with her and to take her out into the gardens, to play chess and to read books. Only one limitation was imposed on me: there were to be no erotic advances, no attempt to make 'proposals'. As we walked in the gardens I felt occasionally that I was being watched from the windows of the hospital; that my lips were being carefully read for signs of (what had been clumsily defined to me as) *zärtliche Wörter.* Yet if I had touched Ania with these 'sweet nothings' she would have asked the doctors that my visits be discontinued. As it was, the visits were conducted in almost complete and wilful silence, without gestures and without generosity.

The summer became slow, hot and overripe; the town became quieter and more desolate. In the evenings I walked up to the lowest ski-station and back in shirt-sleeves and tennis shoes, unnoticed by the stream of lovers. The station would be filled with young people eating ice-creams and playing harmonicas and guitars, Hansel-like blond and bare-chested boys from the summer camps and Gretel-like girls in cotton dresses, their hair in braids. The foothills had changed colour in the evening light: they were no longer lushly dark but hard and burnt, the colour of brown sugar. The grass on mountains is always green . . . but I saw the hills as burnt-brown, glabrous and metallic. The sun had razed them and the fat blue sky of August had absorbed their moisture. The air had become dry and spiced with chemicals, the evaporated essences of resin, decaying wood and heated earth. My walk to the ski-station became slower, I breathed with greater difficulty – the same paralysis I had felt in Italy – and could not smoke during my rests by the roadside without being overcome by nausea and sudden fatigue. (Towards the end of the month I gave up the walks altogether, preferring to remain supine in my room with the shutters closed and to drink iced water.) The gardens by the road had also changed: some of the roses were already flaking, the petals crinkled and slightly stained, the trees dark green and flowerless, the fences dusty and peeling. The verandas – exceptional pools of shadow, even at twilight – contained the quiet motions of old men, but the lawns were empty, the mothers and children had retired elsewhere. In the silence of the deserted gardens the moth-wings buzzed around the paraffin lamps, harsh and monotonous, and fell against the shutters and log walls. The dogs were quiet, stretched out on the porches, the streets were empty of vehicles, a thick solitude had descended upon the houses.

I had with me two photographs of the hospital of St Lazare at Laon, small indistinct images in which I could piece together rows of windows, straggling flower-beds and fragments of the wood. I had ringed her window with a blue crayon. Within the cubes formed by the lattice, the darkness was broken only by a pale vertical line, a plastic tube connected to a bottle. I had one full photograph of Ania, taken in the gardens, in a wheelchair. Drawings and books were jumbled in her lap, a small paint-brush held behind her ear. Her face, blurred by a dazzling stroke of sunlight, was almost unrecognizable. As always, it was a face distorted and made tense by the presence of something hidden. Her hands were interlocked over her lap as they had been at the lakeside lodge, and her neck was still stained with the bruises I had seen at our first meeting, a faint grey ring barely visible above the brightly crossed lapels of her dressing-gown: I had forgotten how noticeable her frailty had once been.

My longest visits were on Sundays, when I was permitted to remain at the sanatorium for most of the afternoon. At the end of the month Ania seemed crushed by the heat and would not walk about in the sun. I tried to cajole her into the garden, telling her that it was no cooler in the building, and she explained.

'It's a different heat in here. The sun is scalding, it makes me want to die. Everything is hot outside, the grass is hot, the air is hot. It burns me to go out there. It burns my inside too, it gets into my throat. I'll cough if I go out now. I went out with Nurse Masleczyńska and I nearly fainted because of the burning. Look at it now.'

We were sitting by the windows and she pointed down to the dusty tracks and dry lawns. It was the fourth day of the heatwave, and the road and gardens were softened by the refraction of an intense light through the thin dust, the imaginary smoky haze that envelops the distant, receded landscape of summer. In full view of the window two gardeners were working on the gates, filing off layers of rust from the scrolls and applying a glittering black paint to the hinges. The click of the brushes and files against the iron rang with the clarity of tiny bells in the faded quietness of the sun-world, but the melting and sinking of elements under the pressure of a supernatural heat dissolved the sounds of their conversation into the whisper of insects.

'Many of the girls have become sick from it,' she continued. 'They fainted and had to have a compress of ice. I saw some of them, they looked like Red Indians, and sometimes their hair fell out. Lucyna Ptasińska was ill for a week on her back, and she couldn't take anything except water. I'm thinner and more delicate than Lucyna, the heat will kill me altogether. I'll die if my hair falls out.'

'We could go higher up, in the woods.'

She sighed melodramatically and wiped her forehead with her sleeve.

'It's too far. The exercise would be bad for me. Besides, I hate woods.'

'The summer-house would be cool. If you would sit and read with me . . . '

'The summer-house!' She turned on her side moaning. 'It's like an oven. It even smells like an oven . . . roasting female flesh. I'll be sick if I go there.'

'The nurses said nothing to me. Are many girls sick?'

'No, it only happens sometimes. But most of them are weak, the heat is horrible for them. It's unnatural. Mother brought me here, you know, for the climate . . . it was kind of her to think of it. But now it's freak weather, I have to be sensible. It would be dangerous for me to go out. Please don't make me.'

I promised her that I would not.

'Take out the chess,' she suggested. 'It's easy for me.'

I laid out the board on the bed and we began to play desultorily, our attention wandering during each other's deliberation to the mountains, sharp and gaunt in the sunshine, the emerald ski-run, and the gardeners labouring on the iron gates. As she moved her pieces I noticed that her fingers were chafed and scaling, as if a light eczema had erupted over them, and that the nails had changed colour slightly near the cuticles. She saw me examining them and pulled up her sleeve to show that her arms were not, as I was beginning to imagine, covered with vesicles.

'It was the detergent, they say, when I was scrubbing the floor. My skin is too delicate, something in the chemicals went wrong. It's not a disease.'

She turned the palms towards me, revealing inflamed patches of crimson skin, and then the toes of her feet which were also afflicted with small rashes.

'It's not pretty, is it?'

I shrugged and moved my piece.

'It will heal,' I said. 'It was silly of you.'

'I didn't know. I wanted to clean the floor; it stank.'

'You don't have to clean the floor, someone will do it for you.'

For the past few days I had noticed that her fingers had acquired a new odour – a smell of sour milk – and that this odour belonged to an ointment she had been given to ease the itching of the irritated skin. She now took out the glass tub of white ointment from her drawer and held it up to my face.

'I have this, to help it. The doctors gave it to me when they saw what had happened. It smells awful and makes your nose twitch, but it's a cure.'

The ugliness she hated, which she perceived as the essence of her surroundings, had infected her body in the form of this inconsequential but defacing disorder. The foul smell of the ointment, the bitter 'cure', was only an added irony which – in a perverse way – humiliated her. She smeared some of the ointment on the tip of her finger and offered it to me to smell, extending that humiliation to its furthest limit.

'It's ugly, isn't it? I have to breathe it every morning and evening. I fall asleep with it in the air. Do you think they're playing a joke on me? It seems like a joke to me.'

I shrugged again, pretending to consider my defences.

'It's not a joke, it's medicine. You should use it anyway, it'll stop the itching.'

'I can't bear it,' she muttered, 'it makes me sick, it's like rotten milk. It's an awful joke.'

I ignored her and played my pieces. She wiped her hands clean and then suddenly tipped the board so that the pieces tumbled sideways into irreparable confusion, spilling over the bed and falling on to the floor. She swung her feet round and stood up.

'I can't play, I want to wash my hands,' she said. 'Would you get the bowl for me?'

She was nervous and I did not mention the disrupted game. I brought her the wash-bowl from the dressing table on the other side of the room and filled it with water from a jug made of the same thin metal. She washed her hands greedily and raised them, still wet, to her face to smell them again and again, as if expelling a curse. When she had rubbed them dry she collapsed on the bed, delighted.

'Now they smell like roses, even if they look the same.'

I had to permit this ritual and tamely folded up the chess board and gathered the scattered pieces on my hands and knees.

'I'm sorry,' she said seriously. 'If you want we could go out . . . for a short, a very short walk. I'm sure it's cooler now. In fact, I don't want to stay here now, I can still smell the ointment around me. We could go out for a little while . . . '

She had already, with startling fickleness, sought out a pair of shoes and was rewrapping her dressing-gown. I left the pieces under the bed and picked up the bowl of dirty water, in which floated spots of oil and little mists of diluted blood.

'If it will not "burn" you,' I said, 'we will go and see if the summer-house is empty.'

I emptied the bowl in the washroom at the end of the corridor and came back to find her made up with lipstick and powder . . . accessories she had smuggled in and which now served to denote a symbolic event. She put a finger to her lips.

'They won't notice today, everyone is asleep. Take me down quickly and no one will see.'

She took my arm and lowered her coloured face until we strolled out into the sunlight of the garden.

The summer-house was made of white wood like the other hospital buildings, but pierced by ornamental windows, ogee lancets and apertures in the shape of Greek crosses. The sanatorium was a country villa appropriated by the government, and the relics of its past were left undisturbed: a canal skinned with lily-pads closing off the lower end of the garden and spanned near the summer-house by a picturesque bridge of bare logs, fruit trees in red and yellow boxes cut into animal shapes, an artificial mound – an Arcadian hillock with a statue of Artemis and a holly bush – on the other side of the canal, and small copper bird-houses hanging from the trees. The summer-house was empty and we sat inside, away from the door, out of sight of the main buildings. The other girls had left the garden and through the queer Greek crosses we could see a hot and silent expanse of empty grass and deserted paths.

'Perhaps they are playing games indoors with Dr Nowakowski,' Ania said. 'He invites them in sometimes, if they are too hot or tired. They play cards and drink lemonade.'

Her lipstick and powder now sharpened a slight arrogance and contempt in her.

'Now at last I can take my hair down,' she went on, 'it feels like a stone on top. Will you take out my pins?'

She inclined her head and I pulled out the pins regretfully, one by one.

'Shouldn't you keep them in?' I asked. 'If the nurses see . . . '

'Perhaps this will be my last walk for a long time,' she cut in. 'I don't want these pins to spoil it for me. Every day they make me wear my hair like this, it's killing me. I may as well have it cut off.'

The hair, released from the pins, uncoiled and fell into my hands, slipping between the fingers and unfurling downwards over my arms. For a moment I held it, before allowing it to fall over her shoulders, and she consented.

'No one will come,' she said softly, 'they have probably forgotten about me. Normally I am left to sleep on my own on Sunday. Only the nurse called Ewa comes to see me at five o'clock, to take my pulse and feed me cherry soup.'

She leant back against the wall of the summer-house, holding the ends of her free hair with either hand and twisting them slowly into needle-points. I knew that the releasing of her hair threw her back into her childhood, the period of freedom she had known up to the time of her confinement in hospital. She sat silently, twisting the strands around her fingers and tasting the fragrant, sticky lipstick lovingly with the tip of her tongue. The heat caused the powder on her cheeks to bubble gently and grow waxy as it combined with perspiration, her temples became wet and the newly freed hair began to stick to them in the shape of delicate curls.

'It's hotter than Italy,' she said faintly, closing her eyes. 'Hotter than the castle on the hill. But there's no sea here, of course.'

'There's the canal,' I joked.

'I'm not swimming in the canal,' she answered suspiciously. 'I can only think about the sea and imagine it. You can get cool thinking about water. I think about the sea at night anyway, when it's suffocating in that room. The sea and the hotels . . . even the sound of it.'

'I didn't think that you remembered it. I thought you had forgotten.'

She closed her eyes and brushed her face lightly with the sleeve of her dressing-gown, staining the cloth with its moisture.

'Here you can't breathe,' she muttered. 'There's no wind, no water. You live like a reptile under a stone, conserving energy. You are on the point of passing out.'

I took her arm, and then, resting against her, kissed her neck. 'Do you feel uncomfortable? Do you want to go back inside? We can go anywhere.'

She drew away a few inches and wiped her face again with her sleeve, without opening her eyes. I saw her weariness of me in the subdued twitching of her closed mouth and the sudden trembling of her eyelids. We remained apart and did not speak, our eyes averted. At the top of each eccentric window a slot of blue sky burned within the empty abstraction of a cross, a circle or an elongated arch. Trees rippled under them and made the lower halves of the geometric apertures green and grey. The garden was merged into these simple colours, toneless blue and green, and held together in static harmony by the force of the heat. From time to time the colours seemed to quiver momentarily, as if dilating in the heat, then expand and solidify once more. Within the summer-house there was a subtle blue shimmer, the palpitation of rocking water, and a motionless green glare from the lawns. Far away, we could hear the girls shouting and laughing indoors, and the sound of a guitar. Her powder was bitter in my mouth, and her neck had left a scent of coal-tar, but otherwise she was tangible, folded into herself and enclosed in a knot of tragic privacy. She would not speak and we sat in silence listening to the heat, the flying insects and the droning of the guitar. At last she opened her eyes and stood up.

'It's late,' she said. 'Nurse Ewa comes to my room at five o'clock. I have to go in and wash myself.'

I stood up with her and offered to tell Nurse Ewa to come later.

'No, she must come at five. I'll go in alone.'

We walked over the lawn and the sun burned in my eyes, striking my face and chest with dazzling force, and I could hardly see her ahead of me. At the door she turned and faced me over the threshold.

'Go on, one peck,' she said pulling me playfully. 'Go on.'

I stooped and kissed her and the lipstick tasted of sugar and the mixed juice of flowers. She consented to this act of friendship then stepped back into the shade of the hallway. Her lips were smeared after the kiss, the powder was running in oily streams across her forehead, the skin was drenched and ghostly, veined with a sudden flush and paler beneath, shedding its colour. She did not wave me away with her hand, but hung back, leaning without strength against the frame of the door, and waited for me to turn and leave. I noticed in that instant that, without my seeing her, she had done up her hair again quickly and soundlessly and that it was wound up again in its former bun. Only odd hairs had been left out, revealing her haste, and hung down in a frayed confusion over her ears and cheeks.

6

Early in the morning someone from the sanatorium made a telephone call to the hotel and left a message for Herr Luffkrass, asking him to take a taxi and come and speak with Dr Nowakowski. I received the note – scrawled by the porter with a soft pencil on the reverse side of a registration slip – as I was leaving for a morning walk to Kasprowy. No time was indicated for an appointment with Nowakowski, so I decided to go to Kasprowy first and visit the sanatorium in the afternoon on the way back to Zakopane. If I hiked there directly – without stopping to pick flowers for Ania – I would arrive soon after four o'clock: later than usual, but early enough for a long visit. I knew that the doctor would see me later in the day, that he would wait. For the first time I felt no happiness in the thought of climbing up to the sanatorium and for the first time postponed my habitual matinal visit without compunction or regret.

In the mountains it was dark and rainy. In the space of a week the heat had fallen off and clouds had come in low, sliding down the backs of the mountains and settling midway into a permanent ceiling of grey smoke, tumbling in sudden small storms and spitting rain. The town had become cool and earthy, saturated with water. The roads smelt of grass and soil, the houses of breathing damp and living moss. It rained every day at the end of the morning, the showers softening the forest, dragging down the undersides of the clouds on to the tips of the trees. At Kasprowy the rain fell lazily – warm and fattened by long waiting – and I remained at the lodge where I was eating, until two o'clock, watching it descend in heavy waves over the bare grass and fields of blueberries. When I began walking back the forest was creaking with water, the paths had dissolved into a pale sticky mud and the overhead cables linking up the empty ski-runs held up slippery strings of water that fell into the gorges in slow drops. It was like the wood in Normandy and the Italian hills in winter, flushed with mist. The hiking paths were empty and I descended alone. When I saw the sanatorium from the path several hundred feet above it, the walls were grey and unreflective, absorbing the drabness of the storms. The blue clock was ringing the three-quarter hour: it was a quarter to five.

When I arrived at the gates I found them closed. The gardeners had scattered under the rain and I had to call the nurse on duty at the reception desk by the door. She ran out in her cape, wincing in the wet. She was new and did not recognize me. I looked up at Ania's window . . . the shutters were drawn back. Inside, the corridors were empty as usual. The young new nurse shook herself out cat-wise, showering the parquet with drops. Her face was oval and candy-pink and at the edges the fresh yellow of sweet vanilla. With plump healthy fingers she operated the internal telephone and talked to Nowakowski. Having received instructions, she turned to me and spoke in a rapid Polish which I could not understand. My confusion provoked a peal of twittering adolescent laughter and clapping of plump hands.

'Da,' she mooed in monosyllabic German, pointing to the stairs, 'Da. Drei.'

She held up three fingers. 'Drei!' I was suddenly a child. 'Da, ja!' she pointed to the stairs . . . the stairs to the left this time, stairs I had never explored before. She pushed me gently in the manner of a stern orderly, still laughing. At the bottom of the stairs the voice of Nowakowski came down in clear ringing French.

'Come up, please.'

The nurse detached me and stepped back at the voice of authority. She waved me up and then turned back to the desk by the entrance. I went up and found Nowakowski alone on the third floor . . . a thin, nervous face reminding me in an instant of panic of the face of Kessler, the man I would inevitably return to. Nowakowski's face was anxious and rimmed with perspiration, his mouth wobbled uncontrollably as he told me about an accident in Ania's room.

'Elle a mangé de la faïence,' he said with near disbelief at his attempt to translate the event into a borrowed language. 'Elle a mordu un plat . . . '

I wanted to laugh at these expressions, but I knew that she must be dead.

'Elle a avalé des fragments.'

She had swallowed pieces of broken plate, and she must be dead. It had happened soon after dawn and Nowakowski was still trembling, the perspiration visibly increasing as he explained. I asked to be taken to the room and he refused and then relented. We walked in silence to the wing on the other side and I heard a gurgling mournful sound deep in his throat, like the cluck of a turkey rising and falling as he walked. He said nothing as we passed through the corridors; only the unconscious clucking broke his silence. When we reached the room the door was locked, apparently to keep out the other inquisitive inmates. The doctor opened it quickly, threw it back and allowed me to stare into the room for a few seconds. The cubicle was in perfect order. The sheets had been relaid, tables, chairs and cupboards were in their usual positions – even the pots of freesias flowered under the window. The edges of the blankets were tucked in and the pillow was fresh and unmarked. The room was brightly lit and it was difficult to believe that it was not inhabited by someone who had perhaps momentarily hidden herself in one of its corners, in the cupboard, or under the bed. Only the pale marks on the floor near the bed, like faded ink stains, betrayed the passing of an ephemeral inhabitant.

PART TWO

Ania Malina

Tuesday

Down in the dark I hear the trolleys with their trays of bottles and metal boxes, sheets, plates of soup, syringes in drawers of cotton wool, oranges for treats, chocolates in shapes of rabbits, bears and birds, chocolates with pink softness and the liquid of raspberries, green mint and toffee, lemon essence, hazelnuts, brown cream riddled with brandy and bitter alcohols, cherry and vodka . . . sometimes cups of ice-creams and a wafer, pancakes filled with strawberries, plum dumplings, blueberry soup with sweet blue noodles and apple *szarlotka*. I see them pass by and I smell the moist lemon cake and the marble cake and the cake made from split almonds. There is a damp perfume of hot tea in samovars and the trail of its steam in the small windows, and the butter smell of the biscuits they bring with it, hot biscuits with melted sugar.

Mama brought these biscuits when it was cold, biscuits and stewed apples and milk with honey and brandy, administered with a silver spoon. I held my head up and closed my eyes and she would drop it in with a 'Drink that' and make me suck the spoon. And she would tear up the biscuits and make me swallow the pieces one by one, wetting them in the milk, and I would pretend I could not do it myself so she would feed me and tell stories. She fed me with lemon cake when it was hot and a thimble of vodka, saying, 'Drink that,' and chucked my chin when I swallowed and tears came to my eyes. I had my bed in the kitchen in winter. I watched them cook, and the snow in the garden, thickening on the swing. Her fingers smelt of bacon and salty fat, they left a savoury oil on my cheek . . . sometimes I asked if I could lick her fingers after the cooking, and she would put a piece of sugar on the end of one of them. Her face smelt of flour and butter when she kissed me; the flour stuck to her sweat when the kitchen was hot and fell off into her hair, and she said my hair would cook into a loaf.

From the window I saw the snow tumbling on to the swing, the birds jumping into the snow and striking at the baskets of nuts. The cookers steamed up the windows and I wrote 'Ania, Ania, Ania', within a heart. Babcia brought me pancakes filled with cream and thimbles of vodka, saying, 'Drink that,' and little Malina blushed and blinked her eyes, gulping the hot vodka and cooling it with mouthfuls of cream.

When they made the bread Basia came and sat with her 'infusions' to watch over the oven; she would sit near me and I could smell the lime-tea on her breath. She held my hand, scowling at the snow. She braided my hair, brushed and tied it, and cut my nails saying, 'Be still, cleanliness is pride.'

My cousin Piotr came from Warsaw at Christmas, and during the summer he often stayed in the kitchen and talked with Mama and I watched him make biscuits and whip cream with her. His hair was clipped at the back, but it grew long in August and covered his ears. At Christmas he came in a black uniform, like a cadet's; in summer he came in a straw hat, smoking cigarettes. He rode my grandfather's horses and made houses out of cards, asking me to blow them down. Later he sat on the back of the reaping machine pulled by horses and tied up stooks until nightfall with the other men. I watched in the cherry trees and the blond boy bounced on the back of the machine and waved with his cap. His body smelt of hay when he lifted me down from the tree, and broken straws stuck to his throat and cheeks. I dared to pick them off and touch his chin, and draw them out of his golden hair, and give him the cherries I had picked.

He took me to Nowy Sącz on the train to visit a relative . . . he in the straw hat, I in ribbons. The windows were open and the heat fermenting the barley-fields poured in over us, making my legs wet and my shirt stick to my back. When he slept his face was buried in the curtain by the window, his hands folded over his lap and his mouth open; his sleeves were rolled up and his arms covered in an almost invisible yellow hair, ridged with swollen veins, hard, distended by awkward bones and muscle, his hands huge and red-knuckled and his nails soiled and uneven. He had been digging a flower-bed in the morning and his boots were freckled with whitened mud. I examined him for an hour, going over each part of him again and again. His eyelashes were black, black on blue, resting in sleep against pale bookish skin. I reached out and touched his knee and the eyes did not move – only the lashes dug slightly deeper into the skin and his mouth trembled.

His face was yellow from the glare of the barley, the burning orange tint of the horizon. I touched his hand and the damp came off on my fingers . . . I smelt the salt and the rancid perfume of his skin. His chest heaved slowly under a blue shirt – a silk shirt of light surfaces and light folds – and the open triangle of his throat was filled with a yellow and blue cravat, thin, aristocratic, blue stripes over canary-yellow silk, and a pin held it down – a silver pin with a black head. Everyone in the compartment stared at the cravat and the silver pin. I told my neighbour he was a prince from Tübingen – I had seen the name in one of his books – and they stared at him until Nowy Sącz. He did not wake up and I watched him in the terrible heat, his fingers twining, untwining, and his eyes trembling. At the farmhouse in Nowy Sącz I wrote the first page of my first journal and it began with the words:

I will die,
I will die . . .

In my grandfather's house he rode the white horse named Marshal Ney and the maids came out to look at him, cooing like birds . . . the Young Master wearing gloves on a horse! From my bedroom I saw the compound and the endless parading circles of the horse and the young women along the garden fence. He did not see me on his trotting horse, though he was so close I could make out the silver pin inserted always into the cloth around his throat, and the yellow hairs on his arms. He never looked up and I watched him through the heart-shaped holes in the shutters, slapping Marshal Ney with his leather stick, laughing and ordering, whistling to the animal and bending to kiss its neck. Several times I wrote only one sentence in my journal: 'Today Piotr rode the horse', and I drew the horse with a green crayon underneath. That notebook, with its green drawings and single sentences, was the first thing I possessed which had to be hidden . . . I kept the separate leaves folded up into tiny squares in the bottom of my shoes.

One year he came to my uncle's house in Warsaw. He had to take Sylvia and me to the parks, to the zoo, to the palace at Wilanów. We rode in the trams with him and he brought his friends to amuse us. My last summer there, riding the trams along boulevards with trees and filled with balconies like the streets in Paris. The roads were dusty and the trams rode through a haze. Our ice-creams melted on to our sandals, and our fingers became sticky and burning in the heat. We leant out into the street, rushing between the trees, and the haze filled our eyes and we reeled in the warm air filled with dust and the noise of people under the trees. He held my hand across the tramway and the melted sugar in the cream stuck to his palm. He spat into a handkerchief and wiped my lips, cleaning off the gummy stains, dabbing my chin and forehead. He said, 'You like those things, don't you?' – almost to himself, spitting and dabbing – and I felt his warm saliva smearing my lips. When my hair fell down he tied it up, complaining. 'Run slower, it will stay up. I can't tie it . . . ' But I picked it out as I ran and he would have to do it again, putting his hands in my hair. He twisted it around his fingers, weaving plaits, crossing and recrossing the threads held apart with one hand. 'If you ran a bit slower, they would stay in place.' His wrists and the back of his hands rubbed against my neck, clumsily and unconsciously, and his fingers held my hair so tight that the scalp stung and I winced in his grip. He made me tip my head forward and stand by a bench so that they could sit down while they waited, and I watched the light moving in spots on the smooth earth of the track while he ran his fingers through my hair.

In the gardens – the gardens of Wilanów– they took off their jackets and led us to the river, between giant hedges and rows of statues. The river was wild and green, there were no Łazienki swans, the banks were crowded with crooked trees and the water moved quickly, like the water from a tap. The garden was empty and they made fishing-rods. We lay in the shadow of the hedges, listening to the water. The lines, baited with worms, trailed with the current and we waited in the silence for fish. The men began to speak in French so that we would not understand, forgetting the nationality of our father. I understood but lay on my stomach and did not move or speak. They talked about brothels. I lay face down in the grass sloping down to the water, smelling the blades crushed against my cheek. Piotr was silent and the other two talked, exchanging the names of girls and Warsaw streets. I did not hear his voice and was glad. The conversation descended to anatomy and still he did not speak. I lay quietly and watched his averted face as they discussed hips, legs, necks and breasts. The light reflected by the water lit up the line of his jaw and the shape of his throat, and I watched him absorbed in the drawing up of the fish, evading their questions.

Then the dark one called Tomasz began to consider Sylvia, as a joke, saying that she would grow up 'a flower'. Sylvia enjoyed it: she lay quietly and did not object. They said that I would also be 'a flower' and Piotr turned slyly to look at us, leaning back on his arm. 'Yes,' he agreed, 'they will.' I did not move, pretending to doze. Perhaps he had forgotten Papa and our knowledge of French; perhaps he had been waiting to say this. They tittered together, seeing us lying immobile. Piotr turned back to the fish and threw out his line with its soggy bread once more. My heart was beating against the grass, I waited for another comment but none came. I did not dare move and my face burned. The others changed the subject and reverted to Polish to discuss politics . . . Sudetenland and the Germans in the east . . . refurnishing their primitive hooks and casting them out lazily into the current of green water. Piotr remained abstracted, unaffected by their talk. He rolled up his trousers and dropped his feet into the water, hanging his rod between his legs. Sylvia was sleeping against my arm and I watched him secretly until the heat began to break and the light contracted over the water and the others wanted to take the bus back to the city. I wondered all the time if he was musing about the remark, revising it, refining it and following in his mind, one by one, the consequences it might open up.

Every summer for four years he came to stay with us. The first summer he was thin and arrogant, he wouldn't speak to me because I was a baby. He was rashed with acne and could not be drawn from his mathematics. He could not ride, the maids ignored him. But by the last summer he was lithe and graceful, long-haired and artificially exquisite. His dress had changed from a schoolboy's severe uniform to a student's robes, half-official, half-theatrical. He did not read mathematics during the last summer – we were at Basia's in Kraków and he read Mickiewicz and Pushkin and endless newspapers over coffee and iced *compote*. He had friends in the south and they came to Basia's to read the newspapers together on a cloud of intellectual gloom, long-limbed youths sprawled over the sofas and stretched on their backs over the carpets. Basia brought them their cakes, loving this intrusion and the presence of the young men. They would stay in the apartment until dusk, never going out into the heat, always pale and serious. On his own, Piotr slept and read . . . he slept until midday and read in the afternoon, cutting out pieces from the newspapers and clipping them together in untidy sheaves. As a favour to my mother he took me to Wawel Hill and bought me ice-creams as we went through the town, ambling indifferently – half-asleep and slowed with the heat – between the peeling yellow walls of the old houses. If he slept late and his group did not come to wake him, I could open the door of his room and watch him snared in the sheets, twisting gently in his dreams and arching his body over the bed. In the kitchen Basia would say to Mama, 'Our little officer is fond of sleep,' and Mama would say, 'Sleep and newspapers,' and they would frown in a funny way. Basia made me take in a bowl of coffee and a pastry and I laid them on the table by his head and he rose up on one arm, dimly muscular and flecked with hair, and caught my nose between his thumb and forefinger, saying, 'Good morning, Malina. Did Mama send you in?' and I would nod and hand over the pastry, the crumbs falling over his arm. I wanted to stay and watch him eat but Mama had told me no, not that. He would take the bowl and look at me gaily, feeling my curiosity. I could linger and ask him, 'Is the coffee good?' but when he had answered I would have to go out, my nose burning softly and my fingers slightly stung by the heat of the bowl. I got up early during the vacations for this ritual, grooming myself for an hour beforehand, combing my hair, tying and untying it before the mirror in the kitchen, combing endlessly until it was perfectly straight and fell down in an immaculate line to the middle of my stomach. I washed my teeth until I was sure that the sweetness of my breath would reach out over the three or four feet that would separate us as I laid the coffee on the table by his head.

Piotr took me alone to Łazienki with stale loaves to feed the swans in the canals. I was as high as his elbow but he took my hand to cross the avenue in front of the park. The paths ran up and down through the lawns, and we met no one on them on our way to the palace. We stopped in a garden filled with tropical plants and he positioned me against the flowers and took photographs. I stayed there because he ordered me to, saying, 'Stop there, you're perfect,' and I could not resist this phrase or the outstretched protest of his hand and the blond scalp lowered over the apparatus, the hair divided and smoothed away from a central parting. He was fulfilling his duty to the family in this way and filled his boredom with attempts to tease me. He spoke Russian to me when we were taking photographs in the amphitheatre, and then German, to make me appear stupid, and finally incorrect English.

I was stung by my incomprehension and began to blush, feeling hot in my thick dress. I told him I wanted to see the swans, pretending to be a child. His teasing dissolved and he took my hand, he could not torment a child. We climbed down from the amphitheatre and walked around the canals, admiring the reflections of the palace in the water. He undid his tie, gave his straw hat to me and began to smoke cigarettes drawn from a silver case which he kept in his front trouser pocket. These cigarettes were thin and brown, not like the stubby white cigarettes everyone else smoked in the tram or on the street. These were slow-burning and emitted a fainter smell. I noticed that when he had finished one he did not throw the butt away but kept it until we reached an incinerator, or dug a hole with his heel in the soft earth and buried it with careful and bizarre ceremony. I thought then that this was a gesture his tutors had taught him, a peculiar mark of gentility. He still held my hand – afraid I would fall into the water? – and I could feel its pampered softness (his hands changed character in the city), dry as a piece of felt, unhardened by blisters, unharmed by labour. He pressed with his hand, forgetting me and forgetting the power of his body, and I felt crushed by him, unable to pull away.

We found the swans floating in the still water on the other side of the palace, seeking the shade, and Piotr tempted them over with our quartered loaves soaked in dirty water. As the birds stabbed at the bread he spoke to me, a few words while we waited for them to feed. He told me that his mother was from the Ukraine and that she was a Jewess. He told me that his brothers were in Sweden for the summer with their mother, that his father was in Czechoslovakia for a few weeks and that he stayed with us because he liked Basia and my mother and the claustrophobic apartment on Wierzyniewska Street. I had never seen the mother – no one spoke of her at home – and I had only seen my uncle once, in Warsaw. That the mother was Ukrainian was a surprise. She accounted for the difference in him, his separation from everything. He was unaware of my dumb nodding as he talked and smoked down the long brown cigarettes until the silver case was empty. Only then, as we were feeding the swans, did I see his face empty itself and become a void, telling me that the world was going to end and that beneath the blazers and white shoes and the tie-pins there was no assertive force, but a dissolute state of fear and a consciousness of doom. I knew the fear should not be talked about, that it should not exist. He had revealed it accidentally, allowing it to affect his gestures, and it could not be confessed. When he had given away the last of the bread we walked back quickly to the gates of the park. Suddenly he was haunted and nervous, his hands stayed in their pockets and his tie was corrected. It was the last time that summer that we went out alone. The following year we were all at Zakopane and no one mentioned, or even hinted at, the world to come.

In the south, the day was not divided into equal parts, and each traditional division – morning, evening, night – was rendered vague by the extreme length of our waking hours, the slowness of mechanical activities merging into each other, the laziness of the clocks and the sliding motion of unorganized leisure. He would split logs for the kitchen and work on the garden. There were no newspapers in our house there. Instead of coffee and iced water he ate the blueberry soup with noodles, the almond cake and the *szarlotka* with apples. He was absorbed into the family. He went to Morskie Oko often with my grandfather on a wagon and Grandpapa said he was difficult to walk with when they got there, fast and tireless. Once he was burnt by the sun hiking to the lake and Sylvia and I smeared yoghurt over his shoulders when he returned. It was the only time I touched his body and I shook so that Sylvia tapped my hand, and he didn't see. In my journal I wrote, 'I touched his back and covered it with yoghurt!' and left a long space. The skin was cracked like an assembly of paving-stones, disrupted into irregular brittle squares on a bed of dried blood. He clenched his teeth as we massaged the cold yoghurt into this mesh of little wounds and gripped his arms together under his head. It seemed miraculous that I could cause him pain with my fingertips. I pressed harder, not wanting to increase his suffering but to confirm my touch. My sister saw and held my hand, saying, 'Lightly, lightly, it's broken,' and showed me the torn skin. He was almost asleep and made no sound. I was amazed at his helplessness. The dry blood had softened in places under the shattered surface – simultaneously glazed smooth and cracked as the surface of a painting – and was oozing out into the yoghurt. I had made him bleed . . . I did not dare with my sister near, but I wanted to lick up the blood from his back and keep what I had drawn out. His hair was girlish in the country, the stubble grew out during the summer and covered his ears, his face had outgrown its acne and was pure and infantile. I wanted to kiss his back and the pores of liquid blood created by the burns; I would have kissed him if Sylvia had not remained by the bed, if she had gone out to help Mama for an instant . . .

During the rains I watched them cook and the water dripping from the swing, the round loaves smoking in the oven and the two women rolling out dough into circles, wreaths and ears of corn. Strips of bacon hung over the fire and the cherries were piled up on my bed so that I could pick at them. I drew Mama and Basia with crayons, and the birds on the swing, the fire with the bacon and the loaves in their smoke. I waited for him to come with the wood. The axe hammered in the yard and I could hear the logs cracking and splitting under the blows and the fragments falling on to the earth, his lungs heaving as he swung the axe and the shifting of his boots in the dirt as he brought it down and the blade entered the log and bit it open. The blows were regular, evenly spaced, and the logs flew apart on the third stroke every time; I counted them and waited for the basket to fill with splinters so that he would come in. He would come after thirty blows, tip out the basket by the fire and then disappear again. The axe would recommence and I would start counting once more as if listening to the mechanism of a clock, counting each second individually and adding it to the hundreds that had already passed. The sound of the blade echoed in the garden and around the nearest hills like the hospital clock, the blue clock on the tower, amplified among the trees, made sharper by the clear air and intimate by the sound of the falling wood and the odour of bread rising in the glowing bellies of the ovens.

Thursday

Down in the garden I can see fir trees and bushes of yew, the trees that ringed the other hospital, the same lawns and gardeners and incinerators smoking in the corners, burning leaves and paper. The lawns are not cut in the same patterns, or organized around fountains and empty ponds of streaked stone. There is no wood near the window, the light is bluer, mountain-bright. Here it is open, the light is in a bowl, transparent, unclouded. Looking up, I see snow. It is violent and bright, a confusion of colour. I can see rivers in the mountains, rolling in silence, and wild vertical lawns of flowers. There is nothing decaying or darkened. There is no sound of guns, the sky is empty and rarified. The land rises and falls, there is no stagnation, no stillness of fear. It is a land in motion, in quiet motion. The trees are fanciful now, in pretty boxes, manicured and sculpted in the shapes of birds and fish, clear silhouettes of brilliant green. Here it is vivid and bright, it is my world and I know the colours and the forms, there is no smell of damp wood and dying grass, there is no smoke in the trees. At St Lazare there were no rivers and no snow, the sky came down to a flat earth, unbroken and heavy, rotting and bitter. When I opened the window near my bed the air was sour with burning bark and decomposing leaves, diluted grey and humming with machines high up beyond the clouds, untouchable and invisible. But the big trees were the same, and used to remind me of here. Only the wounded soldiers wandering, smoking and speaking to themselves, made the other place a world apart.

When I arrived at St Lazare, the room was dark. I was pricked with needles and then they left me. They spoke French and I was relieved. I tried to sleep but was too excited, the pricks in my skin ached and I could not move. I waited in the dark and used my ears: the aeroplanes could still be heard buzzing at the end of the corridor, far away, and the nurses walked past the door in twos, whispering together. No one touched my door. I was alone in a cubicle, connected to a bottle and bandaged over my legs, stomach and shoulders. My back was also padded with cotton wool and strips of gauze wound around my torso. The splinters in my back were numb and my bones were light, cracked in places. An oil-lamp by my bed – turned down to a low flame – was the only source of light, picking out shelves of bottles and brown paper packets. I tried to pluck off the feathers that had covered me, white goose feathers, but I was clean, they had removed them already and I was naked under the blanket, clothed only by the bandages. Silence after the explosion: my ears were singing. A dust had fallen into them, irritating the membranes into a musical resonance. I tried to cover them with my hands but I could not stretch my arms so far upward and had to let the singing continue. My body would not revolve, I could not move on to my side. Instead, I could turn my head on to its ear either way, and examine the ghostly walls illumined by the oil-lamp, feeling my way along each shelf through clutters of glass, paper and gauze. On one side, the door, a line of light and the shadows of feet wading through it, throwing deeper shadow into the room. Otherwise I was almost immobile and paralysed in one position. The shattered leg I could not even make tremble or shiver, it had become detached and petrified. I tapped it – a rod of alabaster – and it was hollow.

My pelvis had acquired a terrifying weight and was sucked by gravity to the bed, fixed in one place, unable to obey my will. I tried to push down with my hips, to displace myself, but the effort evaporated in stillness. I lay transfixed and closed my eyes, listening to the feet echoing in the corridor. I had been blinded and knocked over, and the blood had matted in my hair, hardening with the passing hours and dropping out in a dust of coagulated grains. I had pulled it out myself, the feeling in my hair having frightened me, and the nurses had washed me, shampooed my hair, cut off the longer parts, cleaned my nails and scrubbed my skin. Now there was no trace of blood or dirt . . . only the sound remained in my ears, refusing to be drawn out. Perhaps an insect had been hurled into the inner ear and was dying there. I thought about the insect and began to panic. When I closed my eyes I saw the flash and heard the insect at the same time: the flash produced the insect, the insect whined within the flash. In the flash the geese also ran about, screaming, waddling in terror, rushing through clouds of feathers, and I chased them . . . what for? . . . waving my hands as if to gather them together, chase them away, or kill them myself. They were red and white, blood and innocent feathers, and their wings were outstretched in hysteria. Bricks fell among them and they turned in circles like fat old men, crowing and flapping, casually crushed by the debris. I thought: why is it they cannot fly? The sky was pure and blue, like here; above the chimneys the aeroplanes wheeled in emptiness, serene and bird-like. But the geese were caricatures, dummy birds, waddling old men. I lay among webbed and orange feet, crazed and brainless legs, and they cackled over me, lifting up their bills as if swallowing awkward morsels, screaming and running mad.

I could not sleep on the first night and I lay awake with the blue flame of the lamp by my head, naked under the coarse blanket, and the light from the door was visible to my left eye. There was no window and I did not know what time . . . I think it was at night, in the early morning when the footsteps in the corridor were almost extinguished, that the line of bright electric light trembled and flew open, and a man came in holding a leather bag and a hard clipboard. The door opened and closed. With the left eye I could see the doctor with his bag taking off his coat by the door. He smelt of rain and soaked earth. He hung his coat on the door and took his bag to a corner of the room, opened it and took out pieces of metal – I saw them in the ring of faint diseased light from the oil flame – the metal parts of instruments and rolls of bandage. He did not come to the table and turn up the oil-lamp, but remained in the corner, sorting the instruments on a chair. He made no sound – I could not hear his breathing or the movements of his fingers. When he emerged from the corner into the slightly stronger circle of light around the bed, I saw in a haze – I could not raise my head and look at him directly – a white coat, the tube of a stethoscope and the thin outline of his face . . . the face of a bat in the blue light. I pretended to sleep and closed my eyes while he looked at me from the bottom of my bed, and the rubber tube squeaked softly as he rolled it between two fingers over his chest. The lamp hissed very quietly, but louder than our breathing, and I could hear it in one ear and the insect in the other. I was nearly asleep when the lamp flared up and forced my eyes open, brilliantly lighting the red skin over them and causing me to panic. With my right eye I could see his hand still on the tap, regulating the paraffin, resting indecisively on the oily, serrated cog for a moment before turning the flame down once more and restoring the cubicle to its former semi-darkness.

He had seen then that I was awake. He stood by my head, bent down with the tube and its cup-shaped receptacle, approaching my chest, the space between my breasts; then his hand pulled away the blanket gently . . . so lightly I did not feel it . . . and I felt my breasts – unbandaged, unharmed – struck by the light of the lamp and the receptacle, a small cold disk of metal, descending between them and touching the skin, held in position by one hand. If I opened my eyes I would be ashamed; if I pretended to sleep I would be absent, I would endure nothing. (When we were small we covered our eyes when crossing the road, thinking that we had made ourselves invisible, that the cars would not see us and that we would never be hit by them.) But the metal disk did not move and I knew he was listening. He began to speak to me, telling me that he was listening, that I should lie still, that I should not move or try to move. I opened my eyes and dared only to look downward; my breasts were naked and upright in the lamplight, greenish and hard, distorted by the toneless illumination and rough with pimples from the coldness of the sudden exposure. The tube snaked down to the sternum and his hand was at the base near the skin, ceraceous fingers without hair, and one of his nails pricked me inadvertently. When the tube was lifted he moved down to my broken leg. He raised it by the foot, pressed with his fingers every section from the knee to the ankle and laid it back on the bed. He was reading the reports, he knew that the other leg was virtually unscathed and he did not touch it. The blanket was still folded back and the fold lay over my stomach, leaving my breasts exposed. He walked around the room, around the bed, reading the reports, and the lamp burned over my skin. I closed my eyes again and waited. A few minutes of pacing and silence and then a hand came on to my ribs – the same waxy hand that had held the rubber tube, an experienced, untrembling hand. It listened to my organs: the lungs, intestines and the upper portion of the stomach. The hand was knowledgeable and sure.

My heart was beating faster and the hand perceived it, he murmured to me, 'Relax, I am examining,' and moved his hand over to the flat of the stomach and pressed down with the ball of his thumb. My heart was louder and my stomach became hot, quivering with fear. He pressed again and said, 'Be still, I'm busy,' and I tried to breathe slower, more deeply, tensing the muscles of my throat. The hand felt the pressure running the length of my body, originating in the throat and collecting in the stomach, turning that organ into a hard, inflexible ball. The hand moved in a slow circle around the surface of the abdomen, pushing the blanket further down towards my hips. I could not twist away or move my legs. I was afraid of his disapproval, he would think I was a child. I could not raise my head to watch him, I could only feel his hand executing the careful circle and pressing down on the stomach. My hips were tightening, the muscles drawing in and forming anxious knots. The hand broke off from its circles and ran lightly up the ladder of ribs until it brushed one of my breasts – only for a moment, accidentally – and settled on my shoulder. Its fingers were warmer now and partially moist. It advanced into the saddle of the neck and rested under my ear, two fingers sinking into my hair. The breast that he had momentarily touched began to burn as if touched by a tiny flame. I did not dare raise my hands and use my body against him. His hand lay against my neck and I waited in the roar of my heartbeats. I waited and the lamp burned with its awful hiss, touching my eyes and flooding them with light. It was night and there were no echoes of footsteps in the corridor.

The hand was lifted from my throat and he stepped back with a sudden exhalation of breath. I remained paralysed and did not open my eyes. He moved away from the bed and returned to the corner where he had left the leather bag and a heap of instruments. He packed the bag without haste and unhooked his coat. I wanted to open my eyes and watch him but did not dare. By keeping those eyes shut I preserved my detachment, retaining in myself a residue of purity: if I opened them I would destroy the privilege they made possible. I could feel him looking at me again as he paused by the door and unbuttoned his coat; he had forgotten something. Reaching over to the bed, he flicked the blanket back over my breast and then mumbled, 'Good night, Ania,' as if we had been speaking cordially to each other for the last hour. The door opened and the electric light of the corridor burst in once more and then was gone.

When I awoke he was there again. Perhaps it was later that same night, perhaps it was morning and I could not see the daylight in my room, perhaps days had gone by and I had been asleep . . . they could have administered syringes to make me sleep and I had forgotten . . . I did not know; I could not ask the doctor and he himself did not speak to me about the 'last time' or 'the morning' or 'the evening' or 'the night'. This second time he examined the broken leg again and slipped his hand beneath the blanket near my breast and kneaded the flesh gently with his fingers. When his hand closed around the breast I did not look up at him or open my mouth to speak. As I awoke more fully I heard rain falling on windows in another place, tumbling over hollow tin roofs and dripping in streams from window-hoods. His hand remained on my breast, tugging it upward slightly and feeling gradually its inner recesses, changing its shape by the altered pressure of his fingers. I was afraid: he would uproot it and tear it out and if it were night I would not be heard resisting, the corridor would be empty. It was darker now, he had turned the lamp down to its lowest flame – a flat, spluttering U-shaped flame of yellow and purple bands – and when I began to look up I saw only the grey square of the ceiling, the doctor's white coat brushing against me and the squashed flame itself guttering behind its streaked glass. I wanted to ask him, 'Is it night?' but the pressure of his hand made me harden; my throat would not melt into speech and my tongue was flat against the bottom of my mouth, not moist enough to coil, move, or force open my teeth. I longed to drink, and the sound of water, the rain falling from the windows, tormented me. His hand shifted, moving downward, and my mouth ached with thirst. I searched for saliva under my tongue but the cavity had been sucked dry and the tongue touched papery walls of skin, sticky with fear. He told me to be still, that he was working and that I was too tense. The examination was a long one, for when his hand had been withdrawn and I could think once more about the time, I heard that the rain had ceased and that the windows were silent. His fingers had broken something and torn me away from the world. When his hand drew away and left me, I floated back into the imaginary sounds of the garden and the dripping left by the shower. He told me to sleep and extinguished the lamp, leaving me in darkness. 'Sleep now.' I tried to turn away from him but my hips would not move, I was held by the weight of my leg. He knew I could not and stroked my hair saying, 'Sleep,' and I closed my eyes, trying to vanish into the black hole. It was night, I am sure . . . when he opened the door and stepped out into the corridor his steps echoed in emptiness, in perfect solitude.

In the ward he came again, but I was not alone and he could only visit me at night, he could not touch me as he had in the cubicle. Here I could see him better and I heard his name whispered by the nurses. He would still touch my throat and hair and I could not stop him, but now I could move my face away and slip out of his grasp. He examined my leg and ordered a cast. The cast was lifted above the bed by a pulley and left there to ease the leg. He came and examined it every evening, putting a thermometer in my mouth while he massaged my naked foot and probed the top of the leg near the hip-joint. I could see the bruised thigh, yellow and grey under his fingers, and the tiny cuts speckling the skin towards the buttocks. The cuts preoccupied him: 'We have to look at these all the time,' he said, 'sometimes the particles can be left.' They stung when he touched them and I would begin to cry. 'The glass hit you,' he explained. 'Not seriously. But we will have to look at the cuts every day. The nurses will disinfect them and I will check them.' I did not feel them except at night, when the aeroplanes kept me awake. I was afraid he would come to check the cuts during the night as he had in the cubicle, and I lay awake in fear listening to the aeroplanes and the children coughing, thinking of how I might break his fingers or shout to the nurses, but knowing I never would. He had explained the necessity of his visits – the cuts from the glass – and I could not escape him while I was sick. Often he came twice, three times a day, and sometimes for no reason, entering the ward when there were only a few nurses on duty, and coming only to my bed. No one noticed him, or the attention he paid me. My mother used to come every morning at that time and I could not tell her – the words would not form. She would not have believed it, the nurses would not have believed, the other staff would not have believed. I did not speak and made no move to stop him. I knew it would pass: the cuts would heal up, the leg would mend, the war would end and I would escape one day into the wood I had seen through the windows of the ward, a wood thick and dark enough to conceal me.

Jamie came and gave me apples. I remember the apples, withered, brown pitted apples he had stolen or picked up underneath the apple trees in the hospital grounds; and the sugar he gave me – clean, geometric sugar, unlike the grey, irregular fragments my mother used to bring me – and the chocolates in paper bags and the magazines he brought in parcels tied with string. His face was always sickly and anxious, and he stuttered as he spoke. When he spoke French he made every kind of mistake . . . he would say,

'C'est belle,' in talking about the weather and call me 'une petite renégate', which sounded absurd, though I would never laugh, and he would say, 'J'espère que tu t'amuses bien avec les bonbons,' with great solemnity, and I could only nod and take them gravely and thank him. But I did take them . . . I hoped he would discourage the other from visiting me . . . and I took the flowers he brought and kept them in glass jars by my bed so that Kessler would see. I was sorry for the Englishman, he was nervous and fragile. He did not belong . . . he wore his uniform without knowing why and polished his buttons. He was young, with red hair – not beautiful – and thin, made of sticks. I am spiteful, but I disliked his voice. His lower lip moved in a strange way when he talked, and his habit was to look into my eyes too long as he spoke, so that I became embarrassed and feigned fatigue to make him go away. I thought of Mama ('Eat your sugar and keep to yourself') and Sylvia in Paris and felt lonely in his company. In my tin I kept Sylvia's stockings – they smelt of her legs, of her skin – and the wrappers from the chocolate she had sent in the spring. I smelt the pieces of hair that I kept under the sheets, when I should have been sleeping; it smelt of Paris and young men, it had soaked up nights, weeks and whole summers. Even if they were Germans, they had not harmed her, she had not suffered through them. She was the beautiful sister, why shouldn't she? Why should they harm her? One, I know, gave her poodles and shoes. I read the letter myself . . . little permed dogs and fantastical shoes for dancing. They could not have been like Kessler, turning down the flame of the paraffin lamp and dividing me with his wax finger. In the city, with the officers, she must have been happy; they must have played with her hair on a picnic, twisting it in their fingers. She had rolled it up in silver pens, worn it in nets, had it brushed for her in front of the mirror. And it smelt of grass and wine, under my sheets.

Jamie would take me there, as he said, he would take me out of the hospital. I began to like him; I began to go with him into the garden, in a wheelchair, though the autumn was cold and made me sick. His arm was thin and I thought of his body as white and ropy, refined and hairless, and his eyes as sad and pale. I did not want to touch him, only to hold his arm when I could walk with my cast, and take his hand when he sat by me. It was a different touch, different from the other . . . he made me forget the other's examinations and the curiosity of his touch. Jamie's head was soft and irregular like an aubergine, but the other was smooth and symmetrical, like a bullet . . . I could not have touched him or taken hold of him or repelled him – my hands would have slid from his surface and slipped around him. So I liked Jamie's hands and the weakness of his arm. I let him kiss me, a fumbling peck on my cheek as he rose to leave, and did not mind him. He was sad and becoming old and I could not mind him.

But Kessler still came to examine the cuts and the progress of the leg. He came when he could be alone and he had a strange power over me: I could not resist him or be angry with him. He grew more adventurous – staying longer with me and speaking to me in his strong whisper . . . 'Do not be afraid, it is necessary.' 'Put your legs flat and be comfortable. I have spoken to your mother and she is concerned for you. Cuts can go septic, limbs can heal incorrectly.' 'Do you like it here? Shall we move the bed? There is more light by the windows, and you would be more private. Lie back, let your arms rest by your side . . . ' Impossible to disobey. There was no pain and no forced intrusion. At first I used to cry slightly, thinking of my mother. I was aware of shame and I cried. But there was no pain and I began to grow accustomed to the ritual. He was not harsh or brutal, he did not need to break me open. It was a peculiar influence . . . it avoided hatred. I did not exist to him, he passed through me and I did not care. It is true, my flesh recoiled and burned under his touch. But I was distant, folded up, rolled into a ball. When he had gone I would sleep, exhausted and oblivious. Even his odour of mint and disinfectant did not make me dream. I found the black hole and crawled in, dropping down to the bottom of it and remaining hidden. I saw him so often I became used to him; I ceased to flinch when he pulled back the blanket and laid his hand over my belly. I could look at him and – while his hand moved under the blanket – count the freckles on his forehead and explore the lines in his face. What was cruel in him? His face was not cruel, his language was not cruel. Only my fear was cruel. He himself was gentle and colourless. My guilt was mysterious. I was defiled and did not know . . .

On a train I was stopped in the corridor, under an electric light which illuminated the man's face. He had caught my wrist and we swayed together with the train, his breath flowing into my face and reeking of brandy. The light did not reach his eyes, arrested by ridges covered in blond hair, like the eyes of *Ramapithecus* man in the books. I was deafened by the trees whistling past the windows and the sound of the wheels. His other hand had opened a compartment and he tried to step into the gap, pulling me. He was too weak with drink and I ducked away. The carriage was empty and when I shouted he shouted with me, waving his free arm. I could not free the wrist and he pulled me back to him, pouting his lips for a 'wittle kissy', drawing my wrist to his shoulder and forcing me against his chest. The door opened again and he staggered into the open space. His hair had been burned and he was almost bald, his scalp covered with odd cracks. His giant hand began to tighten and I struck his face with my nails. 'Oh-ho. Petite chatte!' His free hand came down over my face – a vague, bleary blow – and I fell against the window. The light made his injured scalp glare, picking out the wisps of surviving hair and the black seams of wounds. His left arm flailed about him, pulling me with it, and I struck the edge of the compartment door and interior windows, unable to pull away. Is blood the sign of defilement? My lip bled and the blood trickled over my shirt and on to his arm. He pasted his fingers with it and brought the liquid up to his nose. I was bleeding now, was I? His face was distorted with disgust. He smelt the blood and stuck out his tongue with horror. I had defiled him. He threw me away from him and tore off his jacket. I ran down the corridor, tumbling and slipping, between the roar of the trees and the air expelled by the motion of the train. I did not look back, though I heard his groans. I had made him dirty with my blood and struck fear into his soul. Luck! He shouted, 'Leave me alone, with your filth!' and I heard him close the door of the compartment behind him. It was night and the train was empty . . . all the compartments were empty . . . I found one at the other end and locked myself inside.

In the spring my bed was moved again, to the ground floor, and I was not confined to that bed as my leg had healed and I could walk. There was a line of hawthorn trees close to the windows and they flowered as it became warm and the white clusters were brilliant against the blue skies. The children began to leave and I was left alone. I was held back for some reason which was never explained to me. My body had adjusted to Kessler and there was now no discomfort.

The nights were quiet for the first time that spring and I could sleep. The stars were heated up by the earth and turned blue and yellow and quivered as if you could see the fire in them. In the summer here, as I remember, they are even brighter and seem to be shaking so violently they will fall out of position and come towards the earth, burning the planets in their way and turning the sky into a continual summer day, burning even the trees and the animals, turning everyone's hair white, and frying the tips of the houses. (I know now, of course, that this was just a story that our grandfather used to tell us.)

Sunday

Today he came with a handkerchief filled with blueberries and a milk bottle filled with white flowers. He was flushed and perspiring and his red hair was made lank and dark with the effort of walking in the hills. A blinding day thick with insects and floating dust. He wanted to take me out and I would not go. I have always thought that he is frail, that he is unhealthy. Irony that I am the one in bed. I am sure the coniferous trees exude a certain chemical in the heat which makes them darker and greener . . . an inky colour, oily and damp . . . as the trees in Italy were dark in the same way when it was hot – perhaps there is a resin that protects the leaves against the sun by making them gummy and wet . . . and the fir trees here are the same as the umbrella pines in the south, thick and impermeable, heavy blocks of green fringed with black. And there are funeral trees there – the thin pointed trees, the cypresses – their darkness has been observed by the Italians, and they are named as death-trees. Do they throw branches from them into the coffins? Their darkness is supernatural and they stand out from the hills like holes in the earth, or the shadows of old men. And they never move like other trees, they are frozen and unreal. The firs here are not funeral trees, but they are the houses of trolls. Traditionally the trees became sinister in winter. We were told the troll stories then, the Baba-Yaga stories, when we could not go out and look for ourselves. But now that I am imprisoned here and cannot go out to the trees, they are more sinister to me in summer: the sunlight makes them black, the brightness makes them darker. Why should the trolls leave in summer? They are the same woods and Baba-Yaga is always there. I told him all this and he was puzzled. To him, the scene from my window is a happy fresco of primitive colours, fresh forests and purple mountains. He is dazzled by it; it is empty for him, a collection of beauties and novelties, free of memory. He thrust the flowers on me, hoping to divert me. 'Look,' he said, 'that is what the countryside is made of. I found them in sight of the hospital.'

What differs is the heat, the hotness of the air and the stillness of the hottest part of the day – just after noon – into which the world enters with resignation and is crushed. The heat gives me fever, I have explained to him, it causes me to warp. As a child I cowered from the brightness and heat of open places. In the south lemon trees grow out of it and palm trees and flowers . . . but it is more cruel. It was never Jamie's element: sometimes he was a madman, it went to his brain and he could not endure it. Here at least I am free, he does not smother me. If he goes mad in his hotel room, I am not harmed.

I notice now how his weak red hair is falling out and the freckles on his hands are becoming larger. I take his blueberries and flowers and eat the fruit greedily in front of him. While I eat – making my face filthy – he draws up a chair and talks to me, holding my hand. He is trying to be my benefactor once more, my supplier of small luxuries ('I will bring you a lemon next time . . . you live on potatoes here . . . are they trying to purify you?'), but there is almost nothing to say and we sit fanning ourselves, hearing the gardeners under the window shearing rose-bushes and raking the earth of the flower-beds.

When he has gone, I do not move from the bed and wait for the room to darken. When it is true night, I open the windows and shutters and take off the hospital dressing-gown, standing in the cold air near the window until the moon makes everything visible. It rolls up the side of the hill through a bristle of barbed silhouettes and hovers at the peak just beyond their tips. The landscape is globular, the sky arching towards me, and the mass of the mountains the far surface of a concave which is cupped over me, pierced by empty spaces and partially filled in with the black alpine triangles. It is rolled like a curl of plastic, lit from behind by the moon. I peer into the spaces, where the light is purest, and stars are shooting in the vacuum, fizzling and dropping into the fields. (Often, with a shock, I realize that I am already familiar with the shape of the mountains, the positions of the stars at this time of year and the depressions in the surface of the moon.) The aerial light forms a fantastic world; the trees lining the small road, erect as statues, rise up from their own darkness and seem enlarged, as if inflated by excess blood, like insects that have been feeding.

The road lying close to the sanatorium – which I can see clearly if there is a moon – reminds me of the street where Basia waited for her tram dressed in a fancy hat. It is also like the street by the house in Nowy Sącz, a dust track connecting a cluster of lodges. And it is like the street in Paris, the avenue Trudaine, with its silent trees. In some ways these streets must be physically joined up to each other, forming one continuous network that is only accidentally subdivided . . . if I pursue this street I can reach back to all the others in time. And when I see Jamie appear there at midday, struggling uphill in the heat, I imagine that he has just returned from the other streets, passing through all of them on the way here. It is comforting to know that the past is held together by objects, by the simplicity of roads, and I am glad to see him walking there, appearing out of the past. This is why I lean out of the window and wave to him as he comes near . . . but, waving back with blank eyes, he does not, of course, understand me.

Saturday

The heat has broken and rain clouds have come down from the mountains to settle just above us, making the building dark and wet, releasing showers every two hours and scattering the old gardeners with light waves of rain and freak hail. The heat has evaporated for the first time, indicating the end of summer. The lawns are flushed with water, filled with puddles, and the clouds are too heavy, the wind will not lift them. I loathe the drowned look of the ski-run, the descending smoke filled with rain. There was thunder last night, high up, perhaps in Czechoslovakia, booming in the crater of Morskie Oko, rushing in shock waves the length of the valleys into Poland and breaking over the tender plots of the medical villa. There are storms ready to tip over the crests and roll like stones into the gardens of the Polish towns. The next one, the very next one, will probably strike us here, crushing this wooden palace. I wait for it calmly, playing Chinese chequers with myself over and over again, expecting at any moment the timid tap of Jamie's fist on the thin door.

When I leave I will not go to Warsaw, as I have told Jamie, I will go to a bigger city, away from mountains and trees. The possibilities are nearly infinite, given that there are five continents and a thousand cities in a thousand nations. The spitting is beginning to heal, I am told, the quantities of blood will lessen and my fevers are already milder . . . within a month, certainly, I will be able to administer the drugs myself and travel with a suitcase of them to keep me normal – people do it: use syringes on themselves, carry their tablets in jars and prepare their own emetics. I will take Mama with me and we will go off to the tropics. If they entrust the medicines to Mama, they will let me travel; all doctors know the healing properties of sun and sea. I will take Mama to a sea filled with red and yellow fish and lagoons filled with octopus, and then to bars on floating jetties . . . I have seen them crowded with paper lanterns, moving on the water, and crowds of dancers in the open air. We will go to the reefs in a yacht, and I will be oiled and naked as a Polynesian –

the Polynesian queens with flowers for breasts – shells in my hair and smelling of coconut.

My father is buried in the sea. I hear him dancing like a crab on the tips of his bones, walking sideways across the sand. Looking down through the water, I see him: green as an antique coin, on his side, wedged in mud. They have their own sound, objects lost in the sea . . . coins, bottles, masts, prows . . . they move imperceptibly westward, jangling in the current, and he is with them, his bones the sound of drifting metal. He resounds like a bell so far beneath me it is like the bells of another village hidden by a hill, vibrating on a sleepy day. What is his name? The bell says: Antoine. His voice calls his name, which I have forgotten, he waves with his pincers and tangoes across the dunes. The further out I am, the louder his bones are, singing:

> Il était une bergère
> Et ron, ron, ron, petit patapon,
> Il était une bergère
> Qui gardait ses moutons ron ron

beating time with a stick, and rolling a hoop. Now he is shell and coral, corrugated pink and rusted, barnacled and copper-green. You cannot sink a cross in the water, he is invisible in the ocean. Sometimes he is a fish or a floating jelly lying on a cushion of tentacles. He lies on his side to see me and I scoop him up out of the waves, a silver-blue body or a rainbow polyp. The coral is his garden, anemones are his trees. His bones clack on the coral, the sound of ivory dice, the feet of a gentleman who makes no indiscreet noise . . . he was trained as a boy to walk like a mouse . . . and the tapatap echoes in the water. The sea will corrode him too in the end and break up his crustacean body; he will be dismantled and scattered in different places and each part will be torn apart to form another shape, a lower form of shell or clam, and so on, receding without disappearing until he is a nugget of coral or hard sand. Then he will break into crystals and float in the water, a song carried by crystals:

> Qui gardait ses moutons ron ron . . .

Before his descent into the ocean he was an exquisite, fine man, with white hands and velvet lips. He wore gloves in the evening and kept a triangular handkerchief in his front breast-pocket, he was smooth as glass, with the limbs of a bird. He was a fragrant smoker and a carrier of canes, a wearer of golden chains and fur coats. He was himself 'le roi Dagobert' with the great sword in the song he taught me, though his beard was small enough for a child to hold in one hand . . . a Dagobert waxed and trimmed. Only the St Nicholas beard of cotton wool made him a real Dagobert, but buried in the false fleece his thin lips could still be seen, dry and daintily pinched, and his teeth were small, brown and sweet-smelling. They moved within the wool:

Ah, ah, kotki dwa
Two kittens
Fluffy grey

while we held up candles to his red coat, and a yellow light shone in his hair. When I am swimming I hear the kitten song, the kittens 'doing nothing but amusing Aniuszka', and see the candles in the caves. The mermaids stroke him and he observes the flight of ships. He was dropped like a stone at the moment of death and fell to a great depth carried by his inert weight, settling in the sand and lying motionless among the razor-shells. He fell naked and was turned to shell and bone, a basket of seagoing legs and a dish of salty crab-meat.

Mama brought me another photograph when she came to the hospital with my cousins. It was Papa at the beach . . . pale and feline in white shorts, his nose lubricated with oil and his hair solid with brine. He held up a lobster to the camera by its whisker, grinning with pride and casting a sly look down at the ferocious paralysed claws. He had dragged it out of the sea, flailing, still wet, with schoolboy malice. The ocean tilted behind him, sails and sea-birds, grey gulls low over the waves, and children tumbling in the foam of breakers. Mama saying, 'Antoine, hold up your lobster. And smile.' The sun in his eyes, he squinted at her, blinded and bashful. He had wrestled with the monster in the deep and vanquished it – a flabby mythic hero. He would soon re-enter the depths, a lobster himself. 'Your papa,' she wrote on the reverse side of the photograph, and she gave me the oval silver frame. This ocean world has lain by my bed for several weeks, I have seen every night before sleeping and at the moment of waking the wheeling birds and the thickets of sails and his weak hands among the spray of whiskers, legs and claws. He had a seal's body, tender and hairless, babyish and balding. I never saw this body, white as a grub, his round belly and sloping shoulders and his narrow, pappy chest. Why had she given me such a photograph? His costumes had guarded his magnificence. His arm, passing through the bellbind near the aperture in the shutters, was made of other materials. He belongs to another world in his silk cuffs. They singed his face and hauled him out with a gaff, a walking-stick hooked under the chin . . . I have heard the children speaking about the removal of bodies. They drag the cadavers out with walking-sticks to avoid contagion. They could have dragged him easily, he was so light, the system with the stick must have been ideal in his case. Besides, he was too hot to touch, smoking like a coal. And after they had buried him he crawled out and made his way into the sea, his hands were webbed and his back had turned to scales. He has found rest with the starfish and the molluscs, the pink coral hides him.

The change of weather makes me sleepless and restless. I walk in circles around the room in the dark when the wards are sleeping, making the naked boards wince and then turning on the taps for their comforting noise. The bed makes me uneasy: if something comes through the window, I will be trapped on it, unable to move, and I will be seized there. If I spy through the shutters it is Baba-Yaga who comes, dressed in straw, a band of grey hair tied around her waist and her hands made of flax. The witch is like a twist of hemp rope, formless and serpentine, with an irresistible grip. She pulls off the shutters like the wings of a fly and punctures the glass with her fist. Only her arm enters the room, and her opened hand with an odour of wax and turnips. But the arm can unravel like a rope and reach into all corners, and the nails can pass through walls. She has a laugh like a young girl's, innocent and pealing, but the arm is sinuous and frayed, with the uncoiling precision of an insect's mouth. She feels around the room, searching the corners, the mouth licking the walls, and objects stick to her palm . . . papers, books, bars of soap and clothes. Her face is pressed against the glass of the window and her eyes are burning and I run around the room on silent feet, avoiding the arm and the hand smelling of turnips. She has been digging in the earth, her nails are pockets of dirt. We taunted old women:

Baba-Yaga
Baba-Yaga

and she comes for vengeance. In her hut on legs she eats the cadavers she has dug up; she would have eaten Papa before he escaped into the sea, she would have dug him up with her hands and spiced him with garlics. She must have eaten all the others, the soldiers and the old men, but children are sweetest, and the bodies of young girls. And I have seen her before from my bed in the kitchen, creeping under the snow . . . covered with earth and leaves, with the flesh of a carrot and dressed in straw. Therefore I am being stalked, she is waiting. I light a wax pool of a candle under the icon in my room and wait until it is daybreak . . . she will not come in and confront the Virgin and burn her fingers against the blessed image. Nothing taps against the shutters and I sleep on a pillow directly under the icon nailed to the wall just by the basin. The child in the image is made of silver, the mother's halo is painted gold and the candle picks out an oval face of white paint tilted on one side in its bubble of gold, its eyes downcast and empty, its crude smile barely visible.

There was a moment during Mama's visit when she drew close to my bed and asked the cousins to leave the room for a while. She had grown nervous and irritable, dabbing her lips and eyebrows with a handkerchief and resting her hands stiffly on her knees as she talked. She went to the door twice and opened it abruptly, peering savagely into the corridor and listening for the sound of footsteps. 'They are always listening in, those cousins,' she explained with contempt. 'I wanted to leave them at Nowy Sącz, but that would have been rude.' She opened her purse and took out two photographs, the one of Papa and one of Piotr in an army uniform. She gave them both to me and let me examine them for a few minutes: Papa in his bathing-shorts, holding the lobster, and Piotr standing in a dusty summer street with a friend, a Warsaw street lined with trees, holding newspapers and rifles. She leant over and placed her finger on the companion's breast. 'We do not know him,' she said. 'He must be a friend from the regiment. No one in Kraków knows his face.' I did not recognize Piotr either, his high boots and collar were so unfamiliar. The companion was taller, thin and stooping. They were smoking together on a boulevard, the papers open in their arms, and the shapes of the sapling leaves planted along the boulevard fell over their faces. Mama went on, 'I found the photo at his father's. I was asked to sort out his papers and save what had to be saved.

This one was folded in a letter from the father to the mother which was never sent. I will have to give it to your grandmother, she will want to keep it.' I understood then that both the parents were dead. Mama had written on the back of this picture 'Piotr and friend' but had provided no frame. We passed the two photographs back and forth between us, re-examining every detail of them until we learnt them by heart. Then Mama wanted to tell a story about Piotr and crept back to the door to listen for signs of the cousins returning by the corridor. When she was satisfied that we were alone she told the story, hurriedly and incoherently, and kept the small photograph before her on her lap . . . for inspiration. But she did not tell me everything. I told her I did not believe all of her story and made her repeat whole sections of it until they were distorted beyond recognition. And in addition, this story reached me from another source: my aunt Elżbieta wrote me a letter here, telling me about the family. She wrote down everything she knew about the children, including Piotr, things Mama did not know or was afraid to say. It was only from her that I learnt the exact dates and places concerning Piotr. It was only through her that I was able to discover the exact nature of his suffering.

When I am alone at night under the basin with its dripping tap and the candlelit Virgin I imagine what it is like to walk in a sewer, my hands over my head and my feet slipping over the bodies of the drowned. It cannot be darker than my room, there must be the same sound of dripping water. When the Old Town in Warsaw fell to the Germans, Piotr crawled through the sewers to the sector of Grzybów between Żelazna, the Saski gardens, Chłodna Elektoralna and Złota Chmielna near the railway station. He wrote a letter about the sewers to one of his brothers, he described the bodies underfoot and the heat underground from burning houses. In Grzybów he was wounded by a fire in a house during the fighting and taken to an improvised hospital in the basement of a school. Another letter was found, from the basement hospital, dated simply 'September', in which he described the ward. Elżbieta says he was provided with a mattress and a cup of water, a candle and a handkerchief . . . if the ceiling collapsed on to him or he was buried by rubble, he was to urinate in the handkerchief and breathe through it. When the explosions in the streets came near to them, a hot wind rushed through the wards and underground corridors, blowing out the candles. The operating tables would be thrown into darkness and the nurses would scramble around them with electric torches or lighted matches, illuminating the ring of faces around the medical student with his saw and razor blade . . . the operations always found an audience. The medical students were nervous, often dropping things and stammering their orders in faint voices. One day a young girl in overalls came into the ward carrying a pistol . . . she put the pistol against the medical student's chest and demanded that he come to her house to dig her father out of their cellar. The student would not and she cocked the hammer. She swore she would kill him if he did not come. He was cutting out a steel splinter with a razor and refused. The patients shouted at her to put the gun down, they shouted, 'Everyone will die anyway: go home!' At last she put the gun away and disappeared into the street in tears, and the student continued to cut out the splinter from the patient's leg. When he had finished he went to look for the girl, but she had vanished.

There were, Piotr wrote, 300 men on mattresses in the basement. The wall against which he was propped was near the street and he could hear feet passing overhead, either the incoherent pitter-patter of civilians running from house to house, or the stealthy columns of insurgents in heavy boots. The people coming into the ward from the street were flushed and drenched in sweat, so that he knew the days were hot days of sunshine and blue skies. He could hear aeroplanes, even from the basement, and the singing of church services in wrecked chapels and in other basements. The priests toured the wards – Franciscans, Pallottines, Capuchins – like the denizens of catacombs. He wrote that he had not preserved his Bible and that he did not listen to the priests, though everyone else did so. There was no water, but they could lick the condensation from the walls, which was cool and refreshing. His lips cracked and his burns continued to bleed. The walls trembled and bulged when shells fell near and dust poured over the beds, drowning the patients in crumbled plaster and fragments of brick. 'We are buried and suffocating,' he repeats, 'my lungs are full of dust.' In the evening, from five to six o'clock, there would be intensified gunfire from the streets and people shouting from the upper storeys. A fire started in the classroom above the basement and the heat became unbearable. 'First they bury us, then they burn us.' The priests rushed downstairs with a group of children, their coats and shirts in shreds. The children's faces were bleeding and their hair burnt. There was no water to spare for the fire and they had to wait until it had gutted the ground-floor rooms and burned out of its own accord . . . the children fainted in the heat and the patients began swearing: 'Use the water! Use the water!' 'But,' says Piotr, 'the doctors have to wash their razors.' He fainted too, and woke up during the night. The fire had run down but the walls were still warm. The priests and children were asleep in the corridor and the operating table was empty and shrouded in darkness. The doctors had gone elsewhere for a while, or they were asleep from exhaustion. The burns on his abdomen and arms began to sear and he called out to the nurses. No one came and he lay back in impotent fury. The street was quiet and the patients were nearly all unconscious. He thought he could hear the trees in the street above and the sound of families frying pancakes in the apartments on the other side. There was no gunfire and he lit his candle to read a pack of letters (he stored them in the lining of a stolen German helmet).

When he had lit the candle he saw that the girl with the pistol had returned and that she was peering into the ward through the open door, her eyes wide with fright and a bandage tied around her head. She was wilder than before and she held the pistol with both hands, her fingers covered with grease and soot, bony and fanatical. His was the only candle alight and she came up to his bed with the pistol held down towards him, gibbering and shaking. She stood at the end of his mattress and carefully aimed the pistol at his stomach. 'Get up,' she said, 'put your helmet on. My father is in the cellar and I can't dig him out. Get up and come with me or I'll shoot.' His burns made him perspire and he could not lift himself. 'I'll have to shoot you if you don't get up,' she repeated, tapping his burnt foot with her boot. 'He is in a pocket of oxygen and cannot wait. If you don't come he'll as-ph-ixiate' (she pronounced the word with difficulty and accused him with it). 'Put your boots on and the helmet. It's not far.' He reached out for the boots but they were not there . . . if he did not put them on, she would shoot . . . he could only replace the letters in the helmet and place the helmet over his head. 'The boots!' she hissed. 'Put your boots on. You cannot mean to walk without boots.' He shook his head and her lips tightened. She pulled back the hammer of the pistol as she had done before. But now she was alone and would certainly pull the trigger if he did not find his boots. He began, 'The nurses have taken them . . . ' and then changed his mind. 'They must be under the bed somewhere.' He searched by the light of the candle, turning painfully on to his side to probe the floor around him. Somehow he knew that he was dreaming, that the girl did not exist, that she had not come into the ward and was not holding a pistol over him, that probably she was dead already and that this was her ghost . . . but he kept looking for the boots, convinced that he would die if he did not find them. He could hear her breathing and the trigger creaking backwards. 'The boots, the boots . . . they have been requisitioned, the army is in need of boots and they take them from the wounded. I have served by giving my boots. There are no boots here . . . ' When he looked up she had gone and the candle went out as he turned to implore her, extinguished by a sudden gust of air: not the blast of an explosion, but a warm summer draught that had made its way downstairs. He lay back in the dark and listened for her footsteps, but heard nothing. Perhaps she had taken her boots off and run out into the street in bare feet to escape notice, or had climbed out of the building by way of the roofs. He was sure, in the end, that she had not existed. But he waited for her the next night, expecting her, unafraid, hoping that she would come and shoot him. She did not appear again. It was absurd, but he thought that he recognized her from before the war . . . perhaps she had been pushed against him in a tram for a moment or he had crossed her path in one of the parks, feeding swans or sleeping under the trees. He waited every night and she did not reappear . . . he became convinced that she had never come to his bed and that he had dreamt it all. But I know he wanted her to come, I know so, and that he recognized her from before the war. In the end, he was still unsure: he could not tell if she had really come or if he had been dreaming. He kept looking for his boots and was relieved to find they had been taken while he was unconscious. If the girl came again she would have to kill him and he would be at rest.

He hallucinated several times lying on the mattress, waiting for the burns to be treated. Often they were premonitions that he could hear – the sound of German voices and the regular beat of their march. He wrote four letters to his brother and to his mother and father, storing them all in the unused helmet. He could hear crickets in the cracks of the walls, the singing outside in the crevices of ruins in the evenings. At last, a miracle occurred – water fell in heavy drops from the ceiling, a pipe had burst as one of the walls was struck by a mortar shell, and the men were showered by cold water. He thought the war had ended and raised himself up, half-awake. 'Water is coming. They have freed us.' When the pipe was exhausted the men fell asleep in confusion. The water had cooled them off then evaporated, leaving them thirsty and bewildered. It had turned the dust around his bed into cool mud and he leant down to lay his cheek against it. He said he could hear insects coming to life in the mud, activated by the unexpected water, fermenting and multiplying. In the walls he could hear ants and cockroaches scuttling between the dislocated bricks, shifting the powdered cement with their legs. The insects were louder than the guns in the neighbouring streets, and increased gradually until the noise of their wings seemed deafening in the confined space of the ward. 'They should come and kill the insects, they are tormenting us. Does the army not have sprays and chemicals? At night they run over my body and I cannot kill them with my hands, they run too quickly and my hands will not move to catch them. What we need is a good spray . . . ' The last letter, in particular, is filled with details of insects, beetles, centipedes, flies, moths and roaches. He notes each species individually, the sound it makes, the speed at which it moves over his flesh and the colour of its body by candlelight. He even claims to have found new species and varieties of known species. And his hallucinations go further . . . he says he knows the men around him on the mattresses, that they were all at school together and that he knew their names. 'I am glad they have all come and that I find them here. I am among friends.' In one letter he even claims to have seen his brother on the operating table . . . 'They took something out of his head, but he survived, he survived perfectly well' . . . and to have shaken hands with his cousin Alexander Sermov, a Russian.

When the candles had burned down they lay in darkness, the loss of vision intensifying the noise in the street. He says, 'The Germans are in Ochota, in Czyste and in Stawki . . . I can tell by the direction of their shells. I would love to go outside and see the summer night-sky and the shells bursting like stars. There must be flames pouring into the streets and fountains of sparks. It must be beautiful.' A priest came to his mattress and told him that the Polish Red Cross would take them out of the basement in a few days and transfer them to another sector, to a real hospital. He was elated. 'I will have a bed with castors and a dressing-gown, my window will have blinds. They will spray the insects. They will give us jugs of water and cigarettes.' When it was dark, he doubted. Glass was broken in the street, he could hear it cracking underfoot and fragments scattering across the pavements. He began to spit at the flies in the hope of driving them off. 'They are consuming me. Is the army not aware?' He crushed the roaches in the wall with a matchstick and was overjoyed at his success. On the tenth day, however, the man on his left died in his sleep and he records gloomily, 'We too are flies, of course. We are all flies together.' He begins to wonder if the Germans will come to spray them like roaches and, despite his shunning of the Capuchins and Pallottines, he quotes from the Bible left by the dead man:

> . . . them that dwell in houses of clay, whose foundation is in the dust, which are crushed before the moth

adding, 'The moths knock against my face when the candle is lit, they crawl over my belly when it is extinguished. I am afraid of them. They are as hungry as we are . . . ' He was afraid of them as I am afraid of Baba-Yaga, and perhaps Baba-Yaga sent the moths to torment him and carried off the man in his sleep. The ward was a world of insects and dust. (Mama whispered to me, 'He could not drink and the burns drove him mad. He gibbers about spiders and so on, he was a little deranged by then. His own brother told me he was unhinged at the end.') He claims the room was once filled with butterflies – 'They have all hatched from caterpillars in the dust. It is a miracle.' – and that they came and sat on his toes. In his calmer moments, the moments before sleep, he remembers me again, tying up my hair in the park and taking me on the trams. 'She would like the butterflies sitting now on the ends of my toes. I will catch them and send some to her in a jar, their wings stuck together by the heat and the yellow spots on their bodies as big as coins.' But later he claims that they have not moved from his toes and that they are feeding on him, nibbling through the skin and eroding the toes like leaves. 'For them, I am a tree, I am a morsel of vegetation. I cannot move and they are eating me alive.' He shouted to the others to brush away the insects, but no one moved to help him.

The bursting shells came closer and they could hear the wheels of larger vehicles in the streets nearby. The footsteps outside died away and there was some commotion in the upper storeys of the school, the rooms were being filled with men. More medical students appeared in the basement, grim and silent, and more mattresses were brought down. Dust rolled in freely from the congested corridor and the walls began to crack wide open. The noise began to deafen them: 'There is a giant hammering our little box.' There was gunfire from the top windows, high up and distant, and answering fire from the street corners near the wall. The students ran about in confusion, searching for weapons, asking the priests to bless them. The sound of boots on the pavements had changed, the boots were different, but identical to each other . . . the footwear of a systematic army. 'I hope for more gusts of wind, they will blow away the smell of urine and stale air. They will blow away all the filth.' During the night men from the street poured into the ground floor. The students rushed upstairs and did not come back. For an hour the gunfire receded upwards towards the top floors, and from there spread on to the roof-tops. After that hour the building became quiet and the boots came back down from the upper storey, overturning tables, breaking windows. The basement was in darkness and the nurses too had fled. The patients lay silently, listening to the new voices while the classrooms above were being swept out and a powerful voice shouted orders in the chaos.

Boots came down the stairs to the basement and a torch darted over the lines of mattresses, lighting up heads and feet. The soldiers were surprised and ran back up to the classrooms. A man leant over to Piotr, saying, 'They're here. Maybe they'll give us a bath,' and began to laugh. The soldiers returned immediately with a paraffin lamp, which they hung from a beam near the door. No one turned to look at them, but Piotr, leaning on his elbow to watch the group by the door, saw that a Polish priest was conversing with a German carrying a rifle. The rifleman was telling the priest, 'Simply go ahead of me, two paces ahead of me,' and the priest was nodding and agreeing. 'Two paces ahead. If that is how you want it.' The paraffin lamp soon filled the basement with a smell of burning methane and a thin black smoke. The patients woke up slightly to examine the lamps . . . but the priest was speaking Polish in a soft voice to the man nearest the door and they did not find it unusual. The priest went from bed to bed, whispering almost inaudibly, and the soldier followed him, levelling his rifle at the head of the wounded man beneath him and firing a single shot calmly and accurately into a favoured part of the forehead. The shots rang out in clear five-second intervals and the first row was completed in three minutes. The second row was nearer and Piotr could hear the nervous words of the priest more clearly as he went from bed to bed – 'Rest in peace; rest in peace' – and the detonation of the rifle more sharply and precisely. From the corner of his eye he saw the soldier, plump, black-faced from the soot of fires, thick-fingered, squinting awkwardly as he aimed, and perspiring through the grime. 'He must be counting "eins, zwei, drei, vier hop . . . !" and pulling back the trigger of the rifle with a tiny expectoration and a shrug of the shoulders.' At the end of the second row the barefooted priest began to slip in the blood and the soldier prodded him forward with the butt of the rifle, irritated and tired. He swore at him. 'He told him he would give him a bullet at the end if he had one left over, as a keepsake.' The priest finished the second row and wanted to pause before beginning the third and fourth, but the soldier pushed him on. 'This was work, they had no time for coffee and biscuits.' They completed the third row and again the priest began to slip. Piotr finished writing the last letter as they began the fourth row. He folded it and slipped it into the lining of the helmet, then waited for the priest. He lay half-way along the row and could hear the bare feet of the holy man approaching, the whisper of his voice and the report of the rifle following closely behind. As the shots came closer he raised himself up on his elbows, seeing for the first time the face of the priest, an old face as wild as that of Baba-Yaga, splashed with blood and wild-eyed . . . he did not watch as the man behind him shot at the beds. When the soldier fired into the man next to him Piotr sat up and shouted, 'Give me some soap!' and the soldier shot him too quickly without aiming or composing himself, from the foot of the other bed. He was struck above one of his eyes and fell back into the darkness, feeling the blood pour into them.

He woke for a moment in the night, disturbed by his thirst, and the basement was dead . . . the floor was moist, the bed was moist, and his coat was damp with his own blood. The ward was empty and he was alone with the dead men. Rockets were shooting up into the night and there were bonfires in the street, he heard the flames and the hatchets breaking wood. He rolled on to the floor and began to crawl on his elbows, like a mud-skipper, towards the door through the wash of blood flowing from the beds. In the corridor a tray of medicines had been overturned, phials had smashed on the ground and he licked up pockets of liquid from the larger fragments of glass. He passed into unconsciousness again and lay under the tray . . . the guards stealing downstairs to investigate the noises could not see him there. He woke and drank again from the broken phials until his tongue was paralysed.

During the following day the German nurses found him and took him up into the street – a street blackened, gutted and filled with sunlight. He was woken by the light, he says, and they told him he was alive, as if he would not believe it. 'You are alive, lie still. Lie still and only breathe. Breathe softly. Lie still, lie still, lie still.'

I lie myself in the same position, on my back, looking up at the same section of sky. The blue clock goes round and round with its pretty bells, its golden hands changing position, and I hear it ticking, the cogs and spindles revolving and the weights spinning up and down, a small wheel turning within a large wheel and one shaft propelling another, serrated rims locking into other rims and pulling them round tooth by tooth and the spring unwinding like a snake and pushing outwards to mark time, expanding and pushing the mechanism into life, and the tips of the arms scraping the surface of laminated figures lightly, like the wings of birds, and always returning eventually to the same place, if only I lie still and wait.